THE
DESIGNER
BAG
AT THE
GARBAGE
DUMP

THE
DESIGNER
BAG
AT THE
GARBAGE
DUMP

JACKIE MACGIRVIN

DESTINY IMAGE₍₎ PUBLISHERS, INC.

P.O. Box 310, Shippensburg, PA 17257-0310

"Promoting Inspired Lives."

This book and all other Destiny Image, Revival Press, MercyPlace, Fresh Bread, Destiny Image Fiction, and Treasure House books are available at Christian bookstores and distributors worldwide.

For a U.S. bookstore nearest you, call 1-800-722-6774.

For more information on foreign distributors, call 717-532-3040.

Reach us on the Internet: www.destinyimage.com.

ISBN 10: 0-7684-4145-5

ISBN 13: 978-0-7684-4145-1

Ebook: 978-0-7684-8815-9

For Worldwide Distribution, Printed in the U.S.A.

1 2 3 4 5 6 7 8 9 10 11 / 13 12

Acknowledgments

Thanks to all my friends who read and made invaluable comments: Lori Garcia, Linda Sprague (also my technical support person; I'd be lost without you, seriously!) and Sarah Butterfield.

To Julie Kandal, who ministers to orphans in India and who read for accuracy.

To Marsha Foix for doing research on the Indian Mafia and looking up Scripture references.

Special thanks to Jackie McLeod, my go-to person for excellent plot suggestions and feedback. Without you, this book would be much thinner and rather boring!

Thanks to Bob Hartley and the Deeper Water's team for all the great hope teachings from your awesome morning prayer meetings. May they bless others as much as they have blessed me.

Thanks to Ronda Ranalli and the awesome, creative, and unique team at Destiny Image.

Endorsements

Jackie Macgirvin's latest book, *The Designer Bag at the Garbage Dump*, is an imaginative journey of the heart—full of action and surprises. Julie, an unlikely heroine, starts out as a conflicted, self-absorbed, obsessively shallow woman whose world is transformed by an inexplicable event that transports her to a chaotic foreign culture where she finds herself faced with choices that evoke valor and faith she didn't know she possessed. The story is about personal transformation and how one person's change of heart brings redemption, joy, and justice to others. Jackie brings to life the natural and supernatural dimensions of the human dilemma through her characters' journey and most of all through the real power of faith to bring the heart home.

Bonnie Chavda
Senior Pastor, All Nations Church

Touché! Jackie Macgirvin has done it again. *The Designer Bag at the Garbage Dump* is a real page turner that gives you great insight in the very heart of God and His passionate love for every tongue, tribe, and nation!

Kevin Basconi
Author of *The Reality of Angelic Ministry Today Trilogy*
King of Glory Ministries International
www.kingofgloryministries.org

Religion that God the Father accepts…is this: caring for orphans (James 1:27a NCV).

F O R E W O R D

Powerful teaching can be hidden in stories. This is why Jesus taught in parables. You hold in your hand the story that highlights truths we need to embrace in our journey to die to ourselves. Though slow and painful, it is necessary in order to totally live for Him. I have learned through the years that setting our heart to obey Him 98% does not leave us with vibrant spirit. But, giving 100% of ourselves brings 100% of Him. What an incredible exchange!

Learn about the struggle for total surrender by watching Julie's life and read the rich rewards that come to her as a result: intimacy with the Lord, a change in perspectives and priorities, a love for people, a healed heart, relational changes, joy and the alleviation of stress and disease.

The second theme of this book is our attitude toward the poor. Reading this book will give an increased inspiration and vision to touch the poor. I challenge you to grapple with the issue of what it looks like to live a simple lifestyle in our western, affluent consumer-oriented culture. Do our checkbooks distinguish us from our unsaved neighbors? Is most of our time consumed by our work in order to pay for more possessions? Beloved, it is best to settle these issues now, not tomorrow or in ten years. Read, learn, be inspired and be changed by His abundant grace!

Mike Bickle, Director
International House of Prayer
Kansas City, Missouri

CHAPTER

1

MUMBAI, INDIA

A gaily painted dump truck, covered in yellow and red swirls, drove too fast through the pounding rain. The driver held a cup of chai in his right hand along with the wheel and reached to the passenger seat to grab a pastry. He sped toward a narrow bridge over a deep gulf.

In the backseat of the family car, nine-year-old Ravi held his favorite toy, Silly Putty®, contained in a red plastic egg. Next to him was the suitcase his mother had filled with his clothes, toys, homework, and snacks. A large, leather-bound astronomy book was opened to the chapter on the Horsehead Nebula. As the rain intensified, his father kicked the wipers to high.

"Are we there yet?" asked Ravi.

His father chuckled.

"No," replied his mother. "We've been driving for 15 minutes; the drive is 15 hours."

"I don't even remember my uncle."

"That's OK. The last time you saw him you were only four. You will remember this trip. Your cousin Gitika is getting married."

At that moment, Ravi dropped the egg, and it rolled under his mother's seat. On his hands and knees, he reached for it.

"What is my uncle's name? Where does he live?"

"He's your father's brother. He is also a doctor like your father—"

As the dump truck barreled across the small bridge, the cup slipped from the driver's hand and the hot chai scalded his lap. He screamed in pain. The truck swerved into the other lane.

To avoid a head-on collision, Ravi's father turned a hard left just before entering the bridge, and the car became airborne. It smashed on the rocks of the riverbank 40 feet below, where it was obscured from view. It hit nose first and settled right side up. The truck's driver sped down the road unaware.

CHAPTER

2

GARDEN OAKS, NEW YORK

Michael was absorbed in an article, "New York City Waterfront Vision and Enhancement Strategies," when he heard Julie's key in the front door of their flawlessly decorated Victorian home. He dropped his copy of *The Architect's Newspaper* and sprang into action; he fanned the magazines on the coffee table, picked up Logan's toys and tossed them into the antique basket in the corner, and scanned the room quickly to make sure nothing else was out of place.

He sunk back on the floral fainting couch just as Julie burst in the door like a whirlwind. Her shoulder-length brown hair was perfectly styled. Her designer skirt and jacket were perfectly tailored to her tall, slim frame. She removed her leather sandals and gave the room a quick scan. Walking toward the couch, she pocketed the Silly Putty® egg that Michael had overlooked.

She dropped a department store bag in front of the couch, re-fanned the magazines more to her liking, and then held her hands and one foot out for her husband's inspection.

"What do you think?"

"What do you mean, 'what do I think?'" he asked, laying his paper aside.

"Isn't this just the perfect color of pink? I know I was only going to get a manicure, but…pedicures just feel so good. It's such a luxury to have someone fuss over me." She noticed a loose hair on Michael's shoulder and picked it off.

"Well, I don't think I'd want anyone messing with my feet, but I'm glad you're happy," said Michael from his spot on the couch. "What's in the bag?"

"I unpacked this at the store today, and it just called my name," she said as she reached into the purple sack with the gold lettering, "Elegant Fashions by V, Perfection Is Our Standard."

"I'll wear it tomorrow, shopping—"

"You bought an outfit to shop in? Don't you think that's a bit much?" Michael crossed his arms and let out a deep breath.

"Well…." She held up the brightly colored green and yellow dress with a tag that said, "Made in India." "It's casual and comfortable; the colors are almost neon. It will be perfect for the train and traipsing all over New York tomorrow. Feel how light the fabric is, and of course, I took advantage of the employee discount."

Must count to ten. 1-2-3-4-5-6-7-8-9-10. Deep breath, Michael. OK. "Julie, we've been over this before. Employee discounts don't save you money; they cost you money."

"But I would have bought it anyway."

"It's the 24th of the month. Where are you with your clothing budget?"

"Under."

"But what about this shopping trip?"

"It's exempt. I planned it before the budget was in place. It's not frivolous; I need new clothes for work." She plopped down on the couch next to him.

"And tell me again why you *need* more clothes. I designed you a mammoth walk-in," he spread his arms wide, "and it's bulging at the seams."

"Maybe *need* isn't the right word, but you know how everyone at the store dresses perfectly. When I look good, I feel better about myself. It gives me confidence at work, and people seem to respect me more, so," she twisted her hair around her index finger, "I just buy them, and you know we can certainly afford them. It's my little splurge. We've all got our issues."

"But, Julie, you have so many clothes."

"I know. I'll donate some of them. When I wear something too many times I just feel, I don't know, like a bag lady."

"You are definitely the best dressed *bag lady* in the world. Why don't you take up a hobby that's cheaper, like keeping thoroughbred race horses?"

Julie looked wounded.

"I'll get back on budget in August. I promise."

"I've got to pay down some of these remodeling bills and new furniture you bought—"

"Those are one-time bills, Michael. I won't have to buy a couch or bedroom suite for Logan for years." She hugged him. "I don't mean for you to be stressed about the finances. This will be my final splurge. I promise."

"OK, Julie. I'll try to believe you."

"Mommy," shrieked nine-year-old Logan as he ran into the room.

"Hey, buddy! Give me a hug." Julie wrapped her arms around him and squeezed.

"I missed you today. Ran some errands after work. Did you and dad eat?" She tousled his blond hair and looked into his cobalt blue eyes.

"Yep, my favorites. Peanut butter and jelly, macaroni and cheese, and Popsicles®."

"Well, your dad is quite the gourmet, isn't he?" she smiled as she glanced toward Michael, who had conveniently buried his face in his trade journal.

"Did he say 'Popsicles®?'" asked Julie.

"Hey, we all have our issues."

"Read to me, Mommy!" Logan yanked her by the hand, unaware he was rescuing his dad.

"I'll finish the new book we started yesterday, and, Logan," she tossed him the Silly Putty®, "we've had the conversation before—kitchen table *only*."

Everything in Logan's bedroom was decorated around a cowboy theme—lamp, area rug, curtains, artwork, and trinkets. Cowboy hats, lariats, and bandanas were painted on the headboard.

Logan played contentedly with his Legos® while Julie read page after page of an adventure story about a boy Logan's age who escaped from kidnapping pirates.

"...and after the last pirate walked the plank, Mark turned the ship for home."

Logan jumped up, gave a salute, and announced, "I could do that. I'm brave!"

Julie closed the book. "Well, I think you are brave, but maybe you'd need to be a little older before you take on a vicious band of marauding pirates. Dad and I will always be here to protect you as long as you need us. Go take your bath; then come get me. Don't forget, *all* the Legos® *in* the drawer."

"Mom, at Jeffrey's house he gets to leave them out, and we took the sheets off his bed and made a tent over chairs and then slept in it all night." He smiled broadly at the memory.

"If Jeffrey's mom wants to be messy, that's up to her. I feel better when everything's nice and neat."

"And he doesn't have to make his bed in the morning."

She frowned, "Logan, you know the rules."

Logan glanced at her with a mute appeal.

Julie sat on the couch next to Michael. He closed his trade journal again.

"Nine years old, and he thinks he's ready to take on the world," said Julie, sorting the magazines from newest to oldest.

"Huh?"

"Logan. He thinks he's invincible. So sure he could escape from a band of pirates like the hero in the book."

"That's normal. Little boys are all about action and adventure and pirates' treasure. As a former little boy, trust me. My brothers and I played pirates and cowboys and Indians. We even had intergalactic battles to save the Earth from invading Martians. If it wouldn't run away, we'd strategize how to conquer it."

He sighed, lost in his thoughts. "My brothers and I had so much fun together. I wish Logan had a brother to play with. Just think, you could have had three raiding, looting, pillaging, plundering pirates running all over the place! Aaarrg, matey," he said as he pulled his wife close for a kiss. Julie smiled at his antics, but he caught her sad expression.

"I can promise you, little girls are definitely more about playing dress up than saving the planet."

He took her hand and pretended to admire her nails. "So are big girls, too. It's just the perfect color of pink!" he squealed excitedly. Julie pulled her hands away and smiled. She prepared to whack him with the pillow, but he was saved again when Logan called.

"I'm ready."

They both entered his bedroom.

"OK, TV off for the night," said Julie, interrupting the theme song for the Andy Griffith Show. The small, flat screen TV was part of a media center in Logan's room that included all the latest technology.

"Look at you, you're wearing your cowboy pajamas. Maybe you'll dream about riding horses tonight. Jump in, partner," she said as Michael folded back the down comforter, exposing the cowboy sheets. After tucking him in and a little more chitchat, she folded her hands. "Let's pray. Now I lay me down to sleep, I pray the Lord my soul to keep. If I should die before I wake, I pray the Lord my soul to take. Amen."

"Amen," he repeated.

"Amen," said Michael.

She sat on the bed next to him.

"I get extra kisses tonight because I'll be gone when you get up. I'm meeting grandpa for breakfast, and then I'm going to New York. Remember?" Logan nodded.

"You and dad will have a fun weekend. He has all kinds of things planned for you two. And," she said, scanning the room, "you did a great job picking up your toys!" She covered his face with kisses and he grinned.

"Sleep well," said Michael, giving his son a kiss. "Don't forget, it's just you and me," he lowered his voice, "and Popsicles® the whole weekend!" Logan gave him a high-five. Julie gave Michael a look that implied, *Well, maybe I need to talk to you about that.*

Julie and Michael headed for the kitchen. While washing her hands with anti-bacterial soap, Julie said, "I have a surprise. Look in the freezer. Crab and brie quiche!"

As the quiche heated in the microwave, she wiped the fingerprints off the door and quickly wiped the sink and the toaster. Then she washed her hands again.

"Michael, how soon do you think you'll be able to get the mudroom painted?"

Please, not with the paint again! he thought. "Not this weekend. I'll be a stay-at-home dad for the next two days. Got a lot of things planned to keep us busy." The microwave beeped, and she handed him one of the plates.

"Now that I've finalized the decision on the paint color, I just can't wait to see it on the walls."

"Just like the other *two* colors I painted in there?" He crossed his arms.

She was oblivious to his irritation.

"This color will be perfect; the others were close. This is it."

"I've got so much leftover paint in the carriage house I could start a business, Julie."

"Trust me."

"That's what you said about Oyster Shell Grey and Amber Fields," his volume was rising.

"Michael, after living through a major renovation for the last 18 months, the end is finally in sight. Let's try to finish as friends."

He let out a sigh. "A worthy endeavor." He toasted her with his plate.

"I know this paint will be perfect. Lisa painted her living room Mocha Toffee Coffee, and it's beautiful. I looked at the paint swatch while she was out of the room." *At least I hope it will look perfect in my mudroom.*

Michael sat his empty plate on the massive island, and Julie quickly moved it to the dishwasher.

"Ever since Lisa had her home featured in *Victorian Living* magazine, all you girls are trying to out-decorate each other—"

"I know, but my house is just as nice as hers. I sent photos to *Victorian Homes* and *Country Victorian*. I just know they'll call." Julie wiped down the countertops as she spoke.

"Honey, it's really all right if they don't. I'll still love you."

"It has to get painted right away. Everything has to be finished when they call. I don't have a lot of free time with my work schedule."

"Honey, the way it's going, I don't think the house will ever be totally done. Just relax and enjoy the fruits of your labor. You've worked so hard all these months and done an amazing job."

She paused from her cleaning and beamed.

"Julie, the house is awesome. It's authentic right down to the bedpans! I just want you to enjoy it. Remember what you read the other day? 'Work without striving, rest without guilt'"?

Julie's eyes scanned the custom-made oak cabinetry with leaded glass insets, the reproduction 1850 cookstove with nickel trim, and the antique pie safe.

"Do you really like it? Are you really satisfied?"

He gave her a big hug. "Honey, since meeting you, I have a whole new appreciation for the beauty of a plinth block and the elegance of a corbel. I'm more than satisfied. You are awesome."

After her 20-minute routine of skin care, body lotion, and essential oils, Julie climbed in bed next to Michael.

"Smells good. What is that?" Michael snuggled next to her. She relaxed into his arms.

"It's Himalayan geranium and pomegranate oil. It combats premature aging."

"That was going to be my first guess."

"It's imported."

"Yeah, the Himalayan part tipped me off."

Julie sat up and set the alarm clock. "Meeting dad at 7:15 right across from the train station."

"You looking forward to that?" Michael raised his eyebrows.

"Not really. You know how he is."

"Like trying to hug a porcupine."

"Exactly," she said, setting the clock back on the nightstand.

"Well, don't let it ruin your sleep."

"I'll try."

"Something strange happened today," said Michael. "Coming home, I stopped by the bookstore to get my journal, and there was a homeless woman—"

"A homeless person in Garden Oaks? Oh, my gosh."

"Not a person, a family. She had two kids. One about Logan's age. They were so dirty. I just kept wondering how someone ends up like that."

"They end up like that because they don't want to work." She rolled to her side and put her arm around her husband.

"The kids just, well, they seemed so sad. It was like there was no hope or life in their eyes. They should be carefree. Where are they sleeping tonight?"

"They're resourceful. They'll be fine. There are shelters for people like them in other cities."

"I gave them $10 so they could eat."

She kissed him. "You're a soft touch, Michael. Good night."

Julie dozed. She dreamed she shopped in an exclusive New York department store wearing her new, multi-colored dress. The store was chic and glitzy.

I love this blue sequined jacket. She slipped it on in front of the mirror. *It looks even better on. I have to have this. The girls at the store will be so jealous.* She flipped the price tag over. *Yikes, I can't spend that—$1200?* She reluctantly returned it to the rack.

Look at this—perfect for fall. These yummy colors, burnt orange, brown—$1325? I love it, but I can't afford that for one dress. Each highly desirable garment was more expensive than the last. A disappointed Julie continued looking and longing for the clothes she could not afford. *Why am I tormenting myself? I just can't afford these clothes today.* The immaculately dressed salesperson strolled by Julie, eyeing her as if she was a cockroach needing to be stepped on.

"If you see anything you can afford, let me know!" She turned to the other salesperson, and they both cackled. Julie caught a glimpse of herself in the mirror, and her eyes narrowed. Her new dress was dirty and torn. She looked at her hands; there was dirt under her fingernails. Her nose wrinkled in disgust. She looked back at the saleslady, who flashed her a superior grin.

Her cheeks flushed and she fled from the store.

She found herself standing in front of the bookstore back in Garden Oaks. Logan tapped her arm. He wore old clothes and dirt smudged his face. His tired tennis shoes had a rip across the toe.

"Mom, I'm really hungry. I haven't eaten since yesterday. Can I have some macaroni and cheese or a peanut butter and jelly sandwich?"

"I have to get some money first." A businessman walked by, chatting on his cell. Julie took a deep breath and stepped forward.

"Excuse me. My son hasn't eaten. Could you please—"

The man looked irritated and hurried past, dismissing her with a wave of his hand.

She stepped forward, approaching a 20-ish guy walking his dog.

"Excuse me. Can you spare a dollar for a burger? For my son, he hasn't eaten—"

The man cast a pitiful glance and held up his hand as he walked by. "Sorry."

"Mom, I'm really hungry."

"I know, sweetie. I'm working on it." She hugged him as she choked back tears. The next pedestrian was Aunt Bea, from the Andy Griffith Show, who was smiling broadly carrying an embroidered handkerchief. Julie hurried to her side.

"Please, can you help—" blurted Julie, feeling strangely disembodied.

As Aunt Bea smiled, her eyes seemed to dance.

"Of course I'll help you, Julie." She laid her arm on Julie's shoulder. "You look a little down on your luck today."

"Yes, I don't even know what happened, but, yes, I need help."

"Well, let me see what I have in my bag." She rummaged around and pulled out a live baby bird. "I guess this would taste good on the barbeque grill," said Aunt Bea, her face suddenly contorting into a crazed look.

That's totally disgusting!

"Fly away, little birdie," Aunt Bea tossed it into the air. It flapped its wings and was gone.

"What else do I have in here? I know, this could be quite helpful." She pulled out a handful of Legos® and shouted, "Happy New Year," while tossing them like confetti over Logan. Her face flushed with happiness. "Pick them up! Pick them all up!" she shrieked, flinging her arms above her head and dancing the Watusi.

"Don't you have anything that can help us?" pleaded Julie.

"Well, I suppose I do. Where is it?" She rummaged in her bag and pulled out the newest issue of *Victorian Living Magazine*. "Here, on page 37," she said, flipping the pages. "Have you seen Lisa's living room? It's Mocha Toffee Coffee, and it's absolutely gorgeous. It's the cover story, you know?"

3

After several hours, Ravi regained consciousness on the car's back floor, clutching his Silly Putty®. He ached all over, his left arm had a huge gash, he was bruised, but nothing seemed broken. Unaware of what had happened he cried out, "Momma! Daddy! Momma! Daddy!"

His mother's arm was draped over her seat, but there was no life in it. His father was dead, too. All the windows were smashed. With great effort, he pulled himself up on the backseat, and the shattered glass cut into his knees. He placed the astronomy book gently into the suitcase, threw it outside, and climbed out the window.

The sun was going down, and night was already creeping into the valley. The torrential rain continued. The front of the car was smashed into his parents' seats. Ravi slid under the back of the car next to the rear tire to find shelter. He clutched the Silly Putty® egg. His blue shorts and yellow t-shirt provided little warmth, and his teeth chattered. He fell into shock and dozed.

At 2:30 A.M. he awoke with a start. His body ached, his leg was stiff, and the left side of his face was so swollen he could barely see out of that eye. When he remembered where he was, he cried again. Through sobs he pleaded with his Hindu god, "O great Ganesh, rescue me."

Ganesh did not hear Ravi's prayer, but there is one true God who did. He is the Creator of the universe and Ravi's creator. And even though Ravi had never heard of Him, He knew everything about Ravi.

Ravi, before I formed you in the womb, I knew you.[1] You have a great destiny. Now you must leave this place.

Even though Ravi didn't hear his Creator God out loud, he knew he had to walk. To where, he didn't know. Ravi struggled out from under the car, held the back bumper, and pulled himself upright. He cried out in pain. In a few seconds, he was soaked.

He was careful to keep his back turned because of the hideousness that lay in the front seat. Ravi opened his suitcase, carefully placed the Silly Putty® inside, and grabbed his grey cardigan sweater. Pain shot through his body as he stretched his arms behind him to put it on. It was soon soaked and did nothing to warm him.

He looked at the massive hillside looming above him, took a deep breath, and began the climb. Though the rain was subsiding, the hillside was muddy and slick. Each step sent shooting pain through his body, and several times he slid almost back to the bottom, scraping and bumping his chin, knees, and the palms of his hands.

He climbed again but realized he couldn't make it carrying the suitcase. He removed the astronomy book and put the Silly Putty® in his pocket. He let the suitcase go and watched it slide to the bottom of the hill, spilling its contents.

After continuing to struggle, he reluctantly lay the astronomy book among the branches of a bush and ran his hand over the cover. Balancing carefully, he removed his sweater and gently laid it over the book. He patted the egg in his pocket and climbed again.

After a 20-minute laborious climb, he reached the ridge and rolled over onto the flat ground. Dirt was caked under each fingernail, and his new clothes were covered with mud and blood. He'd lost one sandal on the steep bank and left it behind.

He crawled back toward the edge and peered down into the ravine, but the car was obscured from view. With fresh tears in his eyes, he crawled behind a bush beside the bridge, clutched his Silly Putty® and fell asleep.

Ravi woke with a start in the darkness. He sat up quickly and grabbed his head. It and his whole body throbbed. He slowly lay down again, as memories of the bone-jarring accident, his mother's limp hand, and worse played in his mind again and again. He grabbed his Silly Putty® and held it to his heart—the last remnant of his normal life.

Then the rain began again, first a sprinkle, then the lightning and thunder, then the downpour. Soon he was soaked and shivering again. *I want to go home. I want mommy and daddy!* His child's mind could not conceive of what had happened to him in the last 12 hours. His parents were dead. His home was gone. His friends were gone, and at nine years old, he was on his own. It was entirely too much for anyone, especially a young boy, to deal with.

He heard the voice again telling him to "walk."

4

Julie managed to shut off the alarm before it woke Michael. After showering and getting dressed, she fussed with her hair until it was just right. She tried three shades of lipstick before settling on just the perfect one. In her large walk-in closet, she accessorized the colorful dress from India with the perfect bangles and sandals. After looking through her earrings twice, she settled on a shimmering yellow pair. She looked in the mirror — disappointed.

She grabbed her large green designer bag and loaded it with a change of underwear, her makeup bag, hand sanitizer, and her migraine medicine. *I'll just buy something to wear tomorrow so I don't have to take a suitcase.*

I love this bag. She ran her hands over the soft leather. *It's big enough to hold everything.* She put the strap over her shoulder and reexamined herself in the mirror. *Perfect.* She headed to Logan's room.

The sight of her sleeping son brought last night's dream to the surface. *Logan and I homeless, how strange. Aunt Bea! Oh, my gosh!* She shook her head and immediately dismissed it. She smoothed out his cowboy comforter and sat beside him. He awoke, but was still groggy. She kissed him several times and he rolled over and dozed.

She stood up and caught her reflection in his full-length mirror. She paused and analyzed. After fluffing her hair again, she called for a cab.

I think I'll take the paper to read on the train. Going down the front stairs, she heard a squeak so faint she couldn't tell its origin. She paused to listen. *There it is again.* Julie followed the stepping stone path around her English country garden. Tucked between a coiled garden hose and an empty terra cotta pot was a trembling baby bird.

"You poor thing. How in the world? There's not even a tree close." She dropped to her knees. "Well, we can't let Aunt Bea find you, and I have to get you before Patchwork does. You're a little robin, aren't you?" Julie scooped up the little bird. "I'll take care of you; you'll be OK."

She hurried to her parlor. In the corner was an elaborate Victorian birdcage on an ornate wire stand. Julie hesitated, then removed the skillfully arranged silk flowers stem by stem from the cage. *I guess I can re-do these when I get back.*

In a short time the bird was resting in a tissue-lined Lennox cereal bowl in the birdcage, which was now resettled in the kitchen. After printing the results of a quick Internet search on caring for baby birds, she wrote a note for Michael and Logan with the phone number for the nearest wildlife rehab center.

"You don't have to be afraid. I won't hurt you. Here's something for you to eat and drink." She sat a little water and some moist cat food in the cage. "I can't stay and take care of you, but I promise you'll be OK." She washed her hands thoroughly. As she was sanitizing the counter closest to the cage, the cabbie honked.

This traffic is unbearable, she thought as they waited on a red light. *I should have left earlier. Dad hates to be kept waiting. I don't need a lecture before breakfast, or during, for that matter. I've had enough for one lifetime.*

She sighed and distracted herself by stroking the soft leather of her green designer bag, her favorite bag.

Soft as butter. It's perfect. She stopped to admire her manicure as she spread her fingers then turned her attention to the yellow and green colors in her Indian dress and the sparkling bangles. *Looking good, Julie. You're looking really good today.*

After paying the driver, Julie took several deep breaths and walked to the restaurant. Her dad's car was there, and she checked her watch again to make sure she wasn't late. *You can do this, Julie. You can.* She checked her reflection in the window before grabbing the brass handle and swinging open the restaurant door.

Forty minutes later, Julie slunk from the restaurant and crossed the street to the train station.

"The man is incapable of saying anything kind. He never likes what I wear! He didn't even like my bag!" She gritted her teeth in frustration.

As she arrived on the empty platform, the train was pulling slowly from the station. The conductor stood on the steps of the passenger loading platform and called out, "Julie, quick." He held out his hand as the train lurched forward.

I must be late! Without stopping to think why this man would know her name, she ran and he pulled her up.

"Good show," said the distinguished gentleman as he tipped his bowler hat with a flourish and bowed slightly. He pulled out his pocket watch and said, "You're right on time."

He's impeccably dressed in that white suit, thought Julie.

"My name is Mr. Dove, and it is my pleasure to serve you on your special journey today."

"I like your accent. Australian?"

"Heavens no. British." He held open the door and led her through several deserted cars.

Not many people going to New York today, thought Julie.

"The dining car has been specially prepared, and your party is waiting for you," he said. "Please enjoy."

"My party?" Before she could stop him, he was gone. She looked around at the drab interior. *I think it's time for an update.*

One lone man sat in the corner booth. The table was covered in white linen. There was an abundance of food. Three slender burgundy tapers burned in an ornate gold holder.

He motioned to her. Her first response was to immediately decline. *Sure, I'll go sit with some stranger on a deserted train. I don't think so.* She shook her head and turned to go. But without knowing why, she turned back. He motioned toward the empty seat again. She felt drawn. *How strange. It just feels like I need to be here.* Before she realized it, she was walking. He smiled as she approached. She laid her green purse in the booth and slid in opposite him.

What's all this food? Crab legs with butter, mu shu pork, spring rolls, a beautiful garden salad, sliced nectarines, fresh strawberries, blackberry cobbler with vanilla ice cream. My favorite foods! She looked up for the first time and stammered, "H-how could you know this? How?" He smiled as he picked up a large glass pitcher and poured.

Apricot nectar?

She stared at the pitcher containing her favorite drink. "How do you know me? I *demand* you tell me who you are!" She hit her fist on the table for emphasis. She felt exposed, and she didn't like it, but she did not feel endangered. *Maybe I should just leave, now.* But something about the situation was too intriguing.

Her brow furrowed. Her brain scanned and discarded possible scenarios.

"I know! Michael set this up as a joke, right?"

The dark-skinned man with the shoulder-length brown hair, wearing a white robe, smiled the most welcoming smile she'd ever seen. When she looked into His eyes, she felt a new, pure, invigorating sensation—perfect love. It seemed to radiate into every cell. She not only felt disarmed, she felt captivated. *So peaceful.*

Julie, I not only know everything about you, but I created you. My Father and I planned when you were to be born before We created the world.[1] I've walked down the corridor of your life and seen the very end. Every day of your life is recorded in your heavenly book.

When He spoke her name, she recognized Him. She stared in unbelief. *This can't be happening.* At first she thought her heart might stop beating. Then another overwhelming feeling of being loved—truly loved—deeply and fully engulfed her.

"Jesus?"

He smiled warmly and spoke, *103,542.*

She didn't understand and continued staring as she reveled in the incredible feeling.

Of course, after you brush, you'll be down to 103,401.

She still didn't understand and remained quiet, choosing to bask in the overwhelming feeling of being perfectly loved.

He smiled. *Haven't you read in My Word that I know the exact number of hairs on your head?*

"Yes, but I thought that was just...." her voice trailed off.

You thought that was just something someone wrote. Well, it is. Matthew wrote it under the inspiration of the Holy Spirit and I promise you, My Word is life and truth.[2]

She glanced out the window, amazed that each time He spoke, she heard thunder and saw flashes of lightning.

Julie, My Word says that thunder and lightning emanate from My Father's throne,[3] and I assure you, every word is the truth. He paused, and the thunder and lightning did, too.

"How? Why can I see You?"

Let's just say I toned Myself down today. If I appeared in My radiant splendor and matchless glory, you, and everything else, would be consumed. But, Julie, I'm really with you every minute of every day.

He smiled and put His hand on top of hers. She saw the nail scar and was overwhelmed again by another wave of His love for her. It burned like a warm ember in her chest.

I have a favor to ask of you, but your shopping stop is coming up.

"NO," she blurted and grabbed His hand in hers. "No shopping today."

No shopping today?

"No, I want to stay."

If the things you strive for in this world—money, recognition, houses, or clothes, He said with a grin, *don't really satisfy, what does that mean?*

She shrugged and made a questioning gesture, still clasping His hand and feeling totally enveloped in warmth.

It means, My dear one, that you were created for a different world—for My heavenly Kingdom. I planted the seeds of longing for a perfect world inside you. The eternity in Me calls to the eternity in you so you desire to be loved unconditionally. But no person on Earth can do that. Only I can love you perfectly.

I see your wounded heart, mishandled by your father.

Julie bristled. "What's he got to do with anything?"

Julie, I'm not like your dad.

Julie could see something like a movie of herself from the past. She watched as little nine-year-old Julie had dressed herself and walked through the living room headed toward the bus stop. Her dad was in one of his moods.

As a little girl you tried so hard, but the praise and love that you needed never came. It wasn't you, Julie. He was hurting from your mom's death.

"You were supposed to clean this place up last night."

"I had home—"

"And what do you think you're wearing? Those don't match." She could feel her lower lip start to quiver.

"My clothes are dirty."

"Those don't match. You look like Bozo, the clown! Everyone's going to laugh at you, and for good reason."

Little Julie hid in the coat closet, arms wrapped around her knees, rocking and sobbing in the dark.

Outside the coat closet her father pounded his palm against his forehead, then reached for the doorknob—but lost his nerve.

But it crushed you, and inside you're still that little girl just trying to do something right—anything, just to prove your worth.

She nodded in agreement as tears welled in her eyes.

"It drives me."

Since you can't be perfect, you've tried to numb that heart pain by acquiring possessions, and when the newness wears off, you do it all again. I call it the "do-it-wrong-harder principle." But these counterfeits can't fill your longings either. Competing, scrapping, posturing for status, trying to impress are all like fighting for a first class cabin—on the Titanic. This whole world is going down, and the things that people strive and even kill for are going down with it.

I'm here today, Julie, to tell you that your life is a vapor.[4] *It's like the flowers of the field, blooming today, faded and gone tomorrow.*[5] He opened His hand to reveal a beautiful pink tropical flower, and she watched as it wilted, turned brown, shriveled, and turned to dust, which settled gently on the tablecloth. He held out His empty palm for her to see.

Gone. Decades will hurry by. You will turn around a few more times, and your grandchildren will be weeping by your casket. I'm offering you a choice— live unsatisfied with the counterfeits you long for today or learn to live for My eternal Kingdom. When you leave here, you can bring nothing of this world along. Not your Victorian house that you traded 18 months of your life to restore, nor the antiques in it.

One day I will come in the sky to gather My own, and I will tear the veil that separates time and eternity. The veil that separates My eternal home from this temporary Titanic ship you're journeying on. You will live forever, Julie; it's just a question of where.

"I prayed in Sunday school for You to save me when I was seven."

I heard that prayer, but you can't call Me Savior and not call Me Lord.

She looked away. "I can't be good enough. I've tried," her voice dropped, "and I've tried again. Every day and I just can't...." She ran her finger absent-mindedly through the flower dust.

No, you can't be perfect. You'd have to be 100 percent good 100 percent of the time. I'm the only one who did that.

She sighed. As He revealed His holiness and a snippet of His pure shining glory, she became aware of her sinfulness in a way she had never experienced. She felt crushed under a great weight. She turned from Him, compelled to slink away in shame.

Wait, Julie. That's why I left Heaven, put on a human body, and died for your sins. I give forgiveness and salvation to those who trust Me as a free gift. Obedience, through My grace, is your gratitude gift back to Me.

"I told you, I can't. I, I hate myself sometimes...." A tear rolled down her face. He gently wiped it away with a nail-pierced hand.

I know, Julie, He said with great kindness. *It pains Me because you hate yourself all the time. You've taken on the goal of perfection, and you're miserable because you can't attain it. When it's seems almost within reach, it slips away again, leaving you feeling like a failure.*

I want to teach you the difference between rebellion and immaturity. On the outside, they look the same, but inwardly they are very different. I'll show you.

They are standing in a pigpen in front of an old red barn. Julie looks around in surprise and then tries to make sure she doesn't get mud on her sandals. A pig and a lamb are in the mud hole.

Julie, what do you see?

"Um, a pig and a lamb in the mud?"

Jesus waded into the mud, dirtying His hands and garment, and gathered the lamb in His arms, stroking it gently.

The pig and the lamb both ended up in the mud, but the lamb wants to get out, and the pig is planning his next mud bath. You can't see the heart like I can.

He brings the lamb to her; she pets its head, being careful not to dirty her hands.

"Hi, little one."

As He speaks He rubs His nail-pierced hand over the muddied wool and it becomes white as snow.

My darling Julie, you call yourself rebellious, but I see you as immature. I'm overwhelmed with love and enjoyment toward the unattaining yet sincere believer. My heart is also overwhelmed with love toward the rebellious. I love them, but I can't enjoy them. They cause Me great grief because their choices lead to their destruction. As deeply as I love, so deeply do I grieve their unnecessary demise.

He puts the lamb down and Julie strokes it.

But, my darling Julie, He paused to look into her eyes, *you call yourself rebellious. I see you as immature, but lovely.[6] In your immaturity, you'll end up back in the mud hundreds of times, but I made provision for your sin when I died on the cross. I took your punishment as if it was My own. Accept My gifts of forgiveness, mercy, salvation, and grace that I long to give you in exchange for your failures. Come to Me, confess your sins, and I will forgive you. I will help pull you from the mud and clean you up.*

"I want to run and hide when I… choose the mud." She couldn't meet His gaze and glanced at the ground.

Look at Me, Julie. I want to see your beautiful face. That is the biggest lie of My enemy. He wants to destroy you by keeping you away from Me. His voice whispers shame and lies, saying that you can't come to Me until you're perfect. The opposite is true; you can't get free of your sin until you come to Me.

When you are overcome by sin, run, jump on My lap, and say, "Smother me with Your love." Coming to Me for forgiveness and power is the only way you'll ever get free. Wallowing in shame and avoiding Me only sinks you deeper in the mud.

"But there are areas in my life where I can't get free." Stress lines formed on her brow. "I'm a mess. How can You love me?"

Julie, you don't ever have to twist My arm to get Me to care. I love you because I am love, not because you are worthy. I love you because I can't not love you. Love is My nature. It's who I am. All My children are My favorite.

If you spent the rest of your days as a shopping addict, I'd never love you any less. My love is unconditional. It has nothing to do with your performance and everything to do with Me.

"I just can't believe it. But I want to…" she said with a weak smile.

He holds out a bottle with a rubber nipple.

Would you like to feed My lamb? Julie smiles as the lamb enthusiastically drinks. She gently strokes it.

You must renew your mind to replace the lies you believe by reading truth in My Word. Then to get knowledge from your head, He places His hand over His heart, *down to where you believe, it must pass between your lips. Confess this truth over your life, frequently and out loud, to break the lies' stronghold.*

Pray daily, ask Me to tell you what I think about you. Right now, you spend more time in deception, listening to My enemy's accusations that say My love is weak, conditional, and like the love of people who have wounded you. Run to Me in your brokenness and failure. I promise I will never turn you away.

The corners of her mouth curled slightly as she tried to take in this wonderful, new information.

You think that because you just discovered a new place of darkness in your heart that I am also disgusted, because I just discovered it, too. But remember, I saw your whole life, each bad choice you would make, and I still chose you. I know all your future failures that you aren't even aware of. And I still love you. You can't shock Me. As long as you ask for forgiveness and help, we'll get out of every mud hole you stumble into.

And as you call to Me in your failure, you'll learn I'm not like your earthly father. He lacks the ability to encourage and applaud you. His brokenness left you believing the lie that you could never measure up.

Julie, I'm not your opponent. I'm your biggest fan. As you learn more about Me, you'll learn to trust and love Me. I give you My righteousness as a gift, and you don't have to perform to get Me to love you.

Wouldn't you rather go for a walk with Me in the cool of the evening than knock yourself out trying to impress Me with your "good works"?

She again saw His beautiful nail prints as she placed her hands on His. She inhaled deeply as she felt the weight lift.

"Thank You, Lord."

You are so welcome. I'd die all over again, even if it were only for you. A huge crack of lightning hit the weather vane on the barn and she jumped.

I really meant that. They both laughed.

Back on the train when they quit laughing, He picked up a dish and offered it to her. *Let's eat dessert first! Blackberry cobbler, extra blackberries, thickened with tapioca, not flour. Thin crust and vanilla ice cream.*

"My favorite desert as a child. It's been here for an hour, and the ice cream isn't even melted."

You don't like it melted.

She smiled, and they ate and talked and laughed as thunder and lightning ebbed and flowed. After she tried a little from each dish and drank three glasses of apricot nectar, Jesus said, *Julie, it's almost time for you to leave.*

"No, Lord, no!" she grabbed His hands. A stricken look crossed her face.

"No, Lord," is the most common oxymoron I hear. I can be your Lord, or you can tell Me no, but it can't be both.

"Forgive me—Lord. Now that I've found You, I just never want to leave You."

I understand, but you didn't find Me, Julie. I found you. I've pursued you all your life, and I'll never stop. I am always with you.[7] *I promised that in My Word. You just can't see Me like I've allowed you to now. I opened your spiritual eyes for a brief moment, but My presence is always with you. I promise.*

Before you leave, remember I have a favor to ask of you. Do you love Me?

"Yes, Lord."

Then feed My lambs.

"What?"

Feed My lambs.

"What does that mean?"

It means that I have a special group of lambs, My precious orphans. I've spent this time with you to prepare you to feed them physically and spiritually. I am the light of the world,[8] and all My followers are light-bearers.

"Yes, Lord. I'd do anything for You," she said, gazing at His eyes of love focused on her.

I'm giving you this Bible, He handed her a plain-looking black Bible. *Written in the front are some Scriptures in the order you'll need them. My truth will help guide you on this adventure.* He held up a colorful pair of dangly earrings. *I know you like jewelry. These might come in handy.*

"Oh, they're perf—they're wonderful." She puts them on.

It's time for you to leave, but remember, I'll always be with you, Julie.

He walked her to the back platform. She was the only passenger disembarking. After a long hug, she went down the steps backward, still holding His hands and gazing into His eyes. He let go of her hands as the train slowly moved from the station. She followed it to the very end of the platform. "Good-bye," she shouted while waving. She didn't take her eyes off Him until the train disappeared in the distance. "That was amazingly, wonderful, incredible!" She sighed deeply and turned around.

Before she could stop herself, she let out a piercing scream and clamped both hands over her mouth. Hundreds of dark-haired, sari-clad women and Indian men stared at her. The sign above the platform read, "Mumbai."

5

Ravi had been on the road for six days. He was hungry and weak. His wounds were constantly exposed and painful. In an effort to protect the bottom of his feet, he switched his remaining sandal from one foot to the other. It had only resulted in both feet getting cut and bruised.

Spurred on by the voice that told him he must walk, and having no better option, he walked. From morning to night, he walked. Cars flew by him on the country roads, going too fast and passing on hills.

As Ravi limped through the rain, the sun disappeared behind the horizon. A black Mercedes stopped and a well-dressed Indian man, wearing a gold chain, got out and threw his suit jacket over Ravi's shoulders.

"What happened? Let me get you out of this rain. I'm Mr. Shah." He gently picked Ravi up and placed him in the front seat, then turned on the heater and pointed the vents toward him.

"Where are you going on a night like this? Do your parents know you're out?" At the mention of his parents Ravi teared up. Mr. Shah raised his eyebrows and grinned slightly. Ravi anxiously rolled the Silly Putty® egg between his fingers.

"You must be hungry. I'll take you home, clean you up, feed you." They arrived at an average-looking house surrounded by a high wall with an iron gate, a two-car garage, and a shed in the back.

Mr. Shah put his arm gently on Ravi's shoulder as they entered the house.

This is a palace, thought Ravi. The inside of the house was decorated far beyond what the outside would indicate. The first thing Ravi saw was a grand spiral staircase leading upstairs. The walls were rich blue and purple. Ravi gazed at the elaborate crystal chandelier hung from the high ceiling.

It sparkles. In the main hall there was a large carpet surrounded by several leather sofas and chairs. The side tables were elaborately carved teak wood.

He must be rich, thought Ravi, *with carpets in almost every room.*

A small spider monkey, wearing a fez and a vest with several large pockets, leapt from the back of the couch and landed in front of Ravi. It bowed and tipped its hat. It reached in a pocket and handed Ravi a candy. Mr Shah smiled. It reached in another pocket and gave Ravi a coin.

"Why you little...." Mr. Shah swooped down, grabbed the monkey, and emptied its pockets of a carved elephant, reading glasses, pocketknife, and a small screwdriver while the monkey screeched. He grabbed it by the scruff of the neck and flung it into an ornate cage.

"If it's one thing I can't stand, it's a thief! Well, Ravi, let's get you cleaned up. Are you hungry?"

Ravi nodded vigorously. "And thirsty."

Mr. Shah snapped his fingers and the maid appeared.

"Bring a large glass of papaya juice for my friend, Ravi." The maid returned with the juice. Ravi immediately drank it all and let out a deep sigh.

"Well, you were thirsty, weren't you, Ravi?"

He nodded.

"Let's get you cleaned up and then you can eat." Mr. Shah nodded to the maid who escorted Ravi to an upstairs bedroom. The handrail on the wall helped Ravi pull himself up each step, in spite of his pain.

"You'll sleep here." Ravi scanned the room. It was decorated with bright, primary colors, had large pictures of cartoon characters on the wall and several plastic bins overflowing with toys. The thick mat on the floor was in the corner with colorful pillows on top.

"The bath is there," she pointed. "When you're done, you will find clean clothes," said the maid with no emotion.

The bathroom was as beautiful as the bedroom. Blue and orange tile covered the walls and floor. A toothbrush and toothpaste lay on the sink. Ravi took off his blood-stained yellow t-shirt and blue jean shorts and filled the bucket from the sink and stepped into the shower. *I'm covered with bruises.* The warm water stung his wounds, but it was one of the first normal things that had happened to him since the accident. *I am so hungry.* He washed as fast as he could, then wrapped himself in the large, fluffy orange towel. He tried to avoid hitting his open wounds as he patted himself dry.

The new clothes were on the mat. He dressed as quickly as his injured body would allow and limped downstairs, clutching the handrail.

Mr. Shah was already at the table sipping chai.

"Welcome, Ravi. I have a great dinner planned for you." He motioned to the chair beside him, snapped his fingers, and the maid appeared with a bowl of lentil dahl.

So hungry, but I must mind my manners. Ravi put the napkin on his lap and took a modest-sized bite, resisting the urge to pick up the bowl and hurriedly drink it.

"Well, Ravi. I see you are quite the cultured gentleman. Did your parents teach you manners?"

At the mention of his parents, Ravi stared at the soup and fought back tears.

"Where are your parents?"

Tears spilled over Ravi's cheeks as he continued staring in silence.

Good, thought Mr. Shah, *no one to look for you.*

"Ravi," he said, laying his arm around his shoulder, "I'm going to take good care of you. Have some more of that soup. Did you see the toys in your room?" Ravi shook his head and took another bite, while his left hand felt for the plastic egg in his pocket. It wasn't there. He jumped up, wailing.

"Where is it? It's in my old clothes." He hobbled up the stairs, his body aching and his heart pounding. The towel and his old clothes were gone. A wave of despair washed over Ravi, and he hurried, as fast as he could, back down to Mr. Shah. "My clothes, my old clothes. It had my egg. IT HAD MY EGG!"

"Calm down, Ravi. I'll help. What do you need?"

"My egg." He flailed his hands as he shouted. "It was in my old clothes. I need my egg. Please, please, help me."

Mr. Shah rose from his chair and wrapped his arms around Ravi, rocking him back and forth. "Calm down, Ravi. I'll help you." He called to the maid. Ravi continued bawling.

"Will you please bring Ravi's *old* clothes?" Mr. Shah shouted to the maid. "It seems there was something quite valuable to him in the pocket."

The maid disappeared while Mr. Shah tried to reassure Ravi. She entered carrying the red plastic egg.

"Well, don't delay; bring it to the boy. Can't you see he's half mad?"

Ravi clutched the egg to his chest and stood breathing deeply.

"It's OK, Ravi," he hugged him again. "You and your egg are safe. I'll protect you both. You can trust me." As he spoke, he felt Ravi's tight little body relax slightly into his arms. After several minutes, he released him.

"Sit down and eat, Ravi. I know you are hungry. Dry those tears and act like the big boy I know you are."

Each dish the maid brought seemed to taste better than the one before. Ravi ate in silence as Mr. Shah talked on and on.

"My wife and I had three daughters, but Ravi, I always longed for a son. I can tell you're a fine boy.."

When dinner was over Ravi was full. He laid his napkin on the table and loaded the remainder of the flat bread onto it.

"Ravi, what are you doing?"

"For tomorrow," he said, somewhat embarrassed.

"Ravi," said Mr. Shah with a smile. "I told you I'd take care of you. When you wake up, breakfast will be waiting. Trust me. Remember, I promised I will protect you, and I will."

It was hard to do, but Ravi obediently returned the bread. He looked to Mr. Shah for directions.

"Let me take you to your room, son." Mr. Shah gently picked him up and carried him up the stairs. "I saw you limping." He opened the door and set Ravi on his feet.

"There are plenty of toys to keep you busy. Here are some crayons and paper and a few books on the shelf."

"I like to read," whispered Ravi, who stared at the floor.

"What did you say?"

"I like to read," he spoke a little louder as he perused the bookshelf for an astronomy book.

"From the time I laid eyes on you, I said to myself, 'Now here's a smart boy.' You stay in your room tonight and I'll come get you for breakfast. Good night, Ravi, sleep well," said Mr. Shah as he shut and locked the door behind him.

Nothing in the toy box was appealing. He picked a comic book off the shelf and climbed on the mat. As he read the first page, he carefully mashed the putty flat and pushed it on the main character. He peeled it off and smiled. "Tall," he stretched the putty vertically. "Fat," he stretched it horizontally. After copying several more characters he wadded the putty back into a ball, put it in the egg, and clutched it to his heart. He was soon asleep, his body battered and exhausted and his soul even more so.

Ravi was in a deep sleep when the maid knocked on his door the next morning.

"Time for breakfast. Get up," said the maid with a terse voice. She unlocked the door and tossed Ravi's old clothes inside. "Put these on and hurry down to breakfast."

Even though his hurting, exhausted body wanted to stay under the fluffy comforter, Ravi forced himself to get out of bed with the promise of a wonderful breakfast.

Why can't I wear my new clothes? he wondered as he dressed. He transferred his Silly Putty® to the pocket of his dirty, blue shorts. In just a few minutes, he was downstairs. Mr. Shah sat at the table finishing what was obviously a lavish breakfast. He lay a half-eaten pastry on his plate and stood to greet Ravi.

"Good morning, son. Did you sleep well?"

Ravi nodded to the floor, yes.

"My clothes?" he looked toward Mr. Shah. "They still have the...." He pointed to the bloodstains. The maid brought a carafe to refill Mr. Shah's coffee.

"I'm sorry, Ravi; it was the maid's fault." He scowled at her. "You know I told you to get Ravi a new set of clothes today. What happened?" She lowered her eyes and remained silent.

"Well, Ravi, you can wear them for now and change a little later on. Right now I must take care of your wounds, Ravi. Let me have that arm."

Ravi held up his left arm, showing Mr. Shah the long gash.

"The other arm."

"But it's only bruised."

"The gash will be OK. Let's leave it exposed. The air and sunshine will do it good." He wrapped gauze around Ravi's right arm from wrist to shoulder, then lavishly spread Mercurochrome on even the smallest scrapes. Ravi looked at the dark orange stains on his skin. Mr. Shah ripped off a scab on Ravi's knee, then handed him the half-eaten pastry.

"What a beautiful day today. It's too nice outside to keep a fine boy like you cooped up inside. I'm going to take you on an errand today. How does that sound?"

Mr. Shah led Ravi outside. There were two cars. The shiny black Mercedes and an older model green Honda with a crack in the windshield and covered with rust. Ravi looked at the cars. *So different.*

"Jump in, Ravi," said Mr. Shah, pointing to the Honda. As he turned right out of the drive, he put his hand on Ravi's shoulder. "Remember last night, Ravi, I said I would take care of you and protect you? A fine young man like you can't be living on the streets; you'd get killed out there. You wouldn't last more than three days and some gang would get you. You can believe that because it's true," he said, moving the stick shift into second gear.

Ravi reached in his pocket and held his egg.

"You need someone like me to care for you and protect you from the evil on the street, and I'm going to do that just like I promised you, son, but I need something from you in return. I need you to make some money so I can afford to look after you. That sounds fair, doesn't it? I know you'd never expect me to take care of you for free since I'm going to be feeding, clothing, and protecting you."

Ravi stared at the floor, squeezing the plastic egg.

"But don't worry. What I'm asking from you is not hard. I'm going to drop you by this shopping center. A lot of people come here. You're going to ask them for rupees. That's all. It's easy. I'll come back for you tonight before dark." He pulled over and put the car in park.

"Here's a can. Get out now, Ravi. Do what I say. I'll have a hearty dinner waiting for you." Ravi sat, not knowing what to do. Mr. Shah walked to Ravi's side and opened the door. He picked Ravi up and carried him to the sidewalk where he put him down.

"I know you can do this, you're a smart boy. You just come back with the can half full tonight, and everything will be just fine." He grabbed Ravi's egg and held it over his head.

"I'll just hold this for safe keeping, and you'll get it back each evening." Ravi started to cry out and jump for the egg.

"Now get out there and beg." Ravi continued screaming and jumping. Mr. Shah shoved him and sent him sprawling on the sidewalk. "If you aren't here tonight when I come to pick you up, I swear I'll find you and kill you. I can be your best friend or your worst enemy. It's up to you." He got in his car and rolled down the window. "Don't cross me, son. I never forget." He drove away.

Ravi curled into a fetal position and sobbed. His hands sought in each pocket for the red egg that wasn't there. His body ached; several scabs were torn open from landing on the sidewalk. After being stepped over, kicked, and spat upon, Ravi struggled to his feet.

The same voice told him to keep walking. So he did.

CHAPTER

6

Julie frantically pushed her way through the crowd to the front of the ticket line. "Emergency, emergency, excuse me."

She rose onto her tiptoes and pressed her face close to the bars.

"I have to get on that train that just left," she said, pointing to the right. "It's an emergency. More than an emergency!"

"Madame," said the young Indian man, "there is no train that just left."

She squeezed the bars with both hands and pressed her face further between them, trying to get closer.

"It was just here. Check your list."

"Madame, no train just left. That I can assure you of. If a train left that way, it would have a big wreck with the south-bound train coming here any minute."

"But, I just rode it."

"You're going to have to leave now; you pushed to the front of the line."

She fought to regain her balance when the man behind her gave her a shove.

"Two for Delhi," he said. She looked pleadingly at the dark faces in the line.

"Did anybody see the train that went that way?" Most only stared, unable to understand, but those who did agreed with the ticket agent.

"I saw no train."

Then her pleading voice was drowned out by the southbound train pulling into the station. She whirled around and stared. *I'm going crazy!*

Passengers jumped on and off the train before it had stopped. She walked closer. Those scrambling to board and those scrambling to get off brushed by, oblivious to her. She scanned every window, looking. *Are You on here?* When the train left she sat on a bench and wept with her head cradled in her newly manicured fingers.

After several minutes, she felt a shadow over her and looked up to see the bowler hat on Mr. Dove. Before she could suck in enough breath to speak, He smiled and said in an excited voice, *Isn't this brilliant? Here we are in India, and we're looking for lambs!* She jumped up.

"Please, can You help me? I live in New York. I have to get back."

Oh, I'm sorry then. I can't help you get back home now. I thought you were looking for lambs.

"You, You, were sent to help me?"

Well, yes, to help you find lambs.

"Not to get back home?"

No, just lambs. It's your mission.

"My mission?

Yes, feeding the lambs. He did tell you to do that, did He not? Remember, YES, LORD? As He spoke, a huge bolt of lightning struck the top of the train depot.

She wiped her tears with the heel of her hand and nodded yes.

Well, then, I'd be looking high and low for lambs, if I were you.

She thought about this for a moment.

"Do You know where the lambs are?"

Oh, yes, please come with Me.

They exited the train station, and He hailed a yellow and black auto rickshaw. Julie stared at the square-shaped little vehicle resting on three wheels. The top was canvas and the sides were open. A silver pole divided the back and front on each side. The driver sat in a single, small seat. The seat in back looked as if it would hold three.

Get in, said Mr. Dove, motioning. She stepped inside and slid over to make room. He spoke to the driver in Hindi. *He will take you there, Julie.*

"Wait, You're not coming?"

He shook His head. *I was sent to point you in the direction of the lambs.*

"But I don't know anyone."

Jesus is with you.

"What will I eat? Where will I sleep?"

I said, Jesus is with you.

Her body jerked, and she grabbed the metal pole to brace herself as the cab took off. Mr. Dove looked at His pocket watch again. *Impeccable timing.*

Ready or not, Julie was about to encounter Mumbai—legendary, lively, colorful, exciting, chaotic, unpredictable, threatening, dangerous. India's financial powerhouse, rich power-hungry moguls. Bollywood movies, stars, nightclubs, fashion center, discotheques, theatre, music, after-dark romps. Shopping malls, bars, restaurants. Shiny skyscrapers, art deco design, colonial relics, Hindu temples. A study in contrasts. Street bazaars, construction 24/7, honking horns, horrific congested traffic, pollution, humidity, sickening smells. Second most populous city in the world, half living in slums. Twenty-five percent unemployment, grinding poverty. Organized crime, sex trafficking, temple prostitution. Majority religion—Hinduism.

As far as Julie could see, there were vehicles ahead and behind, and none of them seemed to be moving. *Why is everyone honking all the time?* After what seemed like forever, the traffic surged forward.

"Look out, look out," she screamed at her driver as he aimed toward a small gap between cars.

A bus pulled to the curb. Julie watched as people piled on. *They're hanging off the sides. They'll get hit by passing traffic.*

Buses, cars, auto rickshaws, brightly painted trucks, and even an ox cart lined the street with little to no room between them. When the traffic stopped again, those on bikes and motorcycles snaked their way through the small spaces between cars. Because of the horrendous traffic congestion, pedestrians sometimes made faster progress than those in vehicles.

This is unbelievable. The drivers have folded their side view mirrors in so they don't hit each other. This mess makes New York cabbies look courteous!

As the traffic stopped again, Julie watched as an elderly, disheveled, black-skinned man with white hair and beard, limped his way toward the auto. His foot was wrapped in strips of fabric. His hollow eyes were riveted on white, American, affluent Julie. He reached into the auto's open side, displaying an open sore on his arm.

"No, no. Please no! Don't touch me!" She slid to the far edge of the seat as his trembling hand indicated he wanted money.

She curled into a ball and wrapped her arms around her purse. His hand tapped her arm, and she screamed and pushed it away. The traffic moved on, and he was left behind, but trapped like a rat in a maze. He hobbled forward and back, trying to go between the cars to return to the safety of the sidewalk. Julie immediately slathered her palm and arm with hand sanitizer.

It must be 100 degrees. It's so humid; I feel like I'm swimming. She wiped sweat from her brow. She could also feel it trickling from her armpits to her bra. *What's wrong with this country that they don't have air conditioning in cars?*

She coughed and realized her eyes and throat were burning. *What is that smell?* The thick exhaust from a thousand vehicles idling in traffic mixed with gasoline, garbage, human waste, sweat, and industry, combined with the heat and humidity, almost made her nauseous. *Please, not a headache. All I need to make this even more horrendous is a migraine.*

Large buildings towered on each side of the street, making her feel claustrophobic. *I can't even see the sun because of the pollution. I thought New York was bad.*

The sidewalk was packed with vendors displaying their wares—on bicycles, on tables, on carts, and on blankets laid on the ground. Everywhere she looked there were people—people on the sidewalk, people darting between traffic. They all seemed oblivious to their surroundings and in a great hurry to get someplace. This made Julie feel all the more alone. Her heart pounded. *Take deep breaths,* she told herself, but then choked on the exhaust from the city bus that missed her auto by inches.

Driving on the other side of the road was unnerving enough, but being in Indian traffic was like playing bumper cars with the real thing. Trucks, buses, cars, and auto rickshaws moved at a snail's pace when they moved at all. Horns honked constantly. Several times Julie thought they would hit another vehicle.

"Too close, watch it," she yelled to the driver. "Back up! You're tailgating!" She shouted at the rickshaw behind her.

At the next traffic signal, a little girl in a dirty white blouse and with disheveled black hair thrust her hand in the auto.

"Please give to me in the name of God. Please. Please."

"No, go away!" shouted Julie.

"Please. One dollar. One dollar. Please give to me in the name of God."

"No. I don't have any money. Go away. Can't you go?" she shouted at the driver. "I'm getting assaulted back here!" The traffic started, and the little waif darted back to the sidewalk.

After ten minutes of stop-and-go traffic, weaving in and out, they were transitioning, leaving the business district. Skyscrapers gave way to dirty apartment buildings with bricks or lumber piled in front. Tarps and towels hung over the balconies, and outside of each apartment was a clothesline with garments flapping. On one balcony, a man in shorts bathed by dunking a rag in a bucket of water.

Julie was surprised to see nice houses with iron gates and beautiful flowers and palm trees next door to hovels: old boards, cardboard and sheet metal, barely standing, with a tarp for a roof. *Wealth and poverty side by side. That would never happen in the U.S.*

Julie saw multi-storied, expensive homes next to a slum, next to businesses, next to little stalls that serve simple snacks and chai, next to a fish market and tobacco shops.

Half-dressed, filthy children played on the sidewalks. She was too scared to notice the lush green foliage almost everywhere.

The longer they rode and the more she saw, the scarier it felt. She rubbed her burning eyes again and popped a breath mint to soothe her throat. Now the train station seemed like a safe haven that was dwindling away. *Maybe he can take me back to the man in the ticket booth. He spoke English, or maybe he can drop me at a hotel.*

The driver pulled over and stopped.

"No, no, this isn't where I want to be. Is there a hotel around? Ho-tel," she said loudly. "Hy-att, Hil-ton? Close-to-airport?" She held out her arms like wings. "Even a Red Roof Inn?"

The driver shook his head and pointed to the ground.

"Here." He stepped out of the cab, grabbed her hand, and pulled her to the sidewalk. "Two hundred rupees."

She unconsciously wiped her hand on her dress.

"Rupees? I don't have…Will you take American dollars?"

"Yes, yes," said the driver as his eyes lit up. "Five American dollars." In her purse was an English-to-Indian dictionary. "What?" When she opened her wallet she shrieked. The bills were not green, but multicolored. She pulled several bills out to look at them more closely. Gandhi's face was looking back.

"Are, are these rupees?" She hesitated. "Ru-pees?" He nodded, snatched all of them out of her hand, and climbed in the auto.

"No, wait," she yelled as he pulled away. "Don't leave me." She gripped the grab bar and was yanked forward, landing on her face in the street as dirt and exhaust enveloped her. After taking inventory to make sure she wasn't hurt, she muttered, "Welcome to India, home of the world's friendliest people. What is that horrid smell?"

She stood up and dusted off the front of her dress.

"This will never come clean." She brushed it even harder. There were scratches on her palms and both knees. "These will get infected." She applied hand sanitizer liberally, then beat the side of her purse to remove the dust. "Filthy, filthy, filthy!"

On the other side of the street were several vacant lots, which had become the garbage dump for this area. Her eyes scanned the large patch of dirt with one lone tree. Spread out over about 20 feet was a pile of foul-smelling garbage— cans, wrappers, tires, broken furniture, old clothes, plastics, branches, bags of trash, and rusted sheet metal. It was hard to tell what else. Several girls from age 6 to about 11 dug through the pile.

Their clothes were worn and mostly too small. Their charcoal hair, whether long or short, was matted. One little girl was wearing a man's t-shirt as a dress; another, the smallest girl, wore a green dress with one sleeve missing. A young girl, wearing a tattered blue and white print dress, was skeletal. *Her arm and legs are bony like sticks.* The tallest girl wore a grey and yellow dress that was much too small. Another little girl wore a pink dress and shoes, but the toes were cut out.

The boys were in front of a hedgerow that ran along the back, wrestling each other. A littlest boy, missing his front teeth, looked on longingly. Beside him sat a boy wearing a paper hat, made from a newspaper, totally engaged in trying to disassemble some kind of early model cell phone. A medium-sized, emaciated brown dog lay by his side snoozing.

They're playing king of the hill without a hill. Guess the last one standing is the winner. Julie watched as a boy with big ears crept behind the tallest boy and knelt on all fours. The remaining kids charged and toppled him backward over the crouching one. They all cheered.

What a dirty trick. They're behaving like animals. This must be the most disgusting, dirty, rag-tag group on the planet.

A short boy with a scar on his chin yelled something, jumped on the pile, and threw a few punches.

What a bully! They're beyond hope.

She turned her attention to the girls. The little girl wearing the man's t-shirt and a girl wearing a pink dress with ruffled sleeves were in an argument. Julie couldn't tell about what. After a minute, the t-shirted girl bit her opponent's arm, resulting in a loud wail.

The fight ended abruptly when one of the orphans noticed Julie. She pointed and shouted. The sight of a well-dressed, white-skinned American caused a stampede. There had to be lots of money in that purse, and they intended to get it, one way, or the other. Julie watched helplessly as the mob charged across the street with hands outstretched.

The older boys arrived first, shouting what sounded like gibberish. They surrounded her. Dirty hands touched her, pulled her. She was engulfed by the whole group now. She recoiled in horror. She could see a blur of dark skin and hair and white teeth surging in. She felt she was drowning and couldn't break through to the surface. The boy with the scar grabbed her purse and gave a hard yank. A sudden burst of adrenaline coursed through her veins. She managed to hold the strap.

"Stop it! Don't touch me." Dirty hands continued grabbing in slow motion. Desperate pleadings. She couldn't get away. She screamed, "Get-your-hands-off-me! Get back." Panic drove her, and she hit indiscriminately, bringing the purse down hard on several children. She could see angry faces, and she felt her nails dig into flesh.

The littler ones turned to run back across the street. She marched forward as the crowd withdrew, still swinging her purse and screaming, like a crazy woman.

"Don't touch me; you're disgusting." Her body shuddered in revulsion.

Everyone was back across the street, but the littlest girl, barefoot and with the missing sleeve. She had fallen and twisted her ankle. She lay helpless, cowering in the middle of the street. Julie still had her bag raised above her head, ready to strike. Her eyes connected with the soiled little waif who cowered and curled in a ball, sobbing. Julie could see the scratch on her arm was bleeding. The tallest girl, keeping her eyes on Julie, darted into the street, gathered her friend into her arms, and carried her back.

This kind, courageous gesture touched Julie. With her safety no longer threatened, Julie called out, "Wait." she lowered her purse and hooked the strap over her shoulder. "I won't—I won't hurt you." The little girl in the green dress cowered behind her friend. Julie took a few steps, but all the younger children backed away. The older boys glared at her through squinty eyes, daring her over. The one with the scar shook his fist at Julie and yelled.

"Fine, then, I don't want you either!" She retreated to the far side of the street, trying not to watch them as they watched her.

7

*M*y cell phone! I'll call 9-1-1; I'll call Michael!

Julie, you're here to learn to trust Me. I don't want you to call Michael.

"Where have You been? I demand You take me back now. I didn't know what I was agreeing to. I'm not missionary material. I can't be dirty. I don't want lice. I can't—"

Julie, if I can speak through a donkey[1] I can certainly use a fish out of water.

"But, it's too different. I don't speak the language. The whole block smells. It's impossible." She fanned the air as a show of disgust.

Nothing is impossible with Me, Julie. I'm the God of the impossible. Just trust Me. I have this situation under control. I've had it planned for a really long time.

"But, when I don't show up Sunday night, Michael will think I'm dead. I have to call." She opened her phone, and the battery went dead. "It can't be dead.

It was fully charged two hours ago." It took all her willpower not to throw the phone or kick the wooden fence behind her.

Now that that's not an issue, Julie, let's get on with your obedience training. Before the night is out, I want you to read the first two verses in your Bible.

"But You don't understand. I have to go home. I demand that You take me home right now!" She stamped her foot.

There was no reply. Several attempts at yelling and shaking her fists produced no more results.

The orphans watched the one-sided argument from behind the trash pile, exchanging confused looks.

Julie walked down the street to escape their prying eyes. *They're dirty and disgusting. They probably have lice, or worse.* She opened the Bible and looked at the list of handwritten references. At the top was First Corinthians 2:3-5.

I came to you in weakness and fear, and with much trembling. My message and my preaching were not with wise and persuasive words, but with a demonstration of the Spirit's power, so that your faith might not rest on men's wisdom, but on God's power.

She was offended and closed the Bible. "I'm educated at a master's level, and I hold a responsible job. I'm a buyer for the most prestigious boutique in Garden Oaks, New York." She spent the next hour walking around muttering, mumbling, and demanding that the Lord send her home—immediately, if not sooner.

As it started getting dark, an astonished Julie watched the homeless appear from nowhere to sleep on the sidewalk, under bridges, in median strips, anywhere there was horizontal space. As far as she could see, people lay on blue tarps or a worn blanket, and some just lay on the ground. There were men, women, and even whole families.

"They're everywhere. Where did they come from? They're all so dirty!"

Julie, over 10,000 people a day flood into Mumbai in search of jobs. Most never find them. Whole families end up living on the street. It breaks My heart because I love and have a destiny for them. I long for them to know Me as Savior and friend.

Even though she was wearing an Indian outfit, she knew she stuck out like a sore thumb. A chill went up her spine, and she was afraid if she stayed on the street she'd be robbed or worse.

Julie, turn to the left and walk until you find an ivory house with a wrought-iron gate.

Fear of the present had momentarily overtaken fear of what tomorrow would bring. She tiptoed down the street for several blocks, trying to be invisible.

"Ivory house, iron gate. Ivory house, iron gate." On the way a 20-something-old Indian man leaning against a fence noticed Julie. "Madame, you are very beautiful. Come with me!" Julie looked at the sidewalk and picked up her pace. When she passed him he followed. "You are an angel. You are so beautiful." He caught up to her and grabbed her shoulder. "Come with me!" She slapped his hand and ran. She couldn't look to see if he was following because she had to step over bodies. She arrived at the house with her heart pounding. He had not followed. She wiped sweat from her brow.

The house was made of cement, two stories, painted ivory and had a brick fence around the compound. A large iron gate allowed cars out the driveway. There was a cement stairway on the outside of the house that led to the second story. She slipped quietly inside the gate and headed for the door.

Julie, I didn't say you'd sleep inside. See the thick row of flowered bushes? Slide in between them and the side of the house. You will be safe there.

"But, Lord, I can't sleep outside...."

Look around, Julie; thousands of others are. This is My place of refuge for you. If you sleep here, you will be safe. If not, you are on your own.

She looked toward the street, searching for the man. *I can't go back out there!* With no other options, she lay down and belly crawled. "Ouch, ouch." She felt the slight resistance as the thorns caught the lightweight fabric of her dress. Then she heard it tear.

The concrete base of the house had radiant heat left from the scorching day, and she pulled her back and legs away. *I'm sweltering. This heat is oppressive. How do these people survive?*

She struggled to free her purse from the thorns in the confined space, dusted it off, and then laid it in the dirt again. *Maybe I'm losing my mind—some kind of temporary psychotic thing. I'm supposed to be shopping at Bloomingdales now.* She hugged her torso in a failed attempt to console herself. *So much worse than camping! I want my family. I want my bed. I'll never be clean again.* Tears flowed. The light from the window above shined on the row of bushes and offered her a little comfort.

Oh, my gosh! I can catch a taxi to the airport, use my credit card, and in 20 hours I can be out of this nightmare and back in my own bed.

Dragging her purse behind her in the dirt, she backed out of the bushes, stopping frequently to pull her dress free from the thorns. She moved silently across the yard. From her position crouching behind the large, brick gatepost, she saw that many more people were now on the streets. *I'll have to step over them. If I see a taxi, I can just run and be gone before anyone can get me.* She waited 30 minutes, but no taxis came.

Julie, I can hold the ocean in the palm of My hand, yet you think I won't notice if you sneak to the airport? I've been diverting cabs for 30 minutes.

"They'll think I'm dead when I don't show up. Pleeeease just fix my phone?"

This is about learning to trust Me. I promise you, if you take care of My lambs, I'll take care of yours.

Julie kicked the brick pillar and limped back to the house cursing under her breath and beating the dust off. *Look at these snags. It's ruined. I only got to wear it once.* She scooted between the house and bushes and reapplied hand sanitizer. As she lay listening to her breathing, she felt her stomach rumble. She complained to Jesus under the guise of prayer.

"I need to get back home. I'm sleeping on the dirt, and I'm starving. I haven't eaten since the train."

No, Julie. You aren't starving, you're just feeling hunger pangs. Our orphans are starving. Will you feed them? Will you feed My lambs?

Julie had heard enough about lambs for the day and was growing more agitated. She gritted her teeth and thought, *The only lamb I want to see is in a gyros sandwich.* The voice of the Lord left, which even in her anger, scared her.

"Wait, don't leave. I need help...." Her voice dropped in discouragement. Tears flowed. "Jesus, I'm all alone. My family is half a world away. I need to go back. I don't know how to help Your lambs." She twisted her hair around her finger. "I'm filthy, and dirty people keep touching me. It's all too much." She sobbed, her attitude bouncing between discouragement and anger.

She opened the Bible again to First Corinthians 2:3-5. *"I came to you in weakness and fear, and with much trembling."*

"The apostle Paul, intimidated or afraid?"

Julie, I call people to tasks that are far beyond what they are capable of. If you could do this, you wouldn't need to depend on Me. You wouldn't learn that you can trust your life to Me. You can't learn that reading someone else's life story. You have to have your own experience.

She tried to believe what the Lord had shared, but it was out of her grasp. *If I can sleep I can escape this horrid plight for a while.* She used her purse as a pillow. After crying and tossing and turning for 30 minutes, the Lord mercifully sent her sleep.

As the sun's rays fell through the bushes, she awoke. With her eyes still closed, she thought, *What bizarre dreams I've been having lately. First I'm homeless and then....* She stretched her arms and scraped her knuckles on the concrete wall. Her eyes popped open. "No, no, no. What did I do to deserve this?"

If I could transport Philip to the Ethiopian eunuch,[2] why can't I transport you?

"Who's Philip, and what's an Ethiopian-u-nick?"

Check the next Scripture, Julie. Acts 8:26-40. I moved Philip through time and space to have him tell a man about Me. I moved you to tell these children about Me.

But this is the 21st century, and that stuff doesn't happen today, she thought.

You are very much mistaken, Julie, if you think that miracles have passed away. You are very much mistaken.

A shudder went through her body. Until now, she had always found comfort in His voice.

She was startled by footsteps coming up the sidewalk. She took a deep breath and held it. She didn't see anything because she had both elbows over her head and was trying to become one with the dirt. Relief washed over her when she heard them enter the front door. She slowly exhaled. She did, however, resent their cheerful voices. *At least someone has something to be happy about. Uch, I taste terrible.* She rummaged through her purse and was rewarded with a travel-sized toothbrush and toothpaste. She brushed and spit. "Lovely."

Look at the dust. It's settled in all the folds of this bag. She turned the purse upside down and wiped each fold with a tissue.

Then her body let her know that she needed to relieve herself. *Oh great. Just what I need. I'm not going to the bathroom here, that's for sure.* Fifteen minutes later she had found no better option. *I'll never have more privacy than now.* Julie crawled to the far end of the bushes, squatted, and balanced herself by leaning her back against the house. When she put her left hand down to crawl away, she felt the warm liquid.

She jerked her hand away in disgust and tried to wipe it on the house. She squirted out a large portion of the hand sanitizer, but still didn't feel clean. "This is so gross!" Julie brushed herself off with her right hand, ran her pick through her hair, and then felt something wet against her ankle. The bottom of the dress had soaked up a big spot of urine. She clenched her fists and let out a low growl. She searched for something to hit, but the house was too solid. *The last thing I need is to have a broken hand in India. I am dirty and disgusting. I need a bath, and I want to go home. I just want my home, my family, my soft bed, and a hot shower.*

After complaining for another ten minutes, her immense anger was finally overtaken by her hunger. Julie focused on the bushes. They were loaded with berries. *Can these things be edible?* She picked a crimson berry with her right hand and squeezed it between her fingers. The juice smelled sweet. *Should I?*

The Lord's voice came to her. *You may eat them.* She picked berries with both hands and ate as fast as she could while avoiding the thorns. She didn't take time to enjoy the berries' luscious flavor, but ate quickly just to make her hunger subside. In less than three minutes, she had eaten way past satiation and was feeling uncomfortably full.

It still feels better than hunger, she thought.

What are our lambs eating for breakfast?

She gritted her teeth. "I'll take eggs, sunny side up, thanks for asking."

Maybe today they could have berries.

"I don't have anything to carry them in."

Around the corner is a discarded bucket. If you go now, you won't be seen.

She returned with the rusted bucket and let out a deep sigh. About an hour later, the pail was full, and her hands and arms were terribly scratched from having to reach deeper inside the bushes. She blew on her hands to stop the burning. Scooting the bucket ahead, she crawled on her hands and knees to the end of the bushes, ran for the gate, and slipped out, hoping that she wouldn't be seen.

Those who had slept on the sidewalks last night had packed their meager possessions and moved on. *Thank goodness!* The traffic was still horrendous, as were the smells. She turned left to deliver the berries. The breeze alerted her to the dump before she could see it. *How can anything smell so bad? It's a cross between rotting and putrefied.* She buried her nose in her elbow, hid the bucket behind her, and stopped about a half a block away. For the first time she looked, really looked, at the orphans. *I have never seen such skinny, poorly cared for, dirty children.*

Just then a rat scurried out from under the stack of garbage. One of the boys, wearing a blue shirt several sizes too small, grabbed it. He celebrated by doing a little dance while waving it above his head. Then he broke its neck and ran off to build a fire and cook his treasure, hoping no one would take it from him.

She crossed the street and walked cautiously toward the children. She paused, giving them a chance to notice her. They eyed her suspiciously. It was mutual.

Must be kind, Julie. Must be kind. She shouted in her most pleasant voice, "Breakfast. I have berries for you." Then she put the bucket down and turned to walk back across the street, still upset about the urine stain, but feeling somehow pleased about her feeding effort.

A horrible noise startled her and she spun around. The two largest boys had the bucket in a tugging match shouting at each other. As some of the berries spilled, the other children on their hands and knees, frantically picked through the garbage for the precious food. They popped each one immediately into their mouths. The smallest children, including the girl with the missing sleeve, were at the back and received nothing.

The boy with the scar kicked his competitor's leg, gave a big yank, ended up with the bucket, and ran down the street with his prize.

He's bad news, thought Julie.

After the others ate all the berries they could find, the three smallest children crept forward to see if anything was left—the littlest girl with the missing sleeve, a skeletal girl with very dark skin, and a little boy walking with a limp, missing his two front teeth.

Julie was disgusted at the two boys' behavior. *They're in desperate need of manners; I've never seen such a thing.*

Julie, they don't need manners; they need food. While other children are thinking about kid things, staying alive dominates all their actions and thoughts. No one gives them anything; they have to take it. Only the strongest survive.

"They could still be nice about it."

Children from violent families often behave the same way. Those who are abandoned and abused don't know about love, kindness, justice, or security, much less manners. Each day, each hour, the name of the game is survival. The life span of an orphan is short. Lack of appropriate hygiene leads to infections. Children often dodge in between cars to sell or beg and are hit in traffic.

In a few months, unless something changes, some of these young ones will be dead from disease or malnutrition. No one will miss their presence on Earth. No one helps My littlest lambs. What are you going to do about it?

"Me? You just saw my best effort go up in flames. You dropped me in a foreign country with no preparation. I have no idea what to do. What do You suggest?" she snapped sarcastically.

Let Me tell you the parable of the talents, Julie. It's the next passage.

God's Kingdom is like a man going on a long trip. He called his servants together and to one he gave $5,000, to another $2,000 to a third $1,000. Then he left. The first servant worked and doubled the money. The second did the same. But the third man dug a hole and buried the money.

After a long absence the master came back. The one given $5,000 showed him he had doubled the money. His master said, "Good work! From now on be my partner."

The second servant had also doubled his master's investment. "You did your job well. From now on be my partner."

The servant given $1,000 said, "Master, I know you demand the best and make no allowances for error so I found a good hiding place. Here is your money."

"It's criminal to live cautiously like that! Why did you do less than the least? You could have invested with the bank so I could have interest. Take the thousand and give it to the one who risked the most. And get rid of this 'play-it-safe' who won't go out on a limb. Throw him out into utter darkness."[3]

"And that applies to me, how?" she snapped.

Even if you think you have no talent for the task assigned to you, you must try to do something. I'd rather you try and fail than sit and complain. But, I can promise you, Julie, that if you follow My leading, you're doomed to success."

CHAPTER

8

She counted five girls rummaging through the dump. The skeletal girl in the tattered blue and white print dress pulled a can from the trash and ate the leftover contents in two bites.

Julie felt the berries coming, but quenched the vomiting at the last minute. *That is just grotesque. Uch! Unless the Lord rains berries from the sky, I guess I better buy some food. I don't want to do "nothing" and get thrown into utter darkness, whatever that means.*

She remembered a small grocery store she'd seen yesterday and retraced her steps. *There are a lot of stray dogs snoozing on the side of the road trying to avoid this beastly heat. They're so skinny. I wonder if they're pets?*

A young boy grabbed her arm and thrust a small flower at her. She yanked her arm free and tried to walk around him but he blocked her forward movement. "Eat, eat." He moved his arm from his belly to his mouth. "Eat, please." With the other hand he repeatedly tried to get her to take the flower.

If I give him something, maybe he'll leave me alone. She pulled out her wallet and was suddenly surrounded by eight more children all talking, begging, and grabbing. She held the wallet high and with the other hand slipped her purse strap over her head. Then she twisted and shoved her way through the grabbing crowd. They followed her down the sidewalk to the market area until one of the vendors ran them off.

The sidewalk was overflowing with vendors and customers. She took a deep breath and plunged into the crowd. She resented people bumping her in this sea of sultry humanity.

The market was bustling and colorful. Some of these primitive "shops" were just three "walls" of hinged particle board on the sidewalk with wares hanging from the wood. A chai stall stood next to a tobacco stall.

"One cigarette, one rupee," crooned the vendor. Men gathered round smoking. The stench of tobacco mixed with body odor, coconut oiled hair, the fish baskets carried by women, powder and traditional perfumes, and the smells wafting from the vendors' grills turned her stomach. *That smells awful. How does anyone ever get used to this atrocious stench?*

A woman with a cloth spread in front of her was selling leis and gajras, flowers strung together and worn in women's hair. At the next cart, Julie recognized bananas, grapes, oranges, and apples, along with many fruits and vegetables that were unfamiliar to her.

There was cooked and raw meat. The sight of several small blue gill-looking fish that had been deep-fried whole—eyes and all—caused her to turn away. She moved to the next cart and came face to face with several plucked, whole chickens hanging by their necks.

"I think I'm getting a migraine." She hurried to the vendor selling colorful flowers to try to tear the last images from her mind. *I'd really just like a nice piece of salmon with lemon.*

She felt a tap on her thigh and turned to see an elderly man with no teeth sitting on the sidewalk. He was wrapped in what looked like a loincloth, exposing his shriveled, crippled legs. He held up a tin pot to Julie. She gasped and took a few steps backward bumping into a vendor and causing him to drop a plate of chicken on the ground.

He whirled around. "Sixty rupees, sixty rupees!" He grabbed for her but she stepped aside, then turned and ran through the crowd. "Sorry, sorry," she called over her shoulder.

In the midst of these temporary vendors was a primitive grocery store with refrigeration. Inside were beautifully colored fruits and vegetables, gunnysacks with their tops rolled down brimming with legumes, rice, and grains. One long section of shelving lined the store's wall. Glass jars with silver lids in row after row displayed exotically colored spices, but Julie was oblivious to the beauty around her.

She walked the aisles looking for something that wasn't in a can and didn't need to be heated. Finally she settled on prepared sandwiches. She couldn't tell exactly what they were, maybe egg or tuna salad, maybe not. She also bought small bottles of juice, apples, and six small pieces of individually wrapped candies or "sweets," as the cashier called them. The cashier spoke a little English, and Julie was able to learn the words for girls only—*kali ladicl.*

She located a small patch of grass and slathered a large amount of hand sanitizer all the way up her arms. She cautiously sniffed the sandwich, then touched her tongue to the filling. *Cucumber and heavy on the onions. Palatable, but definitely not very enjoyable. I wanted some meat.* A skinny dog ambled toward her, and she tossed the sandwich. Before the dog could get it, an elderly man scooped it up and devoured it, then begged for more. She slapped his hand as he grabbed at her sack. "Leave me alone!"

She returned to the store to find something tastier. After she had eaten, she walked to the dump and stood across the street.

Thank goodness the wind is blowing the other way. I can't take that awful smell.

She yelled for girls only, "kali ladicl," and motioned, "follow me." At first no one moved, so she held up a sandwich. Then everyone, including the boys, charged across the street, all shouting at once, pushing and trying to grab the sack and her purse. The boy with the scar grabbed at her arm, but Julie was too fast.

After the berry experience, she wasn't going to make the same mistake. She yelled, "kali ladicl!" and pushed her way out of the group. When a boy came close, she turned her shoulder and shoved him away. The girls also grabbed at the sack and her purse. After a long scuffle, the boys reluctantly left, one by one. The boy with the scar on his chin stopped to yell and shake his fist, before trotting down the street.

She held the sack high over her head and slapped several hands, as she put her finger to her mouth to hush the girls. Finally, most calmed down, and she motioned them to follow her to a small patch of grass where she sat and motioned for them to do the same. They sat, but not still. When she held out the first sandwich, they were on their feet again, grabbing and reaching for the sack.

"Get back," she slapped the grabbing hands. "Everyone sit down," she yelled as she motioned to them by flailing her arms. After several frustrating minutes, the girls calmed down to the point where Julie could pass out the sandwiches without being mobbed.

Most gobbled them immediately and threw their wrappers on the ground. Several girls hid their sandwiches and tried to pretend that they hadn't received one. Julie had intended to pass out all the sandwiches and juice, sanitize their hands, say a prayer, and all eat together, but she realized how unrealistic that was with starving children. She took a deep breath; *I'll never be able to do this. They're like wild animals. I know dogs that behave better.*

Julie could see the tops of their greasy, dirty heads. One of the girls scratched and Julie caught a glimpse of small white eggs. *Ugggh. Head lice? Keep away from me!* She scrunched up her face and forced herself to look away.

There was one sandwich and juice left. *I know I didn't miscount.* Standing at a distance watching was the little girl in the one-sleeved green dress with the scratched arm. When Julie looked at her, she immediately looked away. Julie stood and took a step toward her and she backed away. *Fine, what do I do now?*

The girl wearing a man's t-shirt and a big frown motioned for Julie to hand her the food and pointed that she would take it to the little girl. When she received it she ran in the opposite direction.

"Stop. Wait. You can't do that!" She stomped her foot. "Unbelievable. I can't trust anyone; they're all savages!"

Julie felt her intestines churning. *Probably those berries.* She opened her sack, and when the girls saw the sweets they let out a cry and mobbed her again. They refused to be seated. Three of the girls grabbed all the sweets and immediately ate them.

"No, no, you were supposed to share." They threw their wrappers on the ground.

"No, pick them up," Julie bent down and grabbed a candy and sandwich wrapper. They all followed her lead and handed wrappers to her hoping anything they did would bring a reward. She didn't realize that they would do whatever was required to get what they needed to survive—and they needed a lot. She had been concerned about manners. Manners? They were fighting for their lives!

Trash was strewn everywhere Julie looked. *Why did I even bother?*

When the girls saw Julie's sack was empty, they all ran back to the dump. *That's gratitude for you.* She went off in search of a bathroom. *I need to find a gas station.*

Stores and gas stations don't provide public toilets in India. The whole outdoors was the bathroom; people even defecated in public, as Julie was about to find out. Desperate to avoid soiling herself, and having no place to clean up, she ducked inside an alley. Julie grabbed several tissues out of her green bag, laid it beside her and squatted. *I've never had such a bad case of diarrhea.* She wrapped her arms around her abdomen and moaned. *Will I ever be finished?*

A short figure darted from out of the shadows. A blue and yellow blur snatched her purse and exited the alley. There was nothing Julie could do. It was over as quickly as it began. She didn't even cry out, not wanting to call attention to herself at that moment. After several more uncomfortable minutes, with her intestines still roiling, she finally finished, wiped with the tissues and after a brief hesitation decided to throw them down. She marched down the street determined to find a short boy with her favorite green designer purse.

Great, Lord, is this why You brought me here, to give me the worst case of diarrhea in the history of the world and to have my purse stolen? Can't You go easy on me? She felt for her bag to retrieve her dictionary. *Great, just great.* Tears welled in her eyes. *I don't even have a passport, a hotel, a ticket home, and now, no money. I can't even believe this.* She flung her arms out in frustration. *I guess I'd better try and find a police station.*

Don't file a report. I'll return your purse.

"If it was all the same to You, I wish it hadn't been stolen."

Julie, this is about you building up your faith muscle. It's very weak. You need to believe I can work this for good.[1] Pray and ask Me to return your purse.

"You know I need it; just bring it back." She stomped her foot and exhaled a long, pained breath.

You need to ask. Obedience is crucial in this situation. You need to depend on Me for everything.

Julie was near her breaking point. Through clenched teeth she choked out, "Return my purse, amen." Turning curtly she walked down the street as if she could leave the Lord's presence behind.

I'd planned to buy a sheet and pillow, more hand sanitizer, some lotions and some snacks. I guess that won't happen now. No TV, cell phone, computer. What's there to do? I can't buy anything but I'm not going back to "bed" until almost dark. Maybe a store will have air-conditioning.

The first shop had touristy knickknacks—intricately beaded patchwork bags, journals, stationery, colorful ceramic statues big and small, linens and beautiful patchwork quilts, but no air-conditioning. Next was the same grocery store she'd been in earlier.

She smelled a wonderful smell and stepped onto the street where a vendor was selling Tandoori kebab, a spicy chicken dish. *I'm really hungry.* The vendor also had roti, unleavened flat bread. *It looks so good.* The vendor plopped a piece of chicken and bread on a paper plate and handed it toward her.

"Fifteen rupees, only fifteen rupees." She shook her head and moved on.

I'd give anything for an iced coffee and a cranberry orange scone. Or a roasted vegetable panini with a caramel brulée and a maple oat pecan muffin. Arrrg! Why isn't there a Starbucks® and why don't I have my gift card?

The next store was full of wooden furniture, mostly functional daily pieces, but toward the back there were some items that caught her eye. She saw several things that she'd like to buy and mentally placed the furniture in her home, re-arranging rooms to accommodate it.

In the very back of the store was a tri-fold wooden screen. *It must be six feet tall.* She rubbed her hand over the intricate carving and the inlaid mother of pearl. *It's not Victorian, but it is exquisite. The craftsmanship is amazing. It would look so good in Michael's office.* The price tag was marked 35,000 rupees. *How much is that? I wonder what shipping costs?* Then she snapped back to reality. *Quit it, Julie, you're not in New York. You're in India with no money and no prospects of getting any.*

It was getting dark, and she wanted to get back to her place beside the bushes before all those homeless people came out. There were lights on at the house, but the curtains were closed. She felt her heart thumping as she reached for the metal latch. She breathed a sigh of relief as it opened. She crawled on her hands and knees between the house and the bushes. The smell of a crushed berry on the ground brought back bad memories.

"Uggh, my intestines are still churning!" She flicked the berry away and tried to make her head comfortable on her bent arm. *Last night my soft leather purse kept my face out of the dirt.*

She was aggravated, more than aggravated, at the little thief who stole it. *I'd like to wring his neck. Now I have no pillow, toothbrush, no money, nothing—not even a breath mint.* Unable to get comfortable lying on her own arm and unwilling to sleep with the side of her face in the dirt, she rolled on her back.

Her stomach growled—an unfamiliar sensation. At home, at the first sign of hunger, or even boredom, she was at the fridge for a meal or snack. Tears ran down the side of her face and into her ear.

The Lord whispered gently, *Julie, over a billion people go to bed hungry every night.[2]*

"Well, I have no prospects of breakfast either, now that I know the effect the berries have on me."

Don't you remember? I asked you to trust Me?

"Just call me 'little faith.' I'm sure that purse, the money, and everything else is long gone. What am I going to eat for breakfast?"

What are our orphans going to eat for breakfast? What are you going to feed them?

"Me? Maybe You can show up with some fishes and bread.[3] You're good with those." The conversation was over.

Julie lay silently cursing this weird *Alice in Wonderland* adventure she was trapped in. She longed for all the comforts of home that she had completely taken for granted. Now a blanket and a pillow seemed like an unattainable luxury. Air-conditioning even more so. *This blistering heat is relentless. I perspire constantly. How will I ever get to sleep? And I was supposed to be home today.* After reviewing her list of grievances, she fell asleep around 3 A.M.

Julie dreamed she was shopping in New York and had caught the train back home. As it pulled into the station, Michael and Logan were waiting. They embraced on the platform.

"I can't wait to show you what I bought." Julie unloaded each bag and showed Michael the contents.

"I know I was supposed to be shopping for work," she said as she held up a plastic garment bag, "but this was marked way down to $200. I just couldn't resist." She pulled the bag off to reveal a black beaded evening gown with a handkerchief hem and V-shaped neckline.

"See," she said holding it up to her. "Whenever I move the whole dress sparkles. Isn't it lovely?"

"It'll look great on you. Red Lobster® here we come," said Michael. Julie didn't answer. She was going through the next sack. After showing off shoes, two suits, three dresses, and a pair of jeans. She handed Michael a wrapped package.

"What's this?"

"It's for your office. Open it."

"Wow. Nice." he rubbed his hand over the elaborately carved wall hanging with inlaid mother of pearl.

"Whoever did this was quite a talented craftsman."

"Do you like it, really?"

"Love it."

"Me too. It was made in India. Two hundred dollars, but I think it's worth it, don't you?" Just as Michael was ready to answer, Julie woke up.

The illusion of being back in her comfortable world was slowly replaced by the horrendous taste in her mouth, along with the reality that she was lying on dirt with a stiff back. She looked at her watch—8 A.M.

What are all those horrid noises? This cacophony of abrasive sounds—honking horns—it never ends. Those rumbling trucks and those constantly chirping birds. How can they be so happy? How can they even breathe in this humidity? It's too early to be this hot.

"Good morning, God," Julie said sarcastically. She was bitterly disappointed that being back home was only a dream. Being stuck in India now was twice as depressing. Her stomach rumbled, and she longed to eat some of the berries just to make her hunger go away, but she didn't dare.

9

R elieving herself at the end of the bushes started the day on a sour note. *Even though no one sees me, this is so humiliating. What would my co-workers think?*

Julie crawled back to the center of the bushes again, crossed her legs, and tried to get comfortable. "Lord, why are the orphans there? Why don't they just leave? There's nothing there for them."

They have no home, Julie, and they receive no help. Not from family, school, or society. None of these children want to live on the street, but they are incapable of escaping. They aren't much different from children anywhere else.

If you asked them what their goals are, they would tell you: eat dinner, school, learn to read and write, have clothes and shoes, a father and mother, a real home. These children never know peace. Their lives are in constant turmoil.

Julie frowned. "But how did they even get there?"

There are many reasons, none of them good: poverty, physical or sexual abuse, parental exploitation, famine, kidnapping.

In the past people lived close to their extended families or neighbors who would help care for the children during tough times. But no more.

Parents who are under stress often end up in arguments. Their anger is frequently vented toward the children, along with emotional or physical abuse. Men turn to alcohol for comfort. Wives and children pay the price.

Home was a place of fear, insecurity, abuse, and misery instead of comfort, nurturing, and provision. Many endured filthy, cramped living spaces and poor hygiene. Some children decide life on the street is better than constant lack, neglect, and abuse.

"But can't they go to the government? Someone has to be able to help."

These precious children are thought of as disposable nuisances, good-for-nothings, troublemakers, thieves, criminals, or a blight on society. But they are of tremendous value, and I cherish and have a dream for each one. See their possibilities, Julie, not their lack.

"Why don't You just feed everyone?" she asked with an accusing edge to her voice.

Julie, I provide enough food to feed everyone in the world, but I didn't distribute it evenly. About half the world's population, over three billion people, lives on less than $2.50 a day.[1] If I give you six loaves of bread and your neighbor no loaves of bread, what does that mean you need to do?

Julie swallowed hard as her face flushed. She shifted her weight, trying to find a comfortable position. She skipped that answer and went on to her next question.

"Well, can't they get a job or something?"

They work hard. All their time goes into surviving. They dig through trash to find something to sell or barter. Any money they make they have to spend on food—no money for a video game or a new shirt. Many work a full day just to buy one meal, but it is not nutritious enough, and they end up chronically tired, malnourished, and sick.

When there is no work, the children turn to begging or stealing. When smaller children beg, the older children frequently beat them and steal their money.

"Why'd they decide to live at this dump?"

Everyone needs to belong somewhere. This group is a surrogate family; it provides a degree of physical and emotional security, identity, self-worth, some protection, friends, and a sense of belonging. Each day My orphans endure challenges that many adults could not endure. They are survivors.

Julie, remember when Logan said he could rescue himself from pirates?

"Yes."

What if Logan was moved to this dump?

She caught her breath and blurted, "No, Lord, he'd get a disease; he wouldn't have enough to eat. He'd be malnourished and possibly die. He'd get molested."

What else?

"He'd have no future. No one would love him or take care of him."

Exactly. Now it's personal for you. But do you realize that I love these children much more than you are capable of loving Logan? Each one of them is My child, just like Logan is yours. It's very personal for Me. Will you help My children?

"But, Lord. I have to get back home to my own child. I can't stay here," she whined while slapping her open palm against her thigh.

Will you feed My lambs? I have plans for each one of them, but step one is to get them out of this dump. They are each a bundle of potential, and they don't even know it. Will you help them reach their God-ordained possibility?

"It is a sad situation, but I can't help them. I know I said I would, but I didn't know what I was getting into. I'm not a doctor or social worker."

You don't need to be; you just need to be obedient. I'll do the rest. I want to help them through you. As you take care of My lambs, I'll take care of yours.

"Jesus, I wish I could help, but I can't do India. It's just too primitive. Please put me on the train now." Tears left rivulets down her dusty cheeks. "I haven't bathed. I haven't changed clothes. I smell bad. I have to go to the bathroom outside. I'm hungry and I don't know where my next meal is coming from—"

Just like My precious orphans.

"That's how they've always lived. I'm not used to it; it's different."

You don't like the inconvenience of not being able to immediately eat something at the first pre-hunger pang or choose from a huge wardrobe or take a hot bath in your Jacuzzi® with aroma therapy oils, scented candles, and your favorite CD.

Her shoulders sagged.

But you are much more equipped than you think. I chose for you to be born in America. You had plenty of food so your body and brain developed normally. You are educated at a master's level. You have a loving husband and a beautiful son picked just for you. Compared to My lambs, you have lived like royalty.

I've asked others to do this task, and they've said no to what they consider a lowly calling. They were greatly deceived. On Judgment Day, they will regret their decision.

The intensity in His words felt like knives stabbing at her. "Why did this happen to me? What did I do to deserve any of this?"

Are you so self-absorbed that you'd turn your back on these precious children? If you want to go home now, tell Me, and I'll find someone who believes my Word—"religion that God the Father accepts...is this: caring for orphans or widows...."[2]

The longing for her family raged against doing the right thing.

"I miss tucking Logan into bed. I miss reading to him and his wonderful hugs and funny knock-knock jokes and having dinner as a family. I miss Michael's phone calls and having his arms around me each night." She also craved the comforts of home: abundant food, temperature control, indoor plumbing, a bed, the routine of her job.

"I want to help, but it's just too hard. I'm not used to any of this, being dirty, the heat, hunger, or the smells!"

Julie, I know it seems overwhelming to you, but I'm here to help. It's not the least bit intimidating to Me. I strongly recommend you see this task to the end, for your benefit as much as the orphans'.

She struggled between doing what she wanted and doing what was right. She bit her lip, afraid if she opened her mouth the words, "send me back now," would automatically spill out.

Remember the story of David and Goliath?

"That's exactly how I feel. I'm up against something that's just too big for me!"

Do you know the difference between David's perspective and the rest of the soldiers'? They looked at Goliath and thought, "He's too big to take." Young David looked at Goliath and thought, "He's too big for me to miss!"

A wrestling match pummeled her mind. She almost felt dizzy. She hung her head and ran her fingers through her hair. It was still all she could do not to beg to be sent back immediately.

"Help me," she squeaked between sobs. "Can You help me to care more?"

Yes, Julie. I just need your willingness.

She wept with her head resting upon her arms and tried to drum up some more resolution. "I don't want to, but I'll try."

You've chosen well, Julie. Fear has you compare the size of the giants to yourself. Faith had David compare the size of the giant to the size of his God.[3] These challenges are bigger than you, but they are not bigger than I am. You don't have to fight them in your own strength.

"But I don't know what to do."

Feed My lambs—

"Lord, I don't have any money. Remember, my purse was stolen?"

Remember, I said I'd see it was returned? Every day is a good day to believe for the impossible. Don't be swayed by what you see.

"But how will I possibly get it back?" She rubbed her red eyes with her saturated tissue.

My part is the how; your part is the obedience. I am totally confident in My abilities. Just go tell the orphans, the girls and the boys, that you'll feed them today.

"But how?"

Agree with Me, not your perceived situation. She heard a rumble of thunder. *Go now, Julie.*

She wanted to trust, but it all seemed so risky. *What if I tell them I'll feed them and don't get my purse back? This might be the first time I've really had to trust God. At home our paychecks cover all our bills and most of our wants. If Logan gets sick, we go to a doctor for advice, medicine, or surgery. I always thought I trusted God, but have I ever really had to? Lord, help me. I choose by an act of my will to trust You. Please bring back my purse. Amen.*

CHAPTER

10

S he spent ten minutes getting her emotions under control.

Deep breaths, Julie. Dry your tears. Then she headed for the dump. She tried not to obsess about her lack of hygiene, but still ended up trying to brush the dust off her dress. *My clothes are dirty, hair's a mess. I stink. I'll probably never feel clean again.*

When she arrived, the girls yelled and the oldest one, wearing a knit grey and yellow dress, pointed toward the boys, yelling something with great fervency. One of the boys, wearing a filthy yellow t-shirt and blue shorts, clung to Julie's purse. A few other boys had tackled him. He squirmed, unable to free himself. The boy with the missing front teeth was afraid to enter the skirmish. He stood near the littlest girl with the missing sleeve, who was also watching cautiously.

I don't think I've seen the boy in the yellow before, thought Julie. Then her face tightened into a pinched expression. *He's the blue and yellow blur who stole my purse—the little thief!*

She waded into the skirmish and grabbed the purse. Not even stopping to thank them, Julie did a quick inventory. *English/Indian dictionary and Bible still here. Credit cards here and only a few rupees are missing.*

"Thank You, Jesus," she shouted,

"Frank Yous Jee-sus," the girls repeated, not knowing its meaning.

As the other boys held Ravi, he resisted. The boy with the scar put an end to his struggling when he doubled his fist and hit Ravi on the side of the head.

Julie flinched. *That had to hurt.* She looked at the boy being restrained. *He has so many injuries; his face is swollen, his chin scraped, and a big gash on his left arm. His clothes are filthy. Nothing new there, but his are also bloody.* Now that she wasn't in such a helpless position in that darkened alley, and now that she had her purse back, this little thief looked pretty harmless, even vulnerable.

Are those tears welling? He's about Logan's age. She remembered Logan's self-assured salute and confident words about escaping the pirates. "I could do that. I'm brave." She knew in her heart Logan would fare no better than this child.

The first pang of compassion she'd felt since she arrived started to stir in her mother's heart. For the first time, she didn't see filthy obligation; she saw a hurting child.

Where are his parents?

As Julie continued to stare, she saw Logan, then the injured boy, then Logan, then the injured boy. *He's so filthy; his wounds need to be cleaned.* To her surprise, she felt tears beginning.

When Julie approached him slowly the other boys holding him scattered. He didn't run; he cowered. Julie spoke gently, "Hello." He continued staring at the ground. She knelt before him, and with her right hand gently lifted his chin until his eyes met hers.

Ravi looked at her for the first time. *My mother's earrings.* His heart leapt in hope, and adrenaline flooded his system. Julie was still speaking, but he didn't hear. He was too busy watching the colorful beads on his mother's favorite earrings swing from side to side.

He remembered his birthday party when she had them on. It was several months ago, but it seemed like an eternity had passed since then.

Ravi had been sitting at the table in the highly decorated dining room. Everyone had sung special "aarti" songs and shared small candies and sweets. As the dishes were cleared, his mother had arrived from the kitchen carrying his birthday cake with one candle burning.

"Blow out the candle, Ravi. Happy Birthday!"

After the cake was eaten, he laughed as the other children sprinkled a few grains of rice on his head for prosperity. Next his father had presented him with a leather book with large, colored pictures of the stars and galaxies.

"Astronomy," his father had pointed to the gold embossed title, "is the study of the sky. When my vacation comes, we'll go see your uncle in the country. We'll leave this city, and at night you will be able to see an abundance of stars."

After the party, Ravi's mother had tucked him in bed.

"I have a special gift for you," she had held up a red plastic egg. "Your father is proud of your good grades and always wants you to study, and I know you love science…but I just wanted you to have this." Ravi had stared, not knowing what to make of it.

"When I was a child, we visited my cousin in England, and she had one— it's called Silly Putty®. I've never forgotten it. I asked her to send me some for your birthday—because even though you're so smart, I know you like to be silly!" She had squeezed the egg gently until it separated, revealing the tan putty inside.

"What's it do, Mommy?"

"It does everything. It bounces like a ball. It stretches. When you fold it, it traps air and pops, but the best thing it does is it copies things."

Ravi's brow had furrowed. She reached for a comic book on his nightstand.

"Take this and press it on the picture of Colossal Man. Now pull it off slowly." She had smiled as her son's eyes lit up.

"Wow!"

"Now for the silly part. Stretch it; watch what happens to Colossal Man."

"He's getting taller."

"Stretch it the other way and he'll get fat."

Ravi had been captivated. "Thanks, Mommy, this is the best gift ever. Can I play with it in bed?"

"Just don't stay up all night. Birthday today, but school tomorrow." When she leaned to kiss his cheek, her dangly earrings had swept across his neck and tickled him, as always.

He heard a voice and was back at the dump. The woman with his mother's earrings was still speaking.

"Julie," she tapped her chest.

"Ravi," he whispered, and before he could stop himself, he dove into her arms, nearly knocking her off her knees. He wept as he flung his arms around her.

Surprised, she steadied herself and held him close. She clung to him like he was Logan, and he clung to her like she was his lost mother.

He reveled with Julie's arms around him, holding and rocking him, like his mother.

But you're different. You don't smell like my mother. You're too skinny. You don't feel like my mother, and you aren't my mother, and she is never coming back. He made no effort to move, but Julie felt his arms go slack.

What just happened? She released Ravi, and he took a few steps backward. When she looked into his eyes, he hung his head, turned and ran until he was out of sight.

She called after him, but he was gone.

I need to find him. Julie forced a smile and waved good-bye to the orphans. Some smiled, some waved, and some just cautiously stared. She headed in Ravi's direction, clutching her purse.

She rounded the corner just as a battered green car with a cracked windshield pulled to the curb and the driver scanned the children.

The driver looked for Ravi, then left in a huff. But then he saw another little boy limping down the sidewalk about a block away. The boy had decided to go for a walk to ponder who this woman was who had showed up at his dump.

Mr. Shah pulled over and rolled down the window.

"Excuse me, can you tell me the way to the market? I need groceries. If you show me, I'll buy you some sweets." He pushed the door open and the little boy missing his two front teeth scrambled in.

"My name's Mr. Shah. What's your name?"

"Sammy," he said, smiling his gap-toothed grin, thrilled at the attention and the chance to ride in a car.

"Sammy, you look like a healthy young man. What is your age?"

"Six."

"Well, Sammy, I will buy you a nice sweet for helping me find the market." He parked the car. "Let's go pick out your favorite kind." Sammy reached up and took Mr. Shah's hand as they entered the store.

"Any sweet you want—you just tell me, and I'll buy it for you," said Mr. Shah, pointing to the brightly colored assortment.

Sammy grinned. *So many choices.* He didn't have a favorite because he never received sweets. That made it really hard to choose.

This looks good, this looks good. What's this one taste like? He finally looked to Mr. Shah.

"Well, Sammy, let's try this," he grabbed the largest package on the shelf and handed the fruit flavored candies to Sammy, who beamed. Mr. Shah tousled Sammy's greasy hair and led him to a small cooler where he pulled out two bottles of cola. After paying for the items, Mr. Shah bought spicy chicken kebabs and flat bread from a street vendor.

"You know, Sammy, I always wanted a son. I just live nearby. Let's go back to my house and eat this chicken and then we'll have our sweets." Sammy nodded. *What a day today was turning out to be.*

Julie searched for an hour, but finally gave up. *Every block I get assaulted by a beggar—or a mob of them. I need to go get food.*

At the market she selected sandwiches made of unknown meat. She also picked up apples and juice boxes. The Lord directed her to the bottle of multivitamins. *I can give them each one, maybe two a day.* Walking back to the dump, she checked her dictionary for the words *girl* and *boy.*

The children saw her coming with sacks, but they remembered what had happened the last time when they had charged her. She had her purse again and obviously wasn't afraid to use it. The children huddled together, each trying to be in the front. The whole group was pushing forward toward her like a slow-moving amoeba.

Julie's heart pounded as she also remembered the previous feeding calamities. *Lord, help me, help me, help me. Please.* Julie slowed her pace; the children were chomping at the bit, but trying to restrain. Julie stopped walking, unsure of what to do next. She knew she couldn't keep the hungry children waiting much longer.

The oldest girl, in the grey and yellow dress, turned to the group and shouted directions. She motioned, and the girls all sat on the ground. Then she turned to the boys and pointed. All of them sat, except the boy with the scar. That scar was the first thing Julie always noticed; his perpetual frown, the second. *He's so young to have that adult-sized chip on his shoulder.*

Knowing they weren't going to get fed until there was order, the other boys wrestled him to the ground, where he resigned himself to sit, but not without crossing his arms and wearing an ugly scowl.

Julie moved closer. She motioned for the first girl to hold out her hand. When Julie squirted a large blob of hand sanitizer on her palm, the girl licked it, made a horrible face, and glared at Julie.

I'll have to teach that lesson later.

Slinging one grocery bag over her shoulder, hopefully out of reach, she handed a sandwich to each child. If the child grabbed, Julie stepped back several feet and waited. When the children realized that grabbing brought the distribution process to a halt, the other children's scowls and jeers were enough to make them obey. When Julie came to the girl dwarfed by the man's t-shirt, she jumped up and tried to snatch the whole bag. Julie moved on to the next seated girl. *Serves you right; you get to eat last since you can't behave and you stole someone else's sandwich yesterday.*

A violent pain shot through her right calf. She screamed. The little girl in the man's t-shirt had bitten her.

You little ingrate. I'll show you. The girl glared back. Julie continued ignoring her until all the children had received their sandwiches. Julie stood at a distance and tossed a sandwich to the "biter." By the time the last child received his sandwich, those who received first had already finished wolfing down their treat. The boy with the dog tore off a corner of bread. The dog immediately sat and was rewarded for his trick.

I have three sandwiches left. One for Ravi and one for the littlest girl. Julie could see her standing at a distance watching. *Who's missing?* Julie started again and passed out the apples. Again, grabbing slowed the process, but there was less of it this time. She took a step back and tossed the apple to the "biter." When she distributed the juice, everyone restrained themselves, and the process went smoothly.

One more time with the vitamins. She gave each child two of the chewable tablets. "Sweets" blurted the first child to eat them. The boy with the dog bit his vitamin in half and, after several attempts, the dog rolled over, to the children's delight, then gobbled the other half of the vitamin.

This girl in the tattered blue and white dress looks like a walking skeleton. I'll give her three. She obviously needs the nutrition.

The children ate the apple, core and all. Then they dropped the sandwich wrappers and empty juice boxes. Julie pointed to the mess and held out her empty sack. Thinking there was more food, they impulsively pushed forward.

"No. Pick this up; don't litter." She pointed to the trash, but received only confused stares. She began to pick up the litter herself. The children watched. Finally the oldest girl helped. Soon the trash was picked up. Julie laid the grocery bag on the main trash pile. She could tell by their faces they weren't getting it. The boy with the dog grabbed several juice boxes, tore them, open then offered the inside to the dog to lick.

The oldest girl, in the grey and yellow dress, approached Julie and pointed to the little waif watching from a distance, "Nilaya." Julie hesitated. *She seems to be the responsible one. She seems to want to help.* Julie let out a breath and handed her the food. She immediately took it to the hungry little girl and returned.

Julie touched the oldest girl's shoulder, trying out the Hindi word for *thank-you.* "Dhanivadha." She beamed at the attention. Julie was riffling through her dictionary, finding the word for *friend,* and motioned for the girl to sit with her.

"Mithra, Julie."

"Mithra, Sashi," replied the girl, eager to earn Julie's favor. Two other girls sat down, and the rest of the children wandered off. Julie learned the other two girl's names, Chavvi and Shoba.

Sashi looked about 11 and was taller than all the children. She had long black hair that was greasy and matted. She was the helper and unofficial leader of the girls. *Her brown eyes are captivating.* Julie noticed that her grey and yellow dress was tight, waist too high and sleeves too short. *She must have been on the street for quite a while; this looks like what might have fit her last year.*

"Sashi, that's pretty," said Julie. Upon hearing her name, Sashi sat a little taller and gave Julie a big smile.

Chavvi was about eight, with short, charcoal-colored hair, and she wore a pink dress with ruffled sleeves and grey trim. *It's dirty, but it doesn't look that old,* thought Julie. *Poor thing, she has shoes, but the ends are cut so her toes stick out. I wish I had scissors; her bangs are over her eyes.* Julie gave Chavvi a big smile, and she smiled back. *She seems a little more mannerly than some of the rest of them. I wonder what her story is?*

Shoba must be about ten. She wore a blue and white print outfit, which looked more rag than dress. Her very dark skin highlighted her white teeth, but her countenance was one of sorrow. Her thin, matted hair fell below her shoulders. *She has to be malnourished; she's emaciated, and her hair is so sparse.* "Mithra, Julie."

"Mithra, Shoba," she smiled and tapped her chest.

Julie noticed the boy wearing the green polo shirt. He was sitting with the dog, cutting different colored plastic shopping bags into strips with a small pocket knife then braiding them into bracelets. *That's clever. I wonder if he sells them. I never see him without that dog.*

The wind picked up, and the stench from the garbage washed over Julie. She put her hand over her mouth, but when she felt herself starting to gag, she jumped up and pointed in the direction that Ravi had gone.

"I have to find Ravi. I still have his food." The girls stood and took a few tentative steps after her. *I can't be dragging three girls along. I can't protect them.* In as kindly a manner as she could she shooed them back each time they tried to follow. Finally, they understood. She smiled and waved. "See you later. Bye, mithra."

After walking for about 30 minutes up and back on the close streets, she kicked a rock and sent it skittering across the road. *Where are you? I'm tired of fighting off beggars—young, old, short, smelly, ugh! You're making my life too hard. I'm a sweaty, worn-out mess.*

Julie. It was the Lord. *He's hasn't been on the streets very long. He needs your protection and your love. How long would you look if it were Logan?*

"That's different, Lord."

Is it? His mom and dad loved him as much as you love Logan, but they're gone now. He has nobody—but you. You're My hands, and your voice is My soothing voice to these abandoned children. No one sees their value. These precious ones are considered a nuisance.

She looked at the ground knowing she couldn't give up, even though she was exhausted and hot.

"Can you point me in the right direction?"

Ravi has fallen asleep behind a heap of trash. Two streets down and then left into the alley. Have his food ready—his first inclination will be to run.

"But I didn't yell at him when I learned he stole my purse. Why's he afraid of me?"

These children live in a totally hostile environment. Nothing is entirely safe. Every meeting with the police, another youth, or an adult can result in betrayal, abuse, or exploitation. They're always on alert. They live with an all-encompassing sense of hopelessness. I want them to hope in the face of adversity. I want them to flourish, not just survive.

Julie walked. *Am I nuts? Do I really believe I'll find him?* Julie turned into the alley and caught her breath at the sight of a large heap of trash. She pulled the food from her purse and tiptoed. There curled up, lying on the filthy ground, was Ravi. The sight was both disgusting and heart-rending.

His body was still covered with scrapes and bruises. His open wounds were filthy. *What if they get infected?* His clothing looked even dirtier than before, if that were possible, and the blood was still visible.

He's just a little boy. How can he survive on his own? She remembered the baby bird she'd rescued. *How can I do less for a child?* She remembered when he hugged her so tightly then abruptly stopped. The memory tugged at her heart.

She sat quietly beside him, giving him enough room to run if he desired, but close enough to hopefully be a comfort.

"Ravi," she whispered. *If I touch him he might startle.* "Raa-vi" she said in a sing-song voice. "Raa-vvi, I have some food for you." His eyes opened, and the first thing he saw was a sandwich in Julie's extended right hand, then the apple and juice in her left, then her smiling face and the earrings. He sat up abruptly, and before he could do anything, he caught the sandwich, the apple, and then the juice that she tossed him. His eyes narrowed with suspicion.

Why would she feed me? I stole her purse. What does she want? He remembered Mr. Shah's kindness. *Look how that ended.* He stood up, his back against the wall, eyes wide. He dropped the apple, and it rolled toward Julie. She put it in the sack with the extra food and handed it to him.

"I only want to help you. Don't be scared." *He has such a lost expression.*

Ravi took the sack cautiously and slowly moved away.

"Ravi, I just want to be your friend. You can trust me." *What was that word? It started with an "m."* She flipped rapidly through the dictionary as he took a few steps toward the other end of the alley.

"Wait, Ravi, don't go. I want to help you. I can feed you every day." She reached for him, but he bolted. "Mithra, mithra," she yelled, "Julie, mithra!" But he was gone. She buried her face in her hands and breathed deeply. Her heart was heavy.

With a grimace on her face, she dug through her purse and found a tissue. She put the strap over her head, squatted, leaned with her back against the wall and hiked her dress. "Lord, I will never get used to this. I think I'm getting a migraine."

The sun was setting, and Julie walked quickly to avoid all the homeless who would soon cover the sidewalk. She entered through the gate and immediately slid between the bushes and the house. She hesitated, then gently lay her bag in the dirt and put her head on it like a pillow. She sighed. The events of the day played through her mind.

I can't believe I have my purse back. Ravi ran from me again. What will happen to him? Where will he sleep tonight? I didn't even get to give him his vitamins. Lord, will You protect Ravi and all the children at the dump? Will You keep them safe? Amen.

It was night, and the children were all sleeping on the ground. Several of the girls huddled together, but most were spread several feet apart.

Convinced that everyone was asleep, Ravi crept back to the dump and lay under a hedge at the back. He was hidden, but close enough to feel the safety of a group. *For the first time since leaving Mr. Shah, I am not hungry.* It was a wonderful feeling. He tossed and turned several times, trying to find a position that didn't put pressure on a wound or a bruise.

Why does that woman have my mother's earrings? Did she know my mother? What does she want from me? Can I trust her? So many big questions for such a fragile little boy.

One moment Julie was lying behind the bushes wondering about the big hug she received from Ravi, and the next thing she knew, it was morning. That was a kiss from the Lord.

She awoke and was immediately aware of her exhaustion—physical and mental. The blistering heat did nothing to help. *The constant noises and the smells, don't they ever go away?* She rolled over and stretched before the demands of the day could impose. Her back ached, her mouth tasted terrible, and her stomach growled. *I hurt all over. I can't believe I'm stuck in this filthy, God-forsaken land—*

Julie, no place on Earth is God-forsaken. India may appear forsaken, but it's only because you don't have eyes to see and ears to hear what I am doing.

Everywhere you look in the natural realm you see lack, but My Kingdom is one of great abundance. Lack is not in My vocabulary. All riches and wisdom dwell with Me. I don't wring My hands wondering how I will provide for My orphans today and how I will manage to do it again tomorrow. I am the bountiful God of abundance. I am totally confident in My plans.

My resources and My love are unlimited. I never grow weary. I am always advancing. Let Me guide each step of your day. Walk in My abundant life, learn to trust Me. Don't worry; cast your cares on Me.[1] *I will carry what is too heavy for you. Switch your thoughts from your problems to your Savior.*

She frowned. "I try, but it's hard not to worry. I'm here, and my family's there. I miss them so much. They must be so worried. Plus, I don't feel like I do any good here,. Everything is messed up."

Your feelings will lead you astray. I want to do a wonderful work through you. Will you submit instead of fighting Me? I breathed out the stars, and I can hold the sea in My palms.[2] Do you think I am unable to care for you and My orphans? Trust is your word for the day. Read the next Scripture.

Julie flipped through the New Testament and finally, in frustration, referred to the index.

"Here it is, Proverbs. Page 900. *'Trust in the Lord with all your heart, and lean not on your own understanding; in all your ways acknowledge Him, and He shall direct your paths.'*[3] It's easy on paper. It's hard in life."

11

Before the sun was up Ravi was awake and walking. He prayed to Ganesh as he moved from one street to another. After walking for a kilometer, the street began to look familiar. A battered green Honda with a cracked windshield backed out of the driveway ahead of him. In the passenger seat was a young girl, missing a hand. Ravi froze.

Mr. Shah looked up, and their eyes met. He threw the car into park, screaming at the girl, and bailed out. Ravi's frozen body leaped into action. He knew his life depended on his ability to escape. As he sprinted through the streets, he could hear footsteps pounding on the cement behind him. "Ravi, come here. I forgive you, Ravi. Please come back, son."

Ravi burst onto the main street by the market. He wove in between traffic, moving and stopping, and finally plunged into the crowd. He ran on, bumping and bouncing off people. His captor cursed and turned back, unable to see Ravi's short frame among the adults.

Ravi finally stopped and hid behind a huge banyan tree, puffing and dry heaving. When he was able to finally calm himself, his thoughts turned to the girl in the front seat.

Run, girl, run. This is your chance.

Mr. Shah gave up and returned to his car to find the passenger door standing open. He cursed his luck, and he cursed Ravi.

"I swear, I'll make that boy pay—twice."

After hiding behind the tree for about 20 minutes, Ravi peeked out and then found the courage to enter the crowd.

Where should I go? He strolled by the vendors, eyeing the food. *Will I eat today?* His thoughts turned to the dump. *Why would they accept me? I can't go back; they'll hurt me again.*

Julie was making her way to the grocery store for the orphans' lunch. The smells and bright colors were still unique to her, and she walked past Ravi without seeing him. Ravi's first instinct was to run, but he decided to follow at a safe distance.

She entered the grocery store, and he trailed her, though he was careful to keep an aisle between them. His stomach growled. He was surrounded by so much food—none of it available. *Until my parents died, I was never hungry; there was always plenty of good food to eat.*

Julie was checking out with her food and drinks. His heart leapt at the thought of eating today. *Who is this woman? What does she want? Can I trust her?* He followed her until the crowds thinned out and then he backed off, ducking behind trees and cars.

Julie arrived at the dump to the orphans' wild excitement. The oldest girl, Sashi, took charge again and directed the boys and girls to sit. Ravi went around the block and watched from behind the hedge. As she passed out the sandwiches, he longed to step forward, but he knew he couldn't.

I stole her purse. Besides, what if she kidnaps kids like Mr. Shah? The desire for safety overcame his hunger—barely. He watched the other children ravenously attack their food. The children put the wrappers in one of Julie's plastic sacks, and she tied the ends and laid it on the trash pile. *But she still had another sack. There was food left.*

She gave Nilaya's food to Sashi, and there were still two servings. She looked preoccupied, staring in the direction of the alley.

After she waved good-bye to some of the braver children, she headed in that direction. Ravi ran as fast as he could back to the alley and lay down on the filthy cobblestone. *What if the food isn't for me? What if she can't remember how to get here?* After waiting for what seemed like a very long time, he heard her voice sing out, "Raaavv-i? Are you here?"

He pretended to be asleep. *Maybe she will leave the food.* His heart beat quicker as he heard her footsteps. He joyfully anticipated food, but what would be required in exchange?

She stood beside him now. *Should I run?* He popped one eye open and looked up at her. She towered over him. Then she held out the sack. He slowly sat up, feeling like a mouse being lured into a trap by the promise of cheese. He could feel his muscles tighten. His body was on alert and adrenaline coursed through his veins. She smiled at him, bent down, and extended the sack further.

Her earrings momentarily distracted him. *Mom's earrings.* They represented the last thing on Earth that reminded him of his lost family. He was briefly mesmerized until his growling stomach snapped him back to the present.

"Here, Ravi, you need to eat to stay strong. I won't hurt you. You can come back to the dump." She turned to take a few steps, hoping to lure him like a hungry cat. When he saw her back away with the food, he leaped up, grabbed the sack, and ran out the other end of the alley.

"Ravi, Ravi, come back." He was gone.

Julie flung her arms above her head in frustration. "Great! What now?"

Julie, if you don't give up, you'll win. I want to lay a foundation for the rest of his life. He's like a wounded, frightened animal. But your consistent kindness will bring him to Me. I have great plans for him, but there is much healing to be done.

"Make my life easier and tell him that he can quit running from me!"

Julie spent the next hour walking the streets calling for Ravi, but there was no reply. *What will happen to him? He won't accept my help.* The anger she had felt toward him for stealing her purse was dissolving. Seeing his wounds in the alley each day caused her stone-cold heart to develop a fissure. He was becoming her surrogate Logan.

At each block she was approached by beggars—old, young, and in-between. A young mother thrust her starving, hollow-eyed baby at Julie while frantically jabbering in Hindi. Julie learned to look at the street and keep walking.

Ravi walked the streets the rest of the day, being sure to avoid the direction of Mr. Shah's house. As the sun sank, he headed back to the hedge. He crawled in from the backside and stared longingly at the children. The girls slept on one side and the boys several yards away. Some of the younger ones were already asleep. A few of the older girls chatted. Madhu was propped on his elbows trying to make a hole in several large dried seeds with a nail.

His heart longed to be accepted, to not be alone another night. He lay down and beseeched his god again. When the last orphan lay down to sleep, Ravi felt totally alone. Being the only one awake was too scary. He tried to force himself to go to sleep, but he was bombarded with thoughts about the accident, being captured again, and his uncertain present and future.

What will tomorrow be like? Will anyone love me again? As he lay there, he picked at several scabs on his knees and cried himself to sleep.

Julie climbed between the house and the bushes. She lay her head on her purse. In a bizarre way, this was starting to seem less weird. The bushes offered a measure of protection that she needed.

She talked to the Lord about her family, although it was really more like complaining. "Lord, I miss Logan and Michael. Can I please call them? I always call if I'm going to be late. They must think I'm dead. The National Guards are patrolling New York by now. My dad must know. I'm upsetting everyone's lives. A simple phone call would solve it all."

She wanted to beg the Lord again to send her home, but Ravi's unknown condition kept interrupting her thoughts. "Lord, will Ravi be safe sleeping in the alley? He's too young to be all alone. Did I blow it today when I backed away with the food?"

Then the tension of the whole situation overwhelmed her. She had to choose. "I can't be two places at once. Lord, help me. It's too hard. I can't do this." For a while she thought she might be physically sick. She put her hands to her temples and massaged. *That old familiar feeling—a migraine again.*

Julie, remember I asked you to trust Me? If you take care of My lambs, I'll take care of yours.

"But, Lord, they must be worried sick. Logan will develop emotional problems from this. Just one phone call could resolve the whole issue. I could tell them where I am, and everything would be fine. They could even pray for me."

Julie, everything would not be fine because you would not learn to trust Me. In addition to blessing the orphans, I brought you here to bless you.

"You're blessing me? It seems like You're killing me."

Exactly.

She fell asleep early in the morning and slept until her aches and pains woke her. She sat up and twisted from the waist in a futile effort to try and alleviate her back pain.

"My neck is so tight," she tried to knead away a large knot in her shoulder, then ran her fingers over the puffy flesh under her eyes. *They're bloated.* "I'm dusty, dirty, and I stink." The smell from her armpits repulsed her. "I need a bath." She pulled a twig from her hair, then fumbled in her purse and pulled out her pick.

Ugh, my hair is greasy; my legs are way beyond stubbly. I don't want to die of some unsanitary disease. Julie climbed from behind the bushes and brushed the dirt from her dress. *Totally disgusting.* Her dress was ripped, and the urine discoloration remained.

Julie, check your verse for today.

She gritted her teeth as she crawled back in the bushes. "*'My ways are not your ways and my thoughts not your thoughts.'*[1] Duh! That's an understatement, Lord. If it was my way, You know where I'd be? Garden Oaks."

Do not let the length or the intensity of this season deter you. Keep your eyes on Me, not the unsettling circumstances that swirl around you. When you are focused on Me, you will begin to view circumstances from My perspective. Nothing happens to you that I don't allow. Do more than just submit to Me; rejoice in My wisdom and care. I just want to remind you that I am taking care of Logan and Michael.

"How?" She almost grinned. "How are You doing that? Did You tell them where I was?"

Release them to Me. Stop fretting. My ways, thoughts, and plans are higher than anything you can imagine.² You must learn to trust Me or you will be in anguish.

"How? I try, but it seems all my mind will do is worry."

First, put on My full armor³ each morning to resist the enemy's fiery darts—temptations. Then you must take every thought captive.⁴ The devil is a liar and the father of all lies.⁵ Train your mind to reject his lies because whoever controls your mind controls you. When a worrisome thought comes, ask yourself, "Where is that from? God, myself, or the devil?" Don't let the lie go unchallenged or it will take root in your brain, and you will believe it as truth.

Visualize yourself marking the cross over it and saying out loud, "I resist and rebuke this lie in Jesus' name, and I replace it with the truth of…." This is how you take every thought captive. Remember, I am the truth.⁶

Every day you have two choices: You can dwell on and magnify Me, or you can dwell on and magnify your problems. If you ruminate on your problems, you give them your worship. You actually meditate on them like you should be meditating on My Word. You actually worship the devil when you worry.

"I don't want to ever worship the devil!" Julie cringed at the thought.

Then take every thought captive.

"It sounds like a lot of work."

It is a lot of work. It's hand-to-hand combat with the enemy, but it leads to truth and peace instead of stress and anxiety. It's well worth the cost. I do not have stress. I laugh uproariously in the face of My enemies.'

"OK, Lord. I rebuke and resist the lie that I will fail at this, and I replace it with the truth that I can do all things through You."

The Lord smiled and sent a bolt of lightning.

12

Ravi was at the market hiding behind a car watching for Julie. He saw her in the distance surrounded by several beggar children. One little girl thrust a flower at Julie, another a bracelet made of braided multi-colored string. Julie kept walking and they kept following. When she entered the market, several of the vendors shooed the children away. Julie forced a smile and entered the grocery store.Ravi followed her at a distance back to the dump; then he hurried around back to the hedge. When the children first saw Julie, several of them let out a shout, which alerted the others. They organized themselves into two circles.

Forgetting protocol, a few of the orphans jumped up. Julie froze and postured her body between the bags and the orphans. Before they reached her, several of the other children grabbed them. The boy with the scar pushed the one wearing the cap before resigning himself to sit.

"Nobody eats until we're all in order," stated Sashi, looking straight at him. Most of them had recognized the pattern. Sashi helped arrange and get them seated while Julie passed out the sandwiches, apple, and juice. The boy with the scar glared at Julie as she handed him his sandwich. Julie glared back. *You are an obnoxious brat, and someone needs to teach you a lesson.*

After they had eaten, Sashi took food to the youngest, Nilaya. *Sashi helps without even being asked. She's so thoughtful.* Julie watched from a distance to make sure that no one took Nilaya's food away. She still wouldn't come near or make eye contact.

At the end, Julie had two sandwiches, two apples, and two juice boxes left. She looked again to make sure everyone had eaten. *I wonder who's missing?* She tried to communicate, but her best charades fell flat.

Ravi had been looking from behind the hedge. He had carefully watched to make sure there was food and assessed the situation correctly when two servings were left.

Which one was missing? Boy or girl? Ravi stared for a long time. *The short boy who walked with a limp. Was he here yesterday?* Ravi strained to remember. He wasn't sure, but he didn't think so. *Where did he go?*

Julie dismissed the mystery of the extra food. *More for Ravi, I guess.*

Some of the orphans seemed to be warming slightly. They thought, *Today she didn't try to hit us with her purse, but just tried to protect the food. Maybe she could be trusted—but just a little.* Julie was thinking the same thing about them.

Shoba, Chavvi, and Sashi stayed around instead of immediately scampering off. Julie moved a little ways from the dump to escape the smell, and when she sat, they did too.

Sapna, the biter, joined them, but looked less than friendly. Julie guessed her about age seven. *Average looks, average everything. Greasy, matted shoulder-length black hair. I guess that was a bob at one time.* The man's t-shirt dwarfed her. The short sleeves came down to her elbows, and the hem covered her knees. *She looks like she's been shrinking.* Julie forced a smile, but Sapna just frowned.

Julie gave wide berth to her. A scab was forming on her calf from Sapna's bite, and Julie hadn't forgotten.

Shoba, Chavvi, and Sashi all looked hopefully at Julie.

They are so starved for attention. She smiled and waved at each of them. They smiled and waved back. "Mithra," each of them replied.

How can I communicate without words? Then she remembered the toddler's game Pat-a-cake. She held up her hands and encouraged Sashi to do the same. Then she performed the motions as she chanted the rhyme. "Pat-a-cake, pat-a-cake, baker's man, bake me a cake as fast as you can. Pat it and roll it and mark it with a 'B' and put it in the oven for baby and me!" Sashi was delighted with the attention and tried hard to follow along with the two-handed claps.

Julie paired Shoba with Sapna and Chavvi to Sashi. The girls didn't quite catch all the motions, so Julie did it again. Each time she sang faster, and each time the children laughed at their attempts. *Is Shoba smiling? Amazing.*

Encouraged, Julie jumped. She sang, "You put your right foot in you put your right foot out. You put your right foot in and you shake it all about." By the time Julie got to "ya put your head in, ya put your head out," the three girls were following like pros. *I guess the "Hokey Pokey" translates into any culture.*

"Good job, you're doing great!" When she clapped for them, they all gave a joyful nod and stood just a little taller.

The girls were having so much fun that Wilson, Madhu, Bhanu, Mahipal, and Praveen all joined them.

Wilson was about eight, had big ears, and was full of rambunctious energy. He wore a filthy white hat and carried a walking stick, which he lay aside to join the dance. On the verse, "ya put your whole self in, ya put your whole self out, ya put your whole self in and shake it all about," he was flailing like crazy. *He dances like he has ants in his pants*, thought Julie, and she flung her head back and laughed at his wild lack of inhibitions.

All the children seem to be having a good time. I guess if you're fed and entertained, that's a good day at the dump.

After going through the songs a few more times Julie waved and left to find Ravi. The children continued playing, enchanted by the "Hokey Pokey." As Julie was leaving she turned and saw Bhanu pick up Wilson's walking stick. Wilson grabbed it so forcefully Bhanu stumbled forward. Wilson shoved him backwards and stormed off.

He's just a little too possessive over that stick, thought Julie, wiping sweat from her forehead. In a flash, Bhanu was on his feet, made a running leap, and landed on Wilson's back. He landed one hard punch before Wilson threw him off. Bhanu yelled something before stomping away.

He's such a bully, thought Julie.

Silently, Ravi ran ahead of her.

Julie's anxiety was building as she approached the alley. *Will he even be there? I really blew it yesterday.*

Ravi sat beside the trash, mulling the situation over. He was "sleeping" as usual and wondered, *Will she give me the food? Is she angry at me for running away? I really blew it yesterday.*

"Raavv-i, are you here? I have food for you." She peeked into the alley and entered more slowly than usual. When he was sure she was there, he opened his eyes. He was pleased to see her smiling. He watched as she slowly sat down and opened the sack.

He hoped there were still two servings of everything. His eyes stared at her face, then the sack, then back to her face. *Is this a trap? I can't let my guard down.* His brow furrowed with concern.

She put a sandwich in front of him. She was sure to leave the bag open so he could see there was more. Without taking his eyes off her, he reached and clutched the sandwich to his chest. To his relief, she gave him the other sandwich, too. He ate, not taking his eyes off of her.

She heard the Lord's voice. *Talk to him.*

Lord, he won't understand.

Julie, don't try to figure things out; just figure out how you can obey. I didn't give Moses the 10 Suggestions.

"Well, Ravi, here we are sharing food in an alley. What a strange place to meet. Here, this is yours," she said, handing him the two apples. "Double rations. I guess someone else found another place to eat today. I'm from America. That's a large country that's far, far away. I have a husband named Michael and a son named Logan. He's about your age. I miss him terribly, and when I look at you, I can sometimes picture him."

"Jesus sent me here to help all the orphans who are living at the dump, including you. It's a strange situation, far too strange to try to fill in all the details. You wouldn't believe it if I told you." She stopped and smiled. He smiled back.

"Ravi, you have a lovely smile. I wish I knew your story. Where are your parents? I wish you would follow me back to the dump, the glorious, foul-smelling dump. How could you possibly resist an offer like that? But at least I could protect you better, and you could make friends. I worry about you. I'm afraid I'll show up one day and," she choked over her words, "you'll be gone forever." Ravi continued eating.

"I wish you could understand me, and I'd ask if you'd be my son while I'm here in India. I could be your temporary mother, and I'd give you big hugs every day." A tear welled in her eyes. "I guess that's not going to happen. Oh, I still have the juice." She passed two cartons to him. She was surprised that he took time to sip the juice rather than guzzling it like the other children.

"I have something else for you," she fished in the pocket of her dress and pulled out two chewable multivitamins. "Here, take these, they're vitamins, they'll help you stay strong and healthy, but they taste like sweets.

"Ravi, as long as I can find you here, I'll bring you food every day, and you won't have to be hungry. I promise." His eyes met hers and held the look for five long seconds. He smiled slightly and finally looked away.

I wish I could do something nice to thank her for bringing me food. Then he picked up the empty sack and put the juice cartons and sandwich wrappers inside, tied the top, and handed it to her.

"Ravi, maybe you understand more than I think you do. Be safe, and I'll be back tomorrow." She wanted to touch him, to pat his shoulder, but decided not to push it. *It's going to take time, Julie; if I don't quit, I win.*

He wanted to hug her again, but fear won out.

She headed back to the dump, oblivious that he followed at a distance. She was also unaware she was humming and that her heart's fissure had cracked a little wider today.

That evening she lay in the dirt, trying to find a comfortable position. Her thoughts bounced between Logan and Ravi; both seemed just out of her reach. She was trying to be positive, *Look on the bright side, Julie; you're making progress,* but discouragement flooded in. *At this rate you'll only be here two or three years before you get to go home.* Despair washed over her, and she wept for her son and husband.

Logan, Logan, how are you? Please don't worry about me. I am coming back—sometime. Michael, I'm here, but I want to be there with you. I miss you. As she wiped her last tear, she heard the Lord's gentle voice whisper.

Julie, you need to practice the discipline of gratitude. No matter how hard your circumstances seem, there is still much to be grateful for. If I didn't give you your next breath, you'd be dead. If I hadn't kept your heart beating, you never would have lived to age 32. I want you to give thanks in all circumstances.

She bristled, "That's not even realistic, and I was expecting a little sympathy given what You're putting me through!"

Since you've been in India, you have realized how comfortable your life was at home, but when you were home, you weren't grateful for running water, flushing toilets, or unlimited food. Many people do not have these, but you never once thanked Me for providing them. How many things can you thank Me for today?

Julie felt her teeth clench. "Ummh? Today I've got no clean water, no flushing toilets, and no food."

You can start by rejoicing that your name is written in the Lamb's Book of Life.[1] You will spend eternity in Paradise covered by My love instead of living in eternal damnation, which is what you deserve. Surely you can be grateful for that.

I guess so, thought Julie, *but eternity is a long ways away; hunger and deprivation are now. And my sleeping condition couldn't get any worse.*

Thunder boomed, lightning flashed, and in several seconds torrential rain was falling.

13

Ravi woke early, concealed under the hedgerow behind the dump. He had a mission today and gave himself a pep talk as he walked to Mr. Shah's house. *You can do this. You must do this.* His heart pounded from his hiding place behind the neighbor's flowering bougainvillea. It was all he could do to stay.

At around 8:00 A.M., Mr. Shah backed out of the driveway in his green car. Ravi could see a small figure in the passenger side, but he couldn't get a good glimpse. The car went down the street three blocks and turned right. Ravi waited. In about ten minutes, Mr. Shah was back, alone. He parked the old green car with the cracked windshield, climbed in his black Mercedes, and left.

Ravi waited another five minutes and then walked the three blocks and turned right. In ten minutes he saw the shopping center. There on the sidewalk was Sammy, the limping orphan with the missing front teeth. Sammy recognized Ravi from the day he was at the dump.

"I can help you escape. Mr. Shah's a bad man. I can feed you if you come with me now."

Sammy considered the invitation. *Mr. Shah's really mean, and I'm really hungry.*

"If you stay, he will hurt you." Sammy's eyes widened.

"He cut off Kumar's arm, he did!" And with that, Sammy followed Ravi back to the alley.

"We will get fed if we stay here. You can't be seen at the dump because Mr. Shah will come looking for you." The young boy nodded, his eyes wide.

Sammy explained how Mr. Shah had offered him a bag of sweets one day, and the next morning he was out begging.

"When he got me yesterday, he was mad. He threw me in the shed. There was a boy blind in one eye, a girl without a hand, a boy with one arm, and a boy without a foot. He leans on a tree branch to walk. Mr. Shah yelled, hit me, and beat me with a rope. I'm hungry.

"The next morning, Mr. Shah gave me a piece of bread and sent me back to beg. He yelled again. That day I made more money, but not enough.

"He hit me with his fists. He didn't feed me. I am very hungry."

Ravi nodded. "I stayed one night, and the first day he put me on the street, a voice told me to leave."

The two orphans chatted a little.

"Raavv-i," came Julie's sing-song voice.

"Fast, fast, lie down and pretend to be asleep." Sammy looked confused, but followed Ravi's lead.

When Julie rounded the corner, she was surprised to see two "sleeping" boys. When she pulled sandwiches from the sack, they simultaneously "awoke." Sammy was not afraid of her like Ravi; he stood and eagerly reached for his sandwich, apple, and box of juice.

Ravi was proud of himself and a little more confident today. He looked at Julie like he might receive a special reward for his bravery.

She frowned. "Ravi, why did you take this boy from the dump? You both need to come back where I can keep a better eye on you." Ravi's countenance dropped, but Julie failed to notice.

Following the Lord's orders from yesterday, Julie talked while Ravi and Sammy ate.

Julie," she pointed at herself and then looked at Sammy.

"Sammy."

"Sammy, that's a nice name. I remember seeing you at the dump. You need to come back. Don't let Ravi persuade you to live in an alley. It makes it so hard on me."

When the boys were done eating, Julie held up the empty sack, and Ravi stared at it with an annoyed look. She motioned several times for him to pick up his trash, but he didn't. Finally she picked up both boys' trash and commented, "Well, someone isn't in a good mood today." She stood and held Sammy's hand.

"Come on, Sammy. If you come back to the dump, maybe Ravi will follow. Let's go."

Ravi jumped up and grabbed Sammy's other hand.

"No, don't go. Mr Shah will come and get you. He'll put you back on the street again. Stay here where you're safe." Sammy pulled his hand from Julie's and took a few steps backward.

"Sammy, it's really OK. Trust me. You can both come to the dump." Sammy took a few steps further back until he was standing next to Ravi, clutching him.

"Oh fine, do what you want! Just be careful. I'll see you both tomorrow." Julie exited the alley, wondering what Ravi had told Sammy to convince him to leave the dump and live in the alley. After failing to come up with a plausible idea, she decided to go back to the shopping district and buy some new clothes. *I am a disgusting mess. I stink.* She gave her armpits a wave. "My dress is torn and worse..." Her voice trailed off as she looked at the large discolored urine spot. She ran her fingers through her hair. "Uggh, so greasy. I wonder where I could take a bath? I'd pay any price."

As she walked, she remembered the year her church had volunteered to work at a homeless shelter in another town. Julie had gone once. Some volunteered in the kitchen and others conversed with the homeless. Julie had made a direct line for the kitchen and stayed there until the bus was loading to go.

When she served mashed potatoes on the line and handed the plates to the homeless, she tried to force a smile, but was mostly disgusted. *Why don't these people take care of themselves? Why do the tax dollars of hardworking Americans go to feed their drug habits?*

Now she walked the street self-consciously. *Who's looking at me? What are they thinking?* She slunk off to the dirt where the sidewalk ended, and sat, more like collapsed, and leaned against a tree. She studied the stains, snags, and rips on her dress and the dirt in the creases of her elbows. Her sandals were not only dusty, but also were stained — with what she didn't even want to know. Her beautifully manicured toes, in the perfect color of pink, were covered in dirt and chipped polish. She held out her hands and really looked at her fingernails. *Disgusting.* She turned them over. *Uchh, dirt.*

She sobbed, but wouldn't put her face in her hands because they were so dirty. She felt sorry for herself and sunk neck high into self-pity. "Why did You pick me to transport to India to live in squalid, disease-ridden conditions? I bring nothing to the table but inexperience and incompetence. Find a social worker and bring her here." She felt in her purse for a tissue and then sobbed again.

Julie, it was the Lord's voice, but she was not necessarily eager to hear it. *My word says that My power shows up best in weakness.[1] You are correct; you need to lean on Me to succeed. By yourself you can produce nothing of value.[2] Trust Me, trust My Word, trust My instructions, and it will be well for the orphans and especially for you. If you hadn't realized it, this trip was not just about changing their lives, but also changing yours.*

"Jesus, if You send me back, I swear I'll volunteer at the homeless shelter — every week. Twice a week. I know now that, given lousy circumstances, almost anyone can end up homeless. I'm sorry I made the comment about them living off our taxes. I'm sorry for everything; just please send me back." She exhaled deeply. "I'll even tithe. I'll work there twice a week. I realize now I had a horrible attitude toward the poor, but I've learned my lesson, really. I can do much more good back home where I have a lot of money and I can speak the language. I'm a changed woman, really." But somehow she knew the Lord wasn't buying it.

There was only one thing to do. She marched directly to the grocery store and picked up a six-pack of cola, a chocolate cake with white icing, and a quart of vanilla ice cream. On the way to the checkout, Julie grabbed a candy bar. There was a glossy Indian fashion magazine featuring a dark, stunning woman in a plunging skin-tight outfit on the front. *Let's see what passes for fashion here.*

She marched with her sack into the nearest restaurant. Out came the hand sanitizer, slathered to her elbows. She pointed indiscriminately to the menu. The waiter brought a heaping plate. She unpacked her food on the table, scraped the plate's contents into her sack, and wiped the plate clean with a napkin. She scooped up half the cake and put it on her plate. *Now for the ice cream on top.* The sound of the popped top on the cola can had her nearly salivating. She scooped up a huge bite of cake with ice cream.

Slow down, Julie, no one's going to take it away. Ummm, oh, so long without good food. So long without a soft drink. She savored each bite, then opened the magazine.

To Julie's surprise, everything was definitely up to date in India's fashion world. By the looks of this magazine, India's answer to Hollywood—Bollywood—was in full swing. *These fashions are different, but totally gorgeous. These fabrics are luscious. They drape so beautifully. Oh, the bright colors.* She turned the page. *Six inches of bangles and stiletto heels—very stylish. Paris has nothing on them.*

Julie took a deep drink of her soda and let out a sigh. *Where are these stores? Not around here.* She continued looking from picture to picture, wishing she could read the text. Fashion and food were doing their job—temporarily numbing her pain.

Julie could picture herself in the model's yellow dress with the draped neckline and slit skirt. Layers of silk wafted in the breeze from the fan that was obviously out of photo range. The stiletto heels featured beautiful embroidery. *These are the prettiest shoes I think I've ever seen.* The matching necklace, bracelet, and earrings of emerald and yellow stones stirred a longing in Julie, which she met by eating more cake, ice cream, and soda.

By the time Julie turned the last page, she had forgotten that she looked like, and was, in fact—a homeless person. On the back cover was a large picture of a glistening perfume bottle. She was jerked back into reality by the smell of her own body odor and the uncomfortable sugar-sick feeling.

She stared at the cake. It was three quarters gone, ditto the ice cream. Candy bar, eaten. *Uggh. I need a glass of milk.* She signaled to the waiter and milked unseen utters in the air. He looked confused. No one else was drinking milk, and there weren't little containers of cream on the table. "Oh, never mind," Julie dismissed the waiter with a wave of her hand.

She finished her soda, grabbed the three remaining cans and her magazine. *They can have the cake.* She turned and left.

That evening in her bushes, she was in great discomfort.

"Urrgh, I don't care if I never see sugar again. Why'd I do that?" Julie massaged her forehead. "Must keep this migraine away." After looking through the magazine several more times, it now bored her. She toyed with trying to find a phone and beg Michael to get her on the next flight out.

Julie escaped into a fantasy of being back home and hosting an elaborate Indian-themed dinner party. She fairly floated across the floor wearing the yellow dress with the embroidered stiletto heels and matching jewelry. All her friends were dressed up, too, but no one was as elegant as she.

"Yes, I picked this up on my trip to India. It's the latest fashion right from Bollywood." She served Americanized Indian food on the new set of stoneware, in wonderful cardamon and curry colors. Everyone raved. The evening was a smashing success and when everyone was gone, Michael swept her up in his arms.

"You look so beautiful tonight, dear. You make this outfit live. It shimmers with your every move. But...why do you smell so bad?"

Suddenly she transformed back to the dirty, smelly, greasy-haired woman lying in the dirt, still a mess, but now she was a mess with a stomachache.

"Lord, I'm so miserable. I'm stuffed, and I'm sugar sick. I feel even worse than I did before I bought all that stuff."

It's a valuable lesson to learn, Julie. Next time you won't even have to go down that path.

"I wish I hadn't gone down it now."

There is a God-given desire for perfection that I have put in every human heart. It's a foreshadowing of what's coming in eternity. That's why seeking perfection in this imperfect world, filled with imperfect people, never works. True satisfaction will not be found in people, things, accomplishments, money, or acceptance. Striving after these things to fill you is idolatry. And as you can see, it extracts a price. I alone can truly satisfy you. Learn to stop striving and rest in Me. Read your next Scripture,

Isaiah 55:1-3.

Julie flipped through the New Testament.

Old Testament, page 963.

Everyone who thirsts, come to the waters; and you who have no money, come, buy and eat. Yes, come, buy wine and milk without money and without price. Why do you spend money for what is not bread, and your wages for what does not satisfy? Listen carefully to Me, and eat what is good, and let your soul delight itself in abundance. Incline your ear, and come to Me. Hear, and your soul shall live....[3]

She pondered for a few seconds. "Wow, now You're getting personal. Do me a favor, Lord. Help me to remember how incredibly lousy I feel now the next time I'm tempted."

CHAPTER

14

Ravi had made his plans and talked Sammy into joining him that morning. They snuck away from the garbage dump unnoticed and headed for the street corner where they had both been rudely deposited by Mr. Shah.

From across the street they could see a little boy holding a can in his right hand. He had no left arm, just a six-inch stump protruding from his shoulder and wrapped with fresh bandages. He shook the can and stepped in front of the people walking by.

"That's him; that's Kumar. Mr. Shah cut his arm off," declared Sammy.

Ravi motioned for Sammy to follow him across the street, and they crouched behind a parked car. Ravi motioned for him to come. The beggar boy, wearing a torn blue t-shirt and dirty shorts, kept walking.

"Come here. We can rescue you. Mr. Shah had us, too, but we got away." The boy heard Ravi, but didn't slow from approaching pedestrians.

"Why isn't he coming?" whispered Sammy.

Ravi shrugged and tried again.

"Hey you, Kumar, come here. We can help you escape." A pedestrian finally took pity on the one-armed beggar and tossed several rupees into his can. It did nothing to alleviate the intense look on his face.

"Remember me? Come with us. We can get you food," tried Sammy. Kumar paid no attention. After trying several more times, they finally gave up.

"Why wouldn't he listen?" asked Sammy.

"I don't know; we can try again later. Let's go back to the alley so we don't miss our food. At least it's a little cooler there."

The boys passed the time chatting and pitching small stones to see who could get them closest to the far alley wall. When they heard Julie's voice, they both looked at each other and fell immediately "asleep."

Julie smiled down at them.

"OK, sleeping beauties, I have some food for you today." She sat down and pulled out sandwiches, apples, and juice boxes. Sammy made a lunge for them, but Julie was too quick. "Nope, manners, manners." Ravi pulled Sammy's hand back then folded his own hands in his lap.

"Well, aren't you the gentlemen today? I'll reward that behavior every time." She handed Ravi his food. Sammy quickly folded his arms and received the same response. Ravi ate half his sandwich and wrapped the other half. Then he spoke to Sammy, who at first looked like he'd been slapped. Sammy grabbed his apple and clutched it to his chest. Ravi motioned to his own wrapped sandwich, and Sammy reluctantly lay the apple aside. They both drained their juice boxes.

"Well, what's going on here? Not too hungry today?" Ravi grabbed his sandwich and stared at Julie. Sammy clutched his apple.

"I'm not going to take them from you." She shook her head in confusion and then pulled out two multivitamins for each of them. Ravi said something to Sammy, who looked dismayed again and ate just one.

Surely Ravi isn't using Sammy to get more food. He seems so sweet, but he did steal my purse. Maybe he's capable of more than just thievery. Could Sammy be in danger? I'll have to keep an eye on him.

With a renewed urgency, she looked at Sammy.

"I wish you would come back to the dump." She held out her hand to Sammy, who looked immediately to Ravi, who shook his head no. She let out a big sigh. *I tried. I don't know what to do. I can't drag Sammy back.* "I'll be back tomorrow." She tried to sound encouraging as she left. "I hope you're both good and hungry then." She flinched. *What a stupid thing to say!*

"Sammy, take your apple and sweet and let's go." Sammy was still hoping to eat his food, but reluctantly agreed. Ravi had to constantly slow down. Sammy's limp kept him from running.

In a few minutes they were crouched between parked cars again waiting for Kumar.

"We've got food for you," said Ravi, holding up his half sandwich. He nudged Sammy, who held up his apple with two big bites removed. Ravi stared at him, and he grinned his gap-toothed smile back.

At the sight of food, Kumar came immediately and crouched between the cars. While he devoured the sandwich, Ravi began his spiel.

"Come with us. We get food every day. I promise. We will help you." The boy finished the half sandwich and began immediately on the apple.

"I'm Ravi."

"Kumar," he said as he finished eating the core.

"I'm Sammy! Remember me?"

Ravi dug in his pocket for his vitamin and handed it to Kumar, who didn't stop to examine it before eating. Ravi turned to Sammy and held out his hand. Sammy dug through one pocket and then the other and with a chagrined look, shrugged his shoulders when he could produce nothing.

I think I'll be the food carrier tomorrow, thought Ravi.

"Come with us, please."

"I can't. If I don't earn enough, I'll get beaten or...something else."

"What else?" piped Sammy, as if he might be missing out on something fun.

"I have to get back to work."

"We'll bring food tomorrow. I promise," said Ravi.

Julie had never gone much past the grocery store. Today she decided to walk farther. In eight more blocks, she came to an area that was more prosperous. These were actual stores, full buildings with locking doors, much more westernized than the primitive shops in Julie's neighborhood.

When Julie had first arrived in India, all the vendors tried to coax or even pull her into their shops. A white woman spelled money. Now ambling down the street, no one noticed her. She stepped into a clothing shop and came face-to-face with her reflection in a full-length mirror. No makeup, greasy hair, her flesh with a thin coating of dust. Her dress was worse. The green designer purse was scuffed, dusty, and stained. Bags under her eyes and five pounds lighter. She recoiled in shock.

What's happened to me? I look haggard, like a homeless person.

Julie was aware the sales clerk was staring at her with the same look she'd given those people reaching for their potato-filled plate back at the homeless shelter. She wanted to explain:

I'm not usually like this. I would be a good customer. I dress well. I value hygiene. I have a good job in America. This is due to circumstances beyond my control. This isn't me. I'm not like this. But today she was. She no longer stood out in the crowd; she was just another poor person to be ignored, looked down upon, or discarded. *No wonder I'm not getting assaulted by beggars anymore.* She exited. Across the street was a barber/beauty shop. The front window had a large drawing of a pair of scissors and written in English were the following services: haircut, facial massage, shampoo, manicure, pedicure, shave, and ear cleaning.

"Oh my gosh, why didn't I think of this before?" Julie felt a little twinge or check when she thought about entering. *If anyone deserves this, it's me.* She squelched the feeling and burst in the door with such enthusiasm that all the clients and workers stared. A look of disgust spread over all the faces. Shame urged her to turn and run, but vanity kept her firmly planted.

Julie walked to the desk, stared at the ground, and waited. She tried not to notice the beauticians looking toward each other hoping someone else would wait on her. She felt her face flush.

Finally an older woman approached, but her act of acceptance was not believable. Julie pantomimed shampooing her hair, painting her nails and toes, and washing her face. The woman motioned for her to sit in an empty beautician's chair and wait.

I'm surprised they even let me in the shop. I'm a disgusting mess. Julie spun the chair away from the large mirror in front. It was too close, too big, and revealed too much.

Her thoughts were interrupted by the sound of a flushing toilet. She jumped up, which startled everyone, and almost ran toward the sound. A door opened, and a well-groomed, 40-ish man exited. He walked a wide berth around Julie and entered the back of the shop. Without waiting for permission, she ducked in the bathroom and locked the door.

How long has it been since I've used a sink and a western toilet? To her surprise the hot water spigot worked. She rinsed the sink out then dumped about five tablespoons of hand sanitizer on a coarse brown paper towel and scrubbed. There wasn't a stopper so she wadded the paper towels and plugged the drain. Then she filled the sink with warm water and washed her face.

Look at how brown the water is just from my face. What a luxury. I wish I had some of my Himalayan moisturizer. How can warm water feel so good? Oh thank You, Lord, for warm water. After giving her face a more thorough washing than it had ever had, she drained the sink, refilled it, and began on her hands and arms.

Even though she pushed her sleeves up, they still absorbed a lot of water along with the front of her dress. Julie watched as the dirt reluctantly released from her elbow creases. *I'm really a white person after all,* she mused.

She refilled the sink and managed to lift a foot high enough to plop it in the bowl. After washing up to her thighs she used all the paper towels trying to mop up the water splashed all over the back of the sink and the floor.

The toilet, wonderful! I can't believe I've always taken it for granted. It just feels good to sit here. To sit instead of squat holding my dress up around my neck. Thank You, Lord, for this toilet. It's the nicest one I've ever used.

Julie didn't realize she was actually engaged in worship over plumbing fixtures, but that was exactly what she was doing. But it all came to an abrupt halt when there was a knock on the door. "Just a minute," she cried out in her happiest voice. She hurriedly applied lipstick. It smudged and when she tried to wipe the excess, it didn't come completely off. The more she rubbed the redder the area around her lips became. Her newfound excitement plunged. *I look like Bozo the clown.* There was a harder knock on the door and a stern voice.

Julie exited and all eyes were on her and her glowing lips. She took a deep breath as her cheeks turned the same color as her mouth. The beautician's badge said Indu. She led her back to her chair. Julie lay her purse down while Indu placed a plastic smock on her. Indu led her to the shampoo bowl and began vigorously shampooing.

Ouch, ouch, ouch, thought Julie as she tried not to squirm. *I had so planned to revel in this experience, but this really hurts.* After rinsing, Indu rubbed in conditioner, set her up abruptly, and wrapped her hair in a towel. Julie forced a smile to say thanks. Unable to see the lipstick on her front tooth, she didn't understand the beautician's smirk.

Indu led her to another chair and gave her a selection of four different nail polishes. *Not a wide selection, but the shrimp-colored one isn't bad.* Indu reclined the chair and put a fabric mask over her eyes. Julie felt her feet being lowered into warm water. Next a soothing cream was rubbed on her face while the beautician started on Julie's hands and nails.

Julie luxuriated in the experience. She pretended to be back in her regular spa, except this one lacked the wonderful fragrance that wafted through the air. For the first time she noticed the soft Indian instrumental music playing. *That's kind of nice.* She took a few deep breaths. *I promise to luxuriate in every second of this wonderful experience. As a matter of fact, this part of today will be perfect when I leave here and buy several sets of new clothes. This dress needs to be burned. I can't stand it for even another minute.*

She remembered the styles in the Indian magazine and pictured herself in each one. *I probably don't need anything designer, though before I leave I might buy some outfits to wear out on the town once I get back. My coworkers will be so jealous.*

Her pedicure was done and Indu started on her fingers. *I'm in heaven.* The face cream was starting to get a little warm. *Maybe it's because my skin has been neglected for so long. Maybe it's a spice or exotic ingredient that automatically warms the cream when it is triggered by body heat. That's fun. Maybe I can buy some to take back with me.*

She went back to her fantasy about new clothing. *I don't think I've ever looked forward to a shopping trip more than this one and that's saying something!*

The face cream was still heating up, but it wasn't painful. *It must be a really deep, deep moisturizer.* Julie felt the second coat of polish going on her fingers and was disheartened that this divine experience was almost over. *Oh, they've still have to cut my hair*, she remembered.

The face cream was getting uncomfortably warm and Julie pointed to her face several times but Indu ignored her. Finally, Julie grabbed a towel, ruining her manicure, wiped off the cream, and looked in the mirror. Where the eye mask had covered was her normal skin color. The rest of her face was a ruddy, dark red. Indu, not used to treating white skin, was unaware the Indian cream would burn Julie's fair complexion.

"I look like a raccoon in reverse," she yelled at the beautician, who flailed her arms and yelled back. Julie leaned in close to the mirror and came up yelling again.

Another beautician joined the skirmish. It was two against one and Julie couldn't understand a word.

"My face!" She pointed with both hands. "You BURNED my FACE. BURNED—MY—FAAACE. LOOK IT'S BURRRNED."

She leaned in closer for them to see this terrible injustice and the second beautician gave her a shove. Julie stumbled, but was saved when she landed in the beautician's chair. She had never fought before, but the emotional nosedive from euphoria to anger was whittling away her will power. She was on her feet again.

"BURNED—IT'S BUUURRNED. CAN'T YOU SEE? ARE YOU BLIND? YOU BURNED MY FACE."

At this point, the well-dressed man emerged. He looked at Julie and to his employees, who both shouted and pointed to her. The man nodded and with a soothing tone of voice put one hand on Julie's back and the other on her elbow and started escorting her to the door.

"I can't believe this. My face—look at what they did to my face." He nodded, but kept walking. He pushed open the door and motioned for her to exit. In a huff she stepped onto the sidewalk. At that point, Indu pointed to Julie and yelled to the manager. He gave a nod. The man leaned toward Julie as if he were going to tell her something and motioned for her to do the same. *Finally, they're going to take care of me.* When she leaned in, he plucked the towel off her hair and slammed and locked the door.

"NO, NO, NO," she shrieked and then realized all the people on the street were looking at her and her wet hair plastered to her head and her dirty torn dress with water spots all over and her red face.

"Aaaaargh! How can such a good experience go so bad? It can't get any worse! It's impossible." She turned to leave and realized she'd forgotten her purse. She pounded on the door, but no one moved. "MY PURSE. YOU HAVE MY PURSE." When an employee glanced her way she pantomimed the strap over her shoulder. "IT'S GRREEEEN! BY THE CHAAAIIR" she screamed while pointing.

People stopped and stared.

"Who speaks English? Does anyone here speak ENGLIIISH? I need HELP. HELP." A young Indian man about 16 stepped forward.

"I speak English."

"Oh, thank goodness. Thank you, thank you," she grabbed his hands as she spoke. "Well, first they burned my face," she leaned forward to give him a good look and he leaned away. "And then they threw me out of the shop, and my purse is still in there. I have to get it. Can you help me?"

"I'll try." He knocked several times.

"Please keep trying. I have to get it back." After several minutes of knocking, the manager returned. The young man spoke in Hindi and the manager nodded.

"MY PURSE," Julie yelled at him for good measure.

The manager returned with her purse, handed it to the young man, who handed it to Julie. She clutched it to her chest like a newborn.

"My purse, how can I ever thank you?" The young man glanced toward her purse and held out his hand. "Oh, of course. You earned this reward." She rummaged for her wallet. She caught her breath and dug frantically. "IT'S GONE. THEY STOLE MY WALLET. FIRST THEY BURN MY SKIN, AND NOW THEY STEAL MY WALLET!"

Everyone was staring again.

"DON'T GO TO THIS SHOP. THEY'RE CROOKS. THEY WILL BURN YOUR FACE AND THEN STEAL YOUR WALLET. HELP, PO-LICE. HELP, I NEED A POLICEMAN."

The young Indian said, "Madame, you need to calm down."

"Where's a police station? I need to get my wallet back. They are dirty thieves *and* incompetent beauticians! Can you take me to the police? Oh, do you have a cell phone? We can call 9-1-1. Do you have that here?"

"Madame, the police will not help you get your wallet back."

"But I know exactly who stole it. I can bring them right back here."

"Madame, that is not the point. The police do nothing without a bribe, especially from a white woman. If you have no money for a bribe, they will not help you. You are also a hysterical foreigner. Why would they believe you over their own people?"

"Because they stole my wallet. They *really* stole my wallet."

"You cannot prove that, Madame, and even if you could, you have no money for a bribe. No bribe—no service, that is the way it is in India. You must be new."

Julie felt like she would explode. If her face wasn't already bright red, it would have been.

"I'm new here, and I have no money. Please just take me." The young man held out his hand. Julie felt sweat beading on her forehead. Her heart pounded in her chest. She rummaged through her purse in desperation. "I can give you... a bottle of kids' multivitamins," she said, holding up the white bottle with the cartoon bear on the label. The young man's countenance dropped.

"Don't go. I'll find something." She pulled out a plastic Bic® pen. "It's an ink pen. I brought it all the way from America. It writes blue." He rolled his eyes, and she began to cry.

"OK, I don't have anything to give you. I have nothing. I'm totally at your mercy. Please just help me."

"I will take you there, but I will not go in."

"Oh, thank you. Thank you." She grabbed his arm, and he pulled away. The young man walked her three blocks back toward the dump.

"Here," he motioned to a nondescript building. "This is the police station." He held the large wooden door open. Her lip twitched. She clenched her fists, took a deep breath, and stepped inside, which was one big room. Two walls were lined with old green file cabinets. About eight policemen in grey uniforms sat talking at their desks. When she entered, silence fell, and all eyes stared at her.

Why do I feel like I'm on trial here? "English? Does anyone speak Ennng-liish?" they eyed her suspiciously. "I just had my wallet stolen," she pointed in the direction of the shop.

Two officers responded simultaneously. A 30-ish officer in the corner and a plump, older gentleman with a seemingly permanent scowl.

"I speak—" began the muscular officer in back.

"I speak English," interrupted the chief, a gruff older man, to the frazzled woman with wet hair, wet, dirty dress, red face, and lipstick on her tooth.

"Oh, thank goodness," Julie ran to stand in front of him and talked a mile a minute.

"It's my wallet. I went to the beauty shop, and they burned my face, and *then* they threw me out, and *then* I asked for my purse back, and they *finally* returned it, but my wallet was gone." She opened the purse and held it close so the officer could look. He didn't. He remained silent.

"Aren't you going to arrest them? They're thieves. We can go right now, and I know they still have my wallet! It just happened a few minutes ago," she pointed at the door.

The stoic officer translated, and when he got to the last sentence he mimicked Julie's frantic voice and pointed toward the door. Laughter exploded.

"But, you have to help. You're the police, right? OK, I won't press charges because they burned my face, but I have to get my *wallet* back. I'm trying to take care of some orphans, and all my money was there. I won't be able to feed them or me. Please help me."

"Why should I help you, a foreigner? There is much injustice done to my people. Can you pay me?"

"No—YES! Yes, I can pay you when I get my wallet back. We can go now. Let's hurry." She took several steps toward the door.

The chief translated and all the officers burst into laughter again, except for the muscular officer in the back.

"Young lady, *if* they really did steal your wallet—"

"But they did steal it. Just a few minutes—"

"Young lady," his voice was stern. "*If* they had your wallet, the money is gone by now—"

"But I know exactly how much was there. I had my credit card—oh, my gosh my credit card. I have to figure out how to cancel those—and I had exactly—"

"YOUNG LADY," his tone caused Julie to jump. "You're not listening. I said we can't help you. We have many cases stacked up." He pointed to the manila folders on his desk. "We are short of staff. I cannot take this case. I suggest you leave now."

Yeah, you look like you're all over the crime problem in this city, you schmuck! You probably don't ever get out of that chair until it's time to go home. "But I'm an American, and I have rights, and I know those rights, and I demand you to act on my rights," she said, her right fist pounding into her left palm.

"Then I encourage you to go back to America immediately to find your rights."

Julie turned to go. She was glad the tears didn't begin to flow until she was out the door. *Too humiliating to cry in front of this bunch of animals.* She rummaged through her purse looking for her migraine medicine.

As the officers laughed again at Julie's dilemma, the muscular officer in the back did not.

Julie was boiling. She paced the sidewalk, her fists clenched.

"Just when I thought nothing could get worse, then the bottom drops out. My face is burned, and my money is gone, and no one will help me. What am I supposed to do?" She fretted over and over about the ordeal in the beauty shop, then the police station, then back to the beauty shop until she was so frustrated she was ready to punch something. *My head is throbbing.*

Julie, you need an adjustment in your expectations. You live in a fallen, imperfect world. Stop expecting an easy life. Trials are the norm. Ease keeps your focus off of Me. Put another way, "Smooth seas make useless sailors."

"Lord, You don't understand." Pedestrians stared at Julie talking to herself.

I understand, Julie. It's you who needs an adjustment in perspective. Don't waste your time fretting about the circumstances or wishing them changed. You are in an impossible situation. This is the exact place that I want you to be—totally dependent on Me.

Trust Me to work on your behalf. Depend on Me for your every move. When I am active, you can be secure in a season of rest. In this world you will have tribulation, but be of good cheer for I have overcome the world.[1] Remember, this is a great time to take all these intruding thoughts captive; you've just been worshiping the devil.

Julie got the last words in. "But my face is *burned,* and my money is *gone!*"

15

R avi and Sammy waited in the alley for Julie.

"When is she going to get here?" Sammy looked hopeful. Ravi shrugged. Sammy rubbed his tummy to silence the growling.

"Let's see if she's at the dump," said Ravi.

The orphans were restless. Julie always came by lunchtime, and it was early afternoon. From their hiding place in the hedgerow, Ravi could see that several of the children had sat themselves on the sidewalk facing the market so they would be the first to see her.

This is not good, he thought, and then whispered to Sammy.

"She's probably just a little late today." He rolled over on his back. He'd come to depend on Julie, and the thought of going back to days without food terrified him. He drummed his fingers on the dirt.

The more time that passed, the more agitated the orphans became. Several boys got in a shouting match, which turned to shoving, which led to an all-out fight. Most of the girls were sitting on the sidewalk, their muscles tense.

Chavvi and Shoba began to cry. Sapna's face paled. They sat in silence. Sashi finally stood up and rummaged through the dump, looking for something she could sell or barter. Their minds were running away with thoughts of where they would get food if the woman who brings it does not come today, or ever again.

The woman who brings it was not having a good day either. She, being led by her bright red face, had walked the entire market and talked to all the vendors, trying to establish credit, which was impossible to do because of the language barrier. Her red face and stained and torn dress did nothing to instill credibility.

The smells wafting from the grills caused her stomach to rumble. She continued walking among the vendors looking at the tempting fruits and vegetables.

"Arrrrgh! It's at arm's length, and I have no way to get it!"

I can't believe You let them steal my wallet. No one is going to eat today, me included. What else is left to go wrong?

The thought of trying to steal something flitted across her mind, but she quickly apprehended it. *Just my luck, I'd get locked up in the police station and have to listen to those lazy cops complaining about their heavy work load.*

Julie, why are you complaining?

"Duh, maybe because my face is burned and my wallet is gone! And in just a short time, I'm all sweaty again!"

I asked you to trust Me.

"Oh, my gosh. Lord, are You going to return my wallet like You did my purse? That's so awesome—"

No, actually that's not the solution now—

"But, Lord, You know where it is. I have to eat, uh, and I have to feed the kids. I can't do that without money."

You can't, but I can if you trust Me.

"But I don't see any way out of this. Without money the situation is hopeless. I can't do anything."

In Heaven, we call that a setup for a miracle. But there is something you're required to do.

"You're going to tell me, aren't You?"

You need to worship and praise Me. That's the solution to this problem. That's the solution to every problem.

"I'm not exactly in the mood."

Your mood has nothing to do with it. Your heart will follow your head, but it takes an act of your will. Train yourself to think faith thoughts. Where others see giants, train yourself to see grapes.[1]

"What's that mean?"

The children of Israel sent 12 spies to the land I had promised them. The spies returned with grapes so big it took two men to carry them. Ten spies only fixed their thoughts on the giants and said that taking the land was impossible. Joshua and Caleb believed that I would do as I had promised. They focused on the benefits. Where others saw giants, by their faith, they saw grapes.

She spun around, looking for something to kick, and she saw a large pile of grapes on a vendor's cart.

Where others see giants, train myself to see grapes. "I see grapes; I see grapes. I want to eat the grapes. Aarrgh! I can't do it, Lord. I'm surrounded by food, but I have no way to get any for me or the orphans. It's impossible."

Julie, take that lie captive.

"OK, I'm picturing the cross over it. I resist and rebuke this lie in Jesus' name, and I replace it with the truth that You can provide food for us in ways that I don't know."

Excellent, Julie. You told me the truth, now I'll tell you the truth. The berries by your house are very desirable. Find a discarded container and go pick them. Then offer to barter for sandwiches at the grocery store.

"Oh, my gosh, Lord, that's awesome."

It was hard to get comfortable picking berries, and it wasn't long until her back and neck ached. *I wish I could just lie down and take a nap,* but her hunger drove her on. After about 40 minutes, she had picked the last berry. *I must have about ¾ of a gallon.* She headed back to the grocery store.

"Lord, help me." Thankfully there were very few customers there. The owner was used to seeing her every day; she was one of his best customers. He stared at her red, berry-stained hands, and her red, burned face as she approached holding up the sack of berries and pointing at it with the other hand like it was a game show prize.

Julie motioned for him to follow. She handed him the berries and picked up 12 sandwiches. She pointed to the berries and back to the sandwiches. Her heart pounded in her ears as she waited for his response. He nodded and smiled. She let out a sigh of relief, stepped outside the door, ripped the plastic off a sandwich and devoured it. *Now, to the dump.*

When she was still about two blocks away, Shoba caught sight of her and jumped up screaming and pointing. That captured everyone's attention, and soon they were all charging down the street toward her. She began to hyperventilate. *It's the mob again. Help me, Lord.*

She wrapped both arms around the bag of sandwiches, turned, and bent over to protect herself. In a few seconds, she was engulfed by bodies and grabbing hands. Anxiety washed over her. She clenched her fists till her nails dug into her palms. *I will not hit. I will not hit. Help me, Lord.* She stood up and twisted right and left and back again. Someone shoved her and she fell.

There was a huddle all grabbing for the sack, but Sashi came up with it and held it over her head. This drew all the attention from Julie, who was still lying on the sidewalk clutching her purse. Sashi shouted commands, and after several minutes the orphans decided to obey because none of them were tall enough to take the bag from her.

The girls first sat on the sidewalk, and when the boys saw them receiving food, they quickly followed. Julie stood up and lay her hand on Sashi's shoulder. She smiled as she took the sack back to make sure she had control over the last three sandwiches.

When it became clear that no more food was coming, no fruit, no drink, the attitude turned sour. Julie couldn't understand the words, but she understood their meaning.

She could only shrug. Sashi took over again, and after several minutes of her instruction, the orphans calmed down. That gave them the opportunity to notice Julie's face for the first time. They pointed and laughed. Julie felt herself blush, but knew it wouldn't show. *I want to hide, but how do I escape from kids who know every inch of this ground?*

She stormed off toward the alley.

"They only care about themselves." She frowned. "The little ingrates, they get food every day, and when it gets cut back, they turn on me."

I know that feeling well, Julie. It reminds Me of someone else. Does it remind you of someone you know? asked the Lord.

She ignored Him. She knew her stomach would be growling in an hour. Her thoughts turned to home. Her refrigerator was stocked with more food than her family could eat. Whatever she wanted, she bought—imported cheeses and chocolates, fruits from all over the world, bottled fruit-flavored water with added vitamins, specialty cuts of grain-fed beef, and as many impulse buys as she had impulses.

Julie, you throw out enough food each week to feed My orphans. Your garbage disposal eats better than half the people in the world.

She flinched. She didn't want to think about it, but knew it was true. *My actions have trained Logan to turn his nose up at leftovers.* It had never bothered her to throw away leftovers or to toss something that didn't taste as good as she'd hoped, or just something she was tired of eating. Her stomach never growled at home. She never went without anything she wanted.

On the way to work each morning, I always stop for a large latte and pastry. I eat lunch out each day. I pick up carryout at least three evenings a week. I never even thought about it before.

Ravi and Sammy had gone ahead of her to the alley and were anxiously waiting.

"I promised Kumar that I would feed him every day. We're only getting one sandwich now."

Sammy considered the situation.

"What are you going to do?"

"I don't know." Ravi chewed on his lip as he fought an internal battle. *I have to take care of myself and Sammy first. Should I save half my sandwich for Kumar? Should I expect Sammy to? I'm so hungry. What if Julie doesn't come with food tomorrow and I gave away half of mine today? Will Kumar get anything to eat?*

Ravi realized that Sammy was staring at him.

"OK. I'm going to give half my sandwich to Kumar. You can decide what you want to do."

They were both startled when Julie was standing over them. She hadn't announced herself with her sing-songy voice. She sat down and Ravi and Sammy immediately folded their hands in their laps. *Can't take chances, when the food is this scarce.*

Ravi noticed her red face, but also her sad eyes as she handed out the lone sandwiches. Ravi suddenly felt sorry for her and tried to force a smile. He ate half his sandwich and reluctantly wrapped the other half. Sammy finished half and wrapped his also, but after a short time he unwrapped it and ate all but the crust. He wrapped them back up and looked chagrined.

"I guess you're saving some for later. That's probably a good idea. Food is harder to get now. I wish you two would come back with me. I worry about you living here in this alley. Each time I approach I get anxious wondering if you're going to be here." She smiled and touched Ravi's shoulder.

"Hopefully I'll be back tomorrow. If there's any way at all, I'll be here with some food. Sleep well, guys," she waved and left.

As she walked, she passed a beggar boy. Not unusual, but this young boy, sitting on the sidewalk, was missing a leg.

"Oh, Lord, how sad. What kind of accident caused that?"

It wasn't an accident, Julie. Hundreds of My young children have their arms and legs amputated each year, the victims of India's "beggar mafia." Others are blinded or have acid poured on their bodies, leaving them with oozing wounds. This suffering is all about money. Children with the worst injuries make the most. A deformed child can make up to ten times what the average person survives on. After work each day, the children are forced to hand over the money to gang masters. If they don't reach their goals, they are beaten and tortured.

Over 44,000 precious children end up victims of the beggar mafia each year[2] and hundreds are deliberately mutilated. Most victims are between two and eight years old. Often they are not fed so that they cry continuously and earn more money. They are taught where to beg, the kind of people to approach, and the kind of mannerisms that make people sympathetic. They beg seven days a week, especially at tourist locations, religious and spiritual sites, near hotels and souvenir shops.

Gang masters cut out the tongues of informers so they are terrified of speaking out. With the beggar mafia making more than $22,000,000 a year in Mumbai alone, there is plenty of money to pay corrupt police officers.

In order to keep the children under control, almost all of the child beggars, mutilated or not, are given solvents, alcohol and powerful hashish, often laced with opium.

Newborns are stolen from hospitals. Many kidnapped children are forced into child pornography and used as sex slaves. Others are killed and their organs sold to wealthy Indians.[3]

Julie felt like the wind had just been knocked out of her. "I know You must be telling the truth, but I can hardly believe what You said. Their limbs are amputated so they can earn more money? Who would do that?"

Many, many evil people do that, Julie, each and every day.

"Lord, I feel nauseous; I might throw up."

This is a very big problem for such a small woman. I wanted to share My sorrow with you. You do not have to solve it. I just wanted you to know.

Your part in this tragedy is these orphans I have given you to love. I am inviting you into a place of deep relationship; stare into My heart and ask for My perspective about My lambs.

What life verse do I desire to give to each of them? What song am I singing over Sashi? How can you celebrate Sammy today? What are My hopeful plans for Chavvi? What aspect of Shoba am I cheering? Which spiritual gift have I given Sapna?[4] What hope-filled promises burn in my heart for Madhu? What key will unlock Nilaya's heart?

Julie, partner with Me in healing these orphans—spirit, soul, and body— that is your mission.

CHAPTER

16

As soon as Julie left the alley, Ravi hurried to the shopping center. Sammy called after him.

"Slow down, Ravi!" Ravi was relieved to see Kumar.

"Kumar," he called from between two parked cars. Kumar's face lit up, and he ran to the boys. Ravi handed him his half sandwich, which he wolfed down and then Sammy, with a smile, held up the crust, which Kumar also devoured.

"My friend didn't bring as much food today. All we got was one sandwich each, but each day that she brings food, I will share what I have." He glanced at Sammy, but didn't wait for an answer.

"Come. Even if we just get one sandwich every other day, you will never get beat. I promise." Kumar stared at him as if he was considering it.

"Mr. Shah said he will find me and kill me if I leave."

"He told me the same thing, and I am still alive. I can help hide you. Come."

"If Mr. Shah drives by and sees me talking to you, he will beat me again to-night." He turned abruptly to approach a lady with a camera around her neck.

Julie was back at the dump trying to communicate. *Looking up words in my dictionary is painfully slow. Lord, I really, really need a translator.* It was easier to engage the girls in games. She taught them hand clapping with a partner — clapping single, then hands together, then going faster until someone broke the rhythm.

The "Hokey Pokey" was still a huge hit. *But I can't get that song out of my head!* She'd seen them play tag, but she was weak and tired. One sandwich wasn't enough to provide much physical energy. *OK, the "Hokey Pokey" it is.*

As she left the dump and headed for the house, Julie didn't notice the muscular policeman from the station on the opposite sidewalk.

He observed the children for a few minutes, then moved on.

"Lord, what am I going to do for food tomorrow?"

Don't go home, go to the market and find a sack.

"But, Lord, the berries are all gone. I picked even the green ones today."

Didn't you just ask what you should do for food tomorrow?

"Well, yes, but, like I said, the berries are all gone."

Julie, I recommend immediate obedience even when it doesn't make sense to you.

"Yes, Lord. Thanks for the reminder. Even though there are no berries, I think I'll go straight to the market and find a sack. Here I go!"

Walking through the market was distracting. The smell from the vendors' carts was more enticing than usual. The chicken, bread, and fish on the grills only emphasized her hunger. She tried not to complain.

Never thought I'd be one of those starving people in other parts of the world that mothers always speak to their kids about to coerce them to finish their peas.

She caught a glimpse of herself in a window and evaluated.

So dusty, so dirty. Face still red, hair not as greasy. My dress—disgusting as ever.

She had used all the hand sanitizer. That meant her hands would never feel the teeniest bit clean. After a minute, she found an empty brown paper sack which appeared clean on the inside.

"Thank You, Lord, for my sack. I think I'll go back to the bushes." Once there, she crawled in her den. *All the berries that are left, and there aren't many, are green. Lord, help me to trust You.*

Julie, I'm going to tell you something, and I want you to think about it for a while before you go to bed. The highest form of worship is rest.

She pictured a choir with all their members slouched in chairs.

"Explain, please?"

If you are resting, then you are trusting totally in Me. You won't feel the need to control each situation, and that eliminates your stress and worry. When you learn to trust Me, that I will provide for you, you can relax, for the first time.

"But India is so demanding—"

I wasn't talking about being in India; I mean you can relax for the very first time. You're stressed at home, you're stressed in India; you carry it with you, in your mind. When your mind stops racing to the problem, you can spend time with Me, and your body and mind will relax. Just let your muscles relax now.

She hadn't realized how tense she was until she let go. Her shoulders relaxed, her teeth unclenched, she felt her face relax.

Take a few deep breaths and really relax because I promise that you and the orphans will eat tomorrow. If you can trust My promise, you can sleep in peace tonight, and every night. Remember, I brought you here, and I promise I have the plan. The quicker you believe that, the easier your life will be. Good night, My dear one. Remember, think about resting in Me. Rest your body and your mind. In My presence there is true peace.

What does it look like to rest? What must it be like to trust? She realized that her shoulders were tight again, and she was clenching her teeth. She took another deep breath and commanded herself, out loud, to relax.

"I renounce and resist the lie that I have to provide food tomorrow. I replace it with the truth that I'm not in charge of food tomorrow. The Lord is providing it. Not me. Him. He's the provider, and I'll be the one who carries it to the orphans. I'm going to have to remind myself about every five minutes." *OK, relax, deep breath....*

She awoke with the same horrible morning breath as always. With her eyes still closed, she stretched her arms and legs and let out a moan. *I'll never get used to sleeping on this dirt, this dirty dirt. Where am I going to get food? Oops, it's not my job.*

"I renounce and resist the lie that there will be no food today in Jesus' name. I replace it with the truth that You will provide. Help me to believe that You will provide." When she opened her eyes she gasped. "Berries, the bushes are loaded, and they're ripe!"

Julie, throughout your life I have performed many miracles, but most of them you didn't notice. I want you to remember this one. Last night no berries; this morning the bushes are groaning under the weight of ripe, luscious berries. Remember when I provided manna each day for the children of Israel?[1] This is a miracle just like that, only on a much smaller scale—but a miracle no less. My Word says not to forget the benefits I provide for you.[2] Write them down and review them if you have to. It will help your attitude and make you a grateful person.

"Thank You, Lord. I can't believe it. I mean, I do believe it. The berries are right before my eyes. You're awesome."

And, Julie, the shopkeeper will give you sandwiches, fruit, and drinks today. There are more berries than yesterday, and I happen to know that these are his son's very favorite. The last ones he took home and enjoyed with his family. He'll do the same thing with these. He'll bless his son, and I'll enjoy watching that. I love that man and his family.

Julie didn't realize it, but as she picked, she was humming. She even ate a few of the berries herself, but restrained from overdoing it. *There must be a gallon of berries. I can't wait to see the shop owner's face when he opens the sack.*

She checked the verse for today and enjoyed reading how the Lord provided for the children of Israel for 40 years.[3] "Whoa, their clothing and shoes never even wore out[4]—bummer for the ladies!"

Ravi and Sammy had slept in the hedgerow behind the dump as usual.

"Let's wait here and see if she comes with food," said Ravi. "I don't want to wait in the alley wondering."

The orphans were agitated again. Yesterday had shaken whatever confidence they had placed in Julie. They wondered if they would eat today if she didn't show. Several of the girls gathered, sitting cross-legged in a circle. Shoba looked at Sashi and asked, "Do you think she'll bring food today?"

"She did yesterday, even though she was late."

"But she only brought sandwiches, and I was hungry all day long," said Sapna, frowning.

"I know, me, too, but remember, we were hungry all the time before she came to help us," replied Sashi.

The girls all nodded.

"Madhu can sell the things he makes, but I don't know how to make things," sighed Chavvi.

"But even if she only comes every other day, we're still better than before. If she comes today, we need to thank her. I don't even know why she brings us food at all," said Sashi.

"Yeah," piped little Shoba. "We'll say thank you."

"She seems a little nicer than at the beginning when she hit us with her purse," said Chavvi.

Nilaya shivered at the memory.

"I think we just scared her. We were all around her grabbing and shoving," said Sashi.

The thought of losing some of their food made these girls grateful for what they had received and hopeful for the future.

"Maybe sometime we can do something nice for her, too," said Shoba.

"What could we do?" they all stared at each other and shrugged. "She likes it when we put the wrappers in her bag," said Sashi.

Several of the other orphans jumped to their feet and pointed.

"She's coming, and she has a sack."

Sashi sprang into action.

"Stay here everyone, get in our circles. Sit down; we can eat quicker if we do." Some of the children had to be guided to the circle, but by the time Julie arrived, they were all seated and squirming with excitement.

"Lunch tiiiime!" shouted Julie, holding up the bag with a huge smile on her face. Restrained pandemonium broke out when she pulled out the sandwiches. The children forced themselves to remain seated, but there was screaming, clapping, shouting, squirming, and smiling.

I wish I could lead them in a prayer of thanks for this miraculous food. God, I really need an interpreter. But I'll thank You on behalf of them all. Thank You for being a God of miracles. Thank You for caring about these children. Thank You for providing for all of us and help me to trust You more. Bless this food to their bodies. And, Lord, help them to smell better or weaken my olfactory senses. Amen.

Sashi gave Nilaya's food to her. After all the children had eaten, it was time for games. Even though they couldn't understand, Julie called out, "OK, today I'm going to teach you a song called 'Father Abraham.' Everyone get in a circle." The boys joined the girls today. Madhu sat out, content to watch the group while working on a toy made from a matchbox and string.

'Father Abraham' was as big a hit as the 'Hokey Pokey,' and they sang both songs several times. Julie caught a glimpse of Nilaya looking out from behind the tree mouthing the words. *That poor little girl, what's it going to take?*

Ravi and Sammy were delighted watching the children laugh and move. Ravi had to clamp his hand over Sammy's mouth to keep him from singing along.

"Shhhh. They can't know we're here."

"Why not?"

"They just can't. I'm not part of this group," said Ravi.

"Maybe someday do you think you can be?"

Ravi looked at the ground, "I don't know. Let's go back to the alley and wait."

They were too excited to waste time falling asleep when they heard Julie's voice. Julie was in a good mood today, and her face lit up when she saw Ravi and Sammy sitting with their hands folded in their laps.

"Look at you two perfect gentlemen. I hope you're hungry because I have...." she paused for effect, "sandwiches, oranges, and juice! Eat up, guys."

As the boys ate, Julie chatted.

"I wish I could communicate. I have such an exciting story about the food today. It's a miracle that you have it." She told the story of the children of Israel.

"Yesterday I had to pick berries and trade them for sandwiches, and last night when I went to bed all the berries were gone and Jesus told me that He would provide the food and that I shouldn't worry. When I woke up this morning, the same bushes were covered with berries. They weren't there last night, not even green ones, and overnight Jesus made them appear just because He wants you to have food today. It's so exciting. I'll never forget it."

Julie stopped talking when she noticed that both boys had only eaten half their sandwich and Ravi hadn't opened his juice.

"What in the world? You only had a sandwich yesterday; you have to be starving." She shook her head. *Maybe he's saving it for later.* "I'll be back tomorrow. I do wish you would come with me to the dump." She waved and exited into the scorching sun. *At least I hope I'll be back tomorrow. You are going to provide food tomorrow, aren't You, Lord?*

She paused by a fence covered with blue vining flowers to wait for an answer.

Julie, do you remember a prayer that goes something like this? "Give us today our daily bread"?[5] If I provided food for a month, where would you store it?

She chuckled. "Good point, Lord. But living day to day is so risky."

That's right, Julie; faith is spelled r-i-s-k.

At that point, Ravi came bursting out of the alley with Sammy doing his best to keep up. They both froze.

"Where are you two going in such a hurry?"

Ravi shrugged and headed back to the alley with Sammy lagging behind.

That's strange. I wonder what they're up to?

Ravi and Sammy waited five minutes and then peeked out. Julie was gone.

When they made it to the shopping center, Sammy's eyes lit up.

"There he is—there's Kumar." They crossed the street and crouched between the cars.

"Give me your sandwich," said Ravi.

Sammy's eyes grew large, and when Ravi looked at him, he smiled his gap-toothed smile and shrugged.

"I forgot it, in the alley."

"That's OK. That gives me an idea."

Kumar ran to Ravi. He reached toward the half sandwich and orange.

"Today you have to come with us. There's another half a sandwich if you do."

"I can't. Mr. Shah will find me and kill me."

"That's what he told me, too, but he didn't. How much is in your can today?"

Kumar hung his head. "Not enough."

"Why would you turn down food to stay and get a beating from an evil man?"

Kumar looked at the sandwich and then at the street. He bit his lip. The silence was loud. Finally Sammy took Kumar's right hand, gave him a big smile and said, "Come on. I'll race you there," as he pointed to his bum leg. Kumar flailed his left stump and laughed. Then Sammy began walking with Kumar by his side. When they arrived at the alley, Kumar devoured his food as a smiling Ravi looked on.

Kumar had been working for Mr. Shah for about three weeks. During that time, he had never once made his daily quota.

"After the second week, he cut off my arm to make me a better beggar, but I still didn't get enough money. I am terrified he will do something even worse."

"You're safe now. Mr. Shah had us, too, but we escaped."

"Ravi rescued me!" chirped Sammy.

"As long as we stay together, we can help each other," said Ravi. "I saw a movie once about cowboys and Indians."

"What are cowboys?" asked Sammy.

"The cowboys take care of cows and they fight the Indians."

His brow furrowed. "Why were they fighting us?"

"They weren't fighting us, they were fighting other Indians."

"There are other Indians, and they have sacred cows?"

"Not sacred cows, regular cows."

"What are regular cows?"

"I just brought up the cowboys because they all stayed together and helped each other."

"I want to be a cowboy," shouted Sammy.

"We are cowboy brothers then."

"What's that mean?" asked Sammy.

"It means," said Kumar, his face brightening, "that we all take care of each other all the time." Sammy beamed.

Ravi entertained the two by telling action scenes from the movie. The boys spent the rest of the afternoon wearing imaginary cowboy hats and acting out the scenes using sticks for guns. Kumar startled with ever sound, especially cars driving by.

After a break from their pretend fighting, Kumar asked, "Do you take turns staying up as guard while the other sleeps?"

"No, we don't need to. We go to the dump. There's lots of orphans there."

"We sleep in the bushes so they don't know we're there," said Sammy.

Kumar looked to Ravi.

"Um, the lady who takes care of us, before I knew her, I, um, I stole her purse."

"And she still takes care of you?"

"Yes."

"So why do you have to hide from her at the dump?"

"I don't think the other kids like me for stealing her purse."

"Do they beat you up when you go there?"

"I don't know. They haven't seen me," said Ravi, looking at the ground. "We just sleep under the hedge where they don't see us. It feels safe."

"Safe," piped Sammy, smiling.

A car door slammed, and Kumar flinched.

"It's OK," said Ravi. "After a week or so you won't be nervous."

"It's getting dark, can we go to the dump?" asked Sammy.

Kumar was hesitant to leave the safety of the alley. They all walked slowly because of Sammy's limp. Kumar turned when he walked, forward, side, and back, scanning the street for Mr. Shah's green car. They approached the hedge from the back and shimmied underneath.

CHAPTER

17

Julie was sitting with the girls painstakingly trying to communicate one word at a time from her dictionary.

All the blood drained from Kumar's face as Mr. Shah's car pulled up in front of the dump. Kumar went fetal, held his knees, and whimpered. Mr. Shah stepped out and scanned the children. Julie and most of the girls were hidden from view by the trash. He carried the monkey, which drew the attention of Madhu, Shoba, and Bhanu, who were playing close to the sidewalk.

"Stay here, both of you. You'll be safe," said Ravi. The monkey handed the kids sweets. Ravi watched Mr. Shah laughing. He produced more sweets, then pointed to his car. All three children headed that way.

Ravi sprang from the hedge and in respectable English shouted to Julie, "Don't let him take them!"

When Mr. Shah saw Ravi, he threw the first orphan into the backseat.

Julie was too startled by Ravi's sudden appearance and by the abduction that she failed to realize that Ravi had spoken in English.

Ravi shouted again in Hindi, and all the children were on their feet headed toward Mr. Shah, who had just thrown the last boy, Madhu, into the car.

"Stop him, stop him," Ravi screamed to Julie. Praveen, the oldest, grabbed a tree limb from the dump. Wilson flailed his walking stick.

Mr. Shah was standing in the street ready to get in the driver's side. Julie was the first to arrive. "How dare you steal these children! I demand you release them now." He slapped her face, then kicked her in the stomach. She fell in the street. A car swerved, but ran over her toes on her left foot. Sashi and Chavvi pulled Julie upright. She leaned against Mr. Shah's car, wincing in pain.

Praveen approached from behind, but Mr. Shah grabbed his branch and sent him sprawling. Wilson hit him across the back with the walking stick, which only served to enrage him. The orphans swarmed him, but he hit, slapped, and easily shoved them to the ground.

When the fight started, Ravi had run to the passenger side of the car and flung open the back door.

"Get out. He will hurt you. He's not your friend." Ravi grabbed Madhu and pulled him out. "Run, run." Ravi leaned into the car and grabbed Shoba, slid her across the seat, and deposited her on the sidewalk. "Run!" He reached to get Bhanu, who resisted.

"No. Leave me alone. He's got sweets and a bedroom and lots of food. Get away." Bhanu's kick connected with Ravi's shoulder.

"He's lying. He'll make you beg." Bhanu kicked again at Ravi, but he grabbed the thrashing boy's leg and pulled him out of the car, being careful to avoid Bhanu's fists.

Ravi stayed on the passenger side of the car, hoping to remain invisible to Mr. Shah. The other two orphans had run and were hiding behind the trash. Ravi looked for Bhanu. *Where was he?*

Praveen approached Mr. Shah, who shoved him to the pavement, sneered, and climbed into the driver's seat. Ravi saw Bhanu had crawled in the backseat on the driver's side. Just as Mr. Shah reached for the door lock, Ravi opened the back door and dove inside. Mr. Shah reached behind and grabbed his arm.

"I'll take two boys any day, especially you, son!"

He stepped on the accelerator. The force swung the back door closed. The car jerked ahead and dropped Julie on the ground. The orphans pursued. Wilson shattered the driver's side window with his walking stick. Mr. Shah let go of Ravi to protect his eyes. Ravi bailed out but couldn't hold on to the squirming Bhanu.

"Don't let him leave," Ravi screamed in English to Julie.

"I'm watching all of you," yelled Mr. Shah. The tires squealed and he was gone. Julie's body trembled; the adrenaline was still flowing. Praveen handed Julie the tree branch and helped her stand. She lay her hand over the side of her face, which was red with Mr. Shah's handprint.

"He steals orphans and makes them beg," said Ravi. "He cut off Kumar's arm. He kidnapped me and Sammy," Ravi pointed to the hedge. Upon hearing his name, Sammy climbed out of his hiding place, grinning as if he was being formally introduced.

"Ravi, you were so brave."

"Thank you," said Ravi in English.

It dawned on Julie, who screeched, "You speak English! Ravi, you speak English. How? Oh my gosh!"

Ravi grinned, enjoying the attention.

"You can be my translator! I can communicate. Oh, this is wonderful." Julie was so excited she hobbled to him, swept him up in a hug, and to her surprise and delight, he threw his arms around her and hugged like he never wanted to let go. *What a difference*, thought Julie as she hugged him even tighter.

"Kumar!" Ravi wiggled out of Julie's embrace, then dove under the hedge. A minute later he emerged from the hedge pulling Kumar behind. Everyone gasped when they saw his stump. Julie stared. *The Indian mafia—it's true.*

Being careful of her foot, she sat and then pulled Kumar on her lap and hugged the frightened boy.

"Ravi, tell him that we will protect him and feed him and he's part of our family." *Family? Where did that come from?* she wondered.

"Oh, you poor thing," said Julie, examining the bandages, "you're shaking." She rocked him as she hummed a lullaby. The same lullaby she cooed holding Logan as an infant. The memory of Logan and the reality of the one-armed boy sitting on her lap combined to stir her to greater depths of caring than before.

Jesus, this is one of Your little lambs who was sucked into the depravity of the human heart. Oh, Lord, help me to care for this one well. She continued rocking him.

"Ravi, did you three escape together?"

"No. I escaped, and then I rescued Sammy, and today we rescued Kumar. We lured him with our food."

After a few seconds a knowing look crossed her face.

"Oh, Ravi, that's why you weren't eating all your food. You were sharing with Kumar! I'm sorry I misjudged you. You're a hero!"

Ravi blushed, but the smile on his face could not conceal his pleasure at Julie's compliment.

Although the other children couldn't understand what Julie was saying, they could tell that she was very pleased with Ravi, and that made them want to be his friend. Plus, he had certainly proved himself by rescuing Madhu and Shoba. Ravi's compassion, manifested as bravery, had changed him from goat to hero.

She was still rocking Kumar.

"Translate for me, Ravi." He nodded. "We have three new family members today. I want you to all be friends and take care of each other. We are a family, and a family loves and cares for each other, and that's what we are!"

She couldn't believe her joy and the affection she suddenly felt for the orphans, and especially for Kumar and Ravi. *And he speaks English. Lord, he speaks English!*

Wilson clenched his walking stick. He spoke, and the faces became serious again. Ravi turned to Julie, "They want to know if you will stay here tonight. They are afraid of Mr. Shah, if he comes back." Kumar's body tensed.

Sashi poked Ravi and whispered to him. Ravi translated, "One time a man came and stole one of the girls. He threw her over his shoulder. She screamed and pounded his back, but he did not stop. They never saw her again."

"Did they tell the police?" asked Julie.

"She says that the police are not our friends. They don't help orphans. Orphans have no money for bribes. I wish you would stay with us. Having you here would make us all feel better."

What could I do to stop a full-grown man from carrying off a young girl? Besides, I feel safer and hidden where I am. Then she heard the Lord's voice.

Angels encamp around those who fear Me.[1] You can do very little to protect the children, but your presence brings My presence to them.

Ravi tugged on her arm and with pleading eyes whispered, "Please?"

I'll miss the sense of security that comes with hiddenness. Although she preferred to feel secure, she knew it was right for her to protect the orphans, especially Kumar. *Out of obedience to You, Lord.* Then she grinned. *The sleeping arrangements that I first thought were so hideous now seem enviable compared to sleeping in the open. I guess I didn't realize when I had it good.*

She let out a deep breath and turned to Ravi, smiling, "I'll stay." Ravi's dusty face lit up. He looked relieved. *I knew you would.* When Ravi explained, a cheer went up! Sapna and Nilaya embraced. Kumar hugged her tighter.

Since she had everyone's attention, she told Ravi to keep translating.

"I am so glad that my God, whose name is Jesus, has provided Ravi as a translator so that we can now communicate and be friends. I am from America, which is a country far, far away. Jesus loves you all so much that He moved me from my home and family...." Tears welled in her eyes; she braced herself and continued, "so I could come here for a while and help you. That is why I am here—to help all of you. Jesus will supply food for you each day.

"I also want to apologize for yelling and hitting you with my purse." She looked chagrined, but plunged on. "I was so scared; I was trying to protect myself. I thought you wanted to hurt me. I realize now that what you wanted was food. You were just so very hungry you couldn't help it." She shrugged her shoulders, "I thought you were all going to beat me up. Will you please forgive me?" She paused and waited for the response as Ravi translated.

Several children looked to Sashi who smiled, then nodded. Julie let out a sigh.

Oh, Lord, what a relief. I've felt really bad about that. She tried unsuccessfully to make eye contact with Nilaya.

"I'm so glad that these two," she pointed to Madhu and Shoba, "are still here, and I'm glad that Ravi was so brave and not only rescued them, but also rescued Sammy and Kumar. They are safe now, and Ravi is our hero!" Julie clapped and everyone followed. "Let's pray for Bhanu's safe return."

The rest of the day most of the children stayed close to Julie, especially Kumar.

Ravi continued translating for Julie.

"What's my name?"

"Auntie Julie" they responded, *Auntie* being a term of respect for an adult woman. They were much mellower than before.

The girls were: Sashi, the oldest girl at 11. *She seems to be the girls' leader. So helpful,* thought Julie. Chavvi, age eight, wore a pink dress. *The only one wearing shoes, and the toes are cut away. They must be three sizes too small.* Julie was still peeved at Sapna, who had bitten her. She was seven and dwarfed by a man's t-shirt. Shoba, age nine. *So skinny. She must be horribly malnourished.* Julie looked at the last girl, Nilaya, age six, who stared at the ground as she whispered her name.

The boys were: Ravi, nine years old, Sammy, age seven, missing two front teeth, Kumar, nine. Julie looked at his missing arm and shook her head. *I need to get clean bandages. I can't even begin to understand his trauma. Lord, will this little one ever feel safe?* Wilson, age eight. *I never see him without his walking stick.* Madhu, age ten, shy. He wore a green polo shirt along with a serious look on his face. *He always seems to be folding something or fixing something,* thought Julie. Mahipal, age 11. *His embroidered Nehru jacket looks as if it was beautiful at one time.* Last was Praveen, 13, the oldest, wearing a yellow tank top with white shorts and flops.

Oh, Lord, I'm going to need supernatural help to remember these names!

Sammy was eager to tell his story, what he could remember of it. Madhu joined the group and listened while he fiddled with several large dried seeds. Julie watched as he produced a nail and meticulously twisted it against one side of the shell, trying to make a hole.

Sammy had no memory of ever having a family. His memories started when he woke up one morning at age six on the street with a head injury.

"I lived behind a grocery store and ate from the trash. Then a bigger boy came and hit me, and I had to leave. When I was walking I saw the other children here and stayed. Later, Mr. Shah drove by in his big car and took me for sweets and then to his home. It was fun at first, but then he turned into a very mean man. Ravi rescued me!" he beamed. "And Ravi is my friend and cow—, what?"

"Boy. Cowboy brother," said Ravi with a chuckle.

"That's good, Ravi," said Julie. Then she turned back to Sammy.

"I'm so sorry, Sammy. Can you remember anything else?" Sammy scrunched up his face and frowned for several seconds before answering, "Nope, nothing else," followed by his toothless smile. Kumar was still on Julie's lap, but she managed to put an arm around Sammy and give him a hug.

"Ravi, what happened to you?"

Ravi looked at the ground and shook his head. Julie noticed the tears in his eyes. *Too tender to go there.* She wanted to draw attention away from Ravi so she asked, "Does anyone know a game we can play?"

"We can play Kabbadi," said Wilson. The children jumped up and divided into two teams. "You can be on our side," said Ravi. He was disappointed when she pointed to her foot and shook her head. Ravi stayed to talk with her while the children played. Madhu's dog was in the middle of the action, causing the children to laugh.

"I can go tomorrow morning and rescue Bhanu. I know where Mr. Shah will take him."

"We'll go together—but you're brave." The sun was setting behind the hedge and Ravi mumbled,

"Not so brave at night."

"What?"

"At night, I wake. Afraid."

"Let's do an experiment. You know that word? X-pera-ment."

"Yes. I like science very much."

"Tonight pray to your god for sleep and tomorrow I'll ask Jesus to help."

"How about you pray for me tonight?" said Ravi, looking hopeful.

"I'd be glad to, my friend," Julie smiled. She reached out and took his hand and he rewarded her with a huge grin.

Julie, if you pray for the group out loud, I will see to it that they all sleep soundly and are safe.

"Ravi, I need you to translate." She winked at him and whispered, "This prayer is especially for you. Jesus said that you will be safe tonight and will sleep peacefully." She was surprised to see tears well up in Ravi's eyes.

"Jesus, You love each child who is here, and You have a good plan for their lives. I ask that You show them how much You love them by letting them have a good, restful sleep and wake up full of energy tomorrow. Amen."

"Ah-meen."

OK, Lord, don't let me down. Julie arranged the guys in one group and the girls in another. She made sure to put Kumar in the middle, surrounded by Ravi and Sammy and the other guys on the outside so he would feel safer. Wilson lay on his side, clutching his walking stick. *I guess that's his security blanket.* Madhu was propped on his elbows, still trying to make a hole in the large, brown seed. *He sure is tenacious,* thought Julie.

Then she slid her way in the middle of the girls. They slid in so close she felt she could hardly breathe. *Jesus, how lonely and frightening it must be for children to be on their own. How lonely to not have someone to love them.*

Julie, you are letting Me love them through you.

"Yes, Lord, but I'll need more help."

That's My specialty, Julie.

There were a few whispers; then the next thing Julie knew, the sun was coming up.

"Thank You, Lord. I certainly slept well." The children were still asleep, so Julie asked the Lord, "What should I do today? I guess I'm a permanent dump resident."

Julie, you are feeding My lambs. I take great joy in you and in the kindness you show to them. I want you to teach them who I am, feed them, and play more games today.

"But, Lord, I'm not a teacher. I don't know how to tell them about You."

How old were you when you were saved?

"About seven."

Do you remember what your pastor told you?

"Yes."

That's all you need to tell the children. I made the Gospel so simple anyone can understand it.

"OK, but help me, Lord."

You can count on it. Every day I want you to tell a short Bible story. I'll tell you which ones. And each morning and each evening have My lambs pray to Me to rescue them from this dump. Then, when I answer that prayer, it will grow their faith.

Julie smiled, "And mine too, Lord; mine too."

As the children woke, they walked a few feet away to relieve themselves. Julie would have drawn less attention if she'd done the same, but everyone was curious what she was doing hiding behind the hedge. She felt her face flush as curious eyes looked around, over, and through the bushes. *Must remember to have Ravi ask them next time for privacy.*

With Ravi's help, it was much easier to get the boys and girls in their circles. The Lord told Julie to give her teaching before eating so she'd have everyone's attention. As Julie stood up, she could feel her body shaking a little. She cleared her throat and, through Ravi's translation, she spoke.

"I am from America, and my God loves you so much that He sent me here to tell you about Him. He loves us, and when we die, He wants us to come and live with Him in Heaven forever, but if we have committed even one sin, then we can't live with Him because He is holy. He has never sinned. What is sin? Sin is the bad things we do that separate us from God. Like lying or stealing or being selfish. He was so sad that we couldn't be with Him, so He solved this problem by sending His Son Jesus to Earth to be punished and die for all our sins. If you believe Jesus paid for your sins and you give your life to Him, then when you die, you will be able to live with Him forever."

Julie picked up a piece of paper from the trash and held up her index and middle finger like a peace sign.

"Let's say this is God," she pointed to one finger, "and this is you," she pointed to the other, "and this is sin." She inserted the paper and brought her two fingers together. "See how sin keeps us from being close to God? But if we trust Jesus and ask Him to forgive all our sins, He takes them away." She pulled the paper from between her two fingers, which were now touching. "Then we can be close to God. Never forget, you can be close to a God who loves you enough to die for you." She paused and looked at the children. No one said anything or even looked like they'd comprehended what Ravi had translated, with the exception of Madhu, who had seemed to listen while he fiddled with the seed and nail. *Well, Lord, I did my best. I ask You to bless it.*

You did, and I will.

Am I picking berries today, Lord?

Yes, and take Ravi with you.

Julie didn't ask the Lord about rescuing Bhanu. She just assumed. So before they went to get the berries, she and Ravi walked to the shopping center. No beggars were there. Mr. Shah, hiding across the street, left unseen.

"We can go," said Ravi sadly. "He will not use this corner again."

Julie sighed. "Let's go pick berries so we can get food."

CHAPTER

18

The berries were back—thick and ripe. The picking was slow because only Julie's berries found their way into the sack. Ravi ate all he picked.

Can't blame him for that, she thought.

"How did you learn English?"

"I completed my fifth standard of school. My father was doctor. I was to learn at school to train also as doctor. In my house was enough to eat. My parents were dead in a car crash. All I had were my clothes. Now I am—" he choked.

Living on the street, thought Julie.

Julie stopped picking and grabbed both his shoulders with her hands. Ravi looked embarrassed. Even though he smelled bad, she wrapped her arms around him and gave him a huge hug. He remained mostly stoic, but Julie couldn't hold back her tears. She held him, like she'd hold Logan, and rocked him back and forth.

Finally she felt his stiff body relax into hers and his arms go around her waist. As she rocked him, she thought of cuddling her son and the myriad multiple hugs she gave him every day. *When was the last time Ravi had any physical affection? He's lived on the defensive, scraping and begging, beginning each day wondering if he's going to eat and how.* Although she felt compassion for him, she couldn't begin to comprehend the danger, rejection, and fear he'd constantly lived in since the wreck.

She finally released her hold on him and wiped her tears away. She didn't know what to say; anything she could think of sounded trite. Ravi reached to touch her earrings. She patted his shoulder and they continued picking.

"Before I slept at the dump, I slept here," said Julie. "Between the bushes and the house."

For a moment, her mind flashed to her king-size bed with pillow top mattress and expensive damask comforter with matching curtains. Air conditioner in the spring and summer, and heat and electric blanket in the fall and winter. Several sets of matching Egyptian cotton sheets with a high thread count and extra fluffy feather pillows. Now she was back to reality. She was ready for Ravi's sympathy.

"This looks safe. It's even behind a fence."

So much for sympathy.

When Julie's sack was full, they headed for the shops.

Mr. Shah and one of his henchmen, Adeel, parked at the dump. Before the orphans noticed their presence, Mr. Shah had grabbed Madhu and Adeel had snatched Kumar. The rest of the orphans scattered, screaming as they left.

"Ravi, what is your favorite food?" asked Julie as they walked. His eyes lit up and a hopeful look flitted across his face.

"Bananas," he said. "Bananas are berry good."

"Are you a monkey?" she asked, laughing as she reached to tickle him. He laughed, too.

"Well, Mr. Monkey, I'll let you in on a secret. I'm a monkey, too. I love bananas!"

"Auntie Monkey," he pointed and laughed.

"Ravi Monkey," she pointed back.

"Let's go get some bananas," she said, as she squatted a little to walk like a monkey and scratched under her arm. Ravi squatted slightly, grabbed her hand, and they shuffled down the street.

They arrived at the grocery store and Ravi grabbed Julie's hand and dragged her through the store until he located the bananas.

"How many do you want?"

"Four."

"Four? You're going to eat with the rest of the kids, too. You won't only have bananas." *Plus you just ate about a quart of berries.*

"Four...pleeease," pleaded Ravi.

A bird in the hand is worth two in the bush, thought Julie. She broke five bananas off the bunch.

"We need to get food for everyone. What's good to eat for the other kids?" Ravi slouched, hung his arms by his side like a monkey, and said, "More bananas."

"Fruit does sound good, but maybe we should get, um...."

"Apples?" suggested Ravi.

"Apples are good." She handed him a basket and said, "Get 14 apples." She held up her fingers and motioned for him to do the same. Then she counted ten fingers and four more. "Got it?"

"Yes," he said, giving her a slightly perturbed look. "Fourteen, I know that, I finished my fifth standard."

"Yes, I'll remember that. You're a smart monkey," she said, striking the slouching pose again. Ravi grinned.

As the cashier examined the berries, Julie looked up in her dictionary the word for toilet. She had a plan. "Pishab?" she inquired. The cashier pointed to the street. Julie broke out in a cold sweat. *I can't keep using the street.* She pointed to the back of the store and the clerk shook his head no.

She turned to Ravi and said, "Tell him I am too shy to use the street. Ask him if I can please, please, please use his toilet. Remind him that I bring his son's favorite berries."

The owner looked surprised, but after a moment pointed to the back of the store. She left the two sacks in Ravi's care and headed for the back.

When she opened the door, her heart sank. There was a hole in the floor with a flat circle of porcelain around it, the same height as the floor. There were imprints for feet on both sides. Next to it was a bucket of water. *It's better than the street. I still have to squat, but at least I squat in private.* She hiked her dress extra high and grabbed the fabric to her chest to keep it out of the way.

Kumar wilted into Adeel's arms, hyperventilating. Madhu put up a fight. Adeel was loading Kumar in the back passenger door so Mr. Shah went to the street side. Madhu's arms were pinned to his side by Mr. Shah's arms wrapped around him, but his legs were loose and he kicked frantically while yelling. "Put me down!"

Mr. Shah managed to restrain Madhu with one arm and open the door with the other. Madhu's dog rounded the corner and chomped Mr. Shah's leg. He screamed in pain and Madhu, taking advantage of the distraction, squirmed free and bolted across the street and down the sidewalk.

Mr. Shah gave a mighty kick and flung the dog into the street.

When Julie arrived at the front of the store, Ravi and the food were missing. *That little thief. I can't believe I trusted him.* She looked at the clerk, who indicated he'd turned left out of the shop. She picked up her pace.

How fast can he run carrying two big sacks? Fast enough to leave me in the dust. What am I going to do now to feed everyone?

To her relief, she saw him standing on the small space on the dirty sidewalk between a woman selling live goldfish in plastic bags and a man selling something deep fried that Julie couldn't identify. He was eating his first banana. He could see by the look on her face that she was relieved.

"I only stole once when I had nothing. I would not steal the other children's food." Julie bent down and hugged him. "I'm sorry. Please forgive me. I remember you were so generous that you saved your food to rescue others."

Ravi beamed.

"Where shall we eat our bananas?"

"Anywhere is good place to eat bananas!" said Ravi, sitting down. He broke one banana off and dropped it by Julie's side. Then he pulled the other three apart and cradled them in his crossed legs for safekeeping. He peeled the banana all the way, threw the skin on the ground, and took a first bite that encompassed a full third of the banana.

"Slow down, slow down. First we have to say a prayer of thanks for our food." Julie bowed her head and spoke, "Dear Jesus, thanks for creating bananas so we can enjoy them, and thank You for providing these for us to eat. And thanks for letting Ravi sleep well last night."

Ravi didn't bow his head or close his eyes. He continued eating and kept a watch on his precious bananas. After he finished gobbling the second banana, he grabbed the third.

"Wait and watch me. Do what I do." She peeled her banana halfway down and explained how keeping the peel on helped keep the germs and dirt off the bananas. For Ravi, dirt had become a fact of daily life.

"Now take a small bite and chew and enjoy. Taste it. Feel the smooth texture. It's your favorite. Make it last as long as possible. When you're done, put the peels in a pile, and we'll throw them away." Ravi looked at her skeptically.

"It's OK. I won't let anyone take your bananas—just enjoy them. They are my gift to you, and Jesus' gift to you."

"Who is Jesus again?"

"Jesus is the real, true God."

"Hindus have millions of gods. Everything is a god."

"Jesus is the One who brought me here to help you. Have any of your gods helped you?" He shook his head no as he savored the taste and texture of the banana.

"I will tell you more about Jesus later. All you need to know now is that He loves you more than your mom and dad loved you, and that's a lot."

Julie finished her banana as she watched the crowds hurry past. Most of the Indian men dressed in western style pants and shirts, but most of the ladies still wore the Punjabis—pants with matching tunic—or the beautifully colored traditional saris. Women who were shopping in the market and running errands were dressed and wrapped in luxurious fabrics. They looked exotic, and many were just gorgeous. *India's beauty is definitely in her people.*

As Ravi finished his last banana, a cream-colored cow with 12-inch-long horns and saggy skin wandered down the street and then on to the sidewalk.

"Someone's cow escaped its pen."

"What is pen?"

"A fence."

This caused Ravi to laugh.

"Cows go wherever they want and do whatever they want."

"Why?"

"We don't hurt them because they are people came back from the dead. It is good Karma to feed and place the flowered necklaces on the cow."[1]

Julie had heard of sacred cows before, but seeing them amble lazily wherever they wanted and the belief that they were people reincarnated made her sad. *So much of India is starving, and the cow is preferred over the people. Guess I won't get a hamburger here.*

Julie had Ravi add his four banana peels to hers in the sack to throw away at the dump.

The taxi braked, but not in time. Madhu didn't stop running when he heard the tires squeal, but the yelp stopped him in his tracks.

Mr. Shah and Adeel were driving away as Madhu ran back. The taxi driver was gone and the dog was lying still on the side of the road, blood dripping from its mouth. In a last herculean effort, it wagged its tail when it saw Madhu kneel beside it, then died.

"Nooooooo! You can't leave me. Don't go!" Madhu buried his face in the dog's side and wept.

Julie questioned Ravi as they walked.

"I have an uncle who lives in another city, but I don't know his name or what city. He probably wouldn't want me anyway," said Ravi, looking down at the sidewalk and shoving his hands in his pockets.

"He's missing out on having a great nephew."

"I don't know if he knows my parents are dead."

"I'm so sorry," said Julie."

"Tell me that again."

"I'm so sorry."

"No, the nephew part."

"He's missing out on a great nephew," said Julie, as she laid her hand on Ravi's shoulder.

"What's it like, Ravi, to live on the streets?"

"Before you came, sometimes I don't eat for days. When I find food, it's not enough. I'm always hungry. Hungry a lot; I hurt, too."

"Do you see a doctor?"

"When I was so hurt from the wreck, I try to find a quiet place to lie down, and I pray to Ganesh for several days until I get up and walk."

Julie shivered. When Logan was sick, she rarely prayed, knowing that a doctor's office was merely a phone call away. In the night, an emergency room and a prescription pad could provide unlimited medicines. The thought of Ravi in pain, curled up under a bush with no one to help him and nothing to eat, calling for help to a "god" that was really a demon, brought tears to her eyes.

She wanted to promise him that she'd take care of him and that it wouldn't happen again, but she didn't have the faith. She put her arm around his shoulder, pulled him tight, and held him there as they walked. His body and skin craved physical affection. *How long can a little boy go between hugs?*

"How'd you sleep last night?" she asked.

"I didn't wake up one time, and my monsters in my mind did not visit." Julie gave him a high five.

"Remember to thank Jesus for that."

As they neared the dump Julie warned Ravi, "Get ready to get mobbed."

Ravi looked ahead.

"Where is everyone?"

They ran to the dump; it was deserted.

"Kumar, Sammy!" yelled Ravi.

"Sashi, Chavvi, Sapna, where are you?" yelled Julie.

"Mr. Shah took them!" screamed Ravi.

"Jesus, no!" shouted Julie, collapsing on the ground. Ravi fell into her arms, and they sobbed together. Devastation overwhelmed him, and Julie felt his body tremble. After several minutes of agonizing grief, Julie ran her fingers through Ravi's hair. Indescribable agony was etched on her face. "I couldn't lose you; you're like my son." Ravi pulled back slightly, looked at her earrings, and hugged her again. She rocked him.

When she looked up she saw Madhu, his face wet from tears, standing over her.

"What happened?" Julie took him into her arms. He began to sob.

"What happened?" she asked again. Ravi translated for her.

"He came back. He got Kumar."

"Did he get anyone else?"

Madhu nodded. "He had me, my dog attacked, I got away. Then…my dog… killed." He broke down sobbing again. "Oh, Mahdu. I'm so sorry." Ravi patted him on the back and silently prayed for him.

"Jesus, will You protect Your littlest lambs? Thank You for keeping Mahdu safe and heal his broken heart. Please keep Kumar safe. Will You bring the others back—?"

"—Yes, Jesus," interrupted Ravi. "You helped me sleep at night. Please hear my prayers." Ravi and Julie continued praying as Julie held and rocked Madhu. Finally Julie lay Madhu on the ground where he went fetal. Ravi continued praying for him. Julie stood and paced, praying under her breath.

Julie prayed louder and finally yelled. "I renounce and resist the lie that Kumar will perish, in Jesus' name. I replace it with the truth that You are responsible for him, and You are able to protect him! Thank You, Lord, You are in control. Not me. You are the miracle-working God, and nothing is impossible with You!"

A tangible peace fell. Ravi looked at her.

"What's that?"

"That's Jesus helping us to not be sad."

"It feels better. And look, Madhu is asleep!"

This is what You meant about choosing to look at You instead of looking to our situation.

"I asked Jesus what we should do," Ravi said, "and He said to wait here and eat our lunch."

"Ravi, that's wonderful. You heard His voice."

"He talked to me before, but I didn't know who He was. He told me two times that I should walk, and now He told me to wait."

"You can trust Him. Always do what He tells you." Julie and Ravi sat beside Madhu, praying for him as they ate their sandwiches. Wilson peeked around the hedge.

"Wilson," cried Ravi, giving him a hug. Wilson took a deep breath, paused, and looked all around.

"It's Jesus, He's helping us not to be sad!" said Ravi.

Wilson smiled. Julie handed him a sandwich. After several bites he said, "After you left this morning Mr. Shah came. Everyone ran. I don't know what happened to—."

"Sammy," shouted Ravi, jumping up and giving him a hug. The stress dissolved from Sammy's face.

"Can you feel Jesus?" asked Ravi.

"He's helping us to not be sad," said Wilson, grinning. Sammy smiled.

After several hours, Sashi arrived with all the girls. Madhu woke and ate with them. Although the orphans were all distraught about the dog, they listened as Julie taught what she knew about peace in the middle of the storm.

Surprisingly, many were able to relax. Some smiled and a few even giggled. By evening, everyone had returned and eaten except Kumar.

"Let's pray for Kumar," said Julie. Each child prayed earnestly.

"Jesus just spoke to me," said Julie. "He said Mr. Shah has Kumar, but if we continue to pray, He will bring His peace to Kumar just like He did here." The children prayed and played until it was bedtime. Julie led the group to pray for Kumar before they fell asleep.

19

Julie prayed each morning for the orphans' salvation and adoption. "Lord, I can see how they would all get saved, but I don't have the faith for how they can all get adopted."

Remember what I said? This is My project; you are merely My mouth and feet. You couldn't imagine that I had the power to make berries appear or get your purse back.

Julie laughed in embarrassment, "Oh, yeah; I'd already forgotten about that. Thanks, but can You do it again with the wallet?"

Good try, Julie, but I have unlimited ways to provide for My orphans.

After Julie's prayer time each morning, she led the children in prayer for Bhanu and Kumar and taught a Bible story.

The afternoon was usually filled with games. With Ravi's help, Julie and the children played hide 'n' seek, which it turns out they already knew by another name, kanha muche attha. The girls were reluctant to leave Julie, but she promised she'd be there all day since she didn't have to leave to feed Ravi. And she'd stay the night.

Julie taught them London Bridge. When a child was caught between two people and "shaken up with salt and pepper," everyone laughed. Julie was so caught up in the games, she was able to forget about her worries. She laughed and enjoyed the orphans as much as they were enjoying her.

"Thank You, Lord, the mood has sure changed around here." Unbeknownst to Julie, that's what the orphans were thinking about her. Her reputation as a purse-waving maniac was fading a little more each day.

Over the next few days Julie spoke with several of the children as Ravi translated. She was able to find out how some had come to call this dump "home." Some were full of shame, refusing to talk or hanging their heads when they did.

Shoba began, "When my mother died, my grandmother took me in. We lived in a shack with holes in the roof. My grandmother was very old and lay on her mat all day. We ate only lentils and were both tired." She spoke in a mono-tone voice, staring, but not focusing. "One day I took her food and she was dead. I left and never went back."

Julie rubbed her hand over Shoba's skinny arm. *Found her grandmother dead? No one to help? Only lentils? No wonder she looks like a concentration camp survivor. Jesus, help Shoba. These children have lived a lifetime of pain in childhood. What will the rest of their lives be like?*

"Praveen, what happened?"

"My parents died while I was a baby, and my aunt didn't want me. She yelled and beat me. One day she took me to my uncle's and left me. He beat me more and said I was a 'good-for-nothing' boy. At school, my teacher made fun of me because I could not read. I wanted to get away from everyone. When I turned eight, I left for school one morning and just walked and walked."

Julie was shocked. *I can't imagine what he's endured. Has he ever had one day when someone loved him well?* She patted him on the shoulder, groping for something to say.

"I'm sorry, Praveen. I really am. I'm glad you came here, and now you have friends who care for you. And me. I'm your friend, too." Wanting to take some of the pressure off Praveen she turned to Wilson.

He fiddled with a knot on his walking stick, then spoke, "I am eight years old. I grew up in an orphanage. The kids teased me about my big ears. When the teachers went to sleep, the other boys would hit me, but never on my arms or legs where bruises would show. Every night was terror; I was very afraid. I wanted to run away, but had no place to go.

"One day the police came and made everyone move out to tear down the orphanage to build a road. I left with my friend Dayasagar. We slept on the streets. He got very sick, and sicker; then he died. I left his body under the bridge where we slept, and I ran and ran for many days. Then I found here with other children, and I stayed." He held out the walking stick for Julie's closer inspection. "This belonged to my friend, Dayasagar."

To Julie each story seemed more heart-wrenching than the last. *Jesus, Jesus, Jesus. I'm beginning to see why You want to help these children.* Wilson looked into Julie's eyes, then glanced toward the ground. Julie put her arm around his waist and pulled him close. Surprisingly, he let her. *Jesus, this rambunctious, fearless child is such a wounded little soul.*

"It's a really nice walking stick, Wilson." She ran her hand over the smooth, honey-colored wood. "A really nice one…." Her voice cracked, she buried her face in the crook of an elbow, and fought tears. Her hand gripped the walking stick until her arm shook. *His friend is dead, and all he has is this dump. This stinking, filthy dump every day and every night. And he's just a little boy, and his best friend is dead.* Tears of compassion flowed.

For several minutes the children stared at Julie and then at each other, as if asking, "What can we do to help?" Madhu pulled an origami butterfly from his pocket and placed it on her lap. Nilaya gently touched Julie's arm. When Julie saw who it was, a new wave of tears overtook her. All the tissues in her purse were used, and more were needed.

Sapna gently patted Julie's knee. She turned to Ravi to translate.

"Sapna says for you not to cry. We are a family, and we take care of each other. You are in our family now. We will help you to not be sad."

Julie doubled over sobbing. Each show of affection gripped her and at the same time convicted her.

How can they be so mistreated and show such kindness? How can they be so sweet when I've been so unsympathetic?

The sobbing continued. Praveen fished a used tissue out of his pocket and offered it to Julie. Even this unsanitary gesture emotionally disabled her.

Oh, Jesus, I repent of my terrible attitude. Please forgive me for despising these neglected ones. Lord, change me, please.

Her sobbing eventually tapered to weeping, then to an occasional whimper. She had no choice, but to wipe her nose and eyes on the sleeve of her dress as she wrestled her emotions for control.

After a few minutes, Chavvi, the eight-year-old in a pink dress, shared in great detail about her family and the happy times.

"I had three brothers and two sisters. My dad worked a job, and we were happy." Her face scrunched in pain and she wept. Julie patted her arm with one hand and rubbed her back with the other. After a few minutes, Chavvi sobbed out the rest of the story.

"I was with my family at a religious festival. There were many people. I stopped to look at flowers, and when I looked up, I couldn't find my family. I screamed and yelled. I looked for days." She sobbed even harder. "They didn't want me anymore."

"Oh, sweetie." Julie pulled her on her lap and rocked her. "Do you know your address?"

Chavvi shook her head.

We lived by a big park; it had a fountain."

"What's your last name?"

"Reddy."

Maybe, thought Julie, *that will help.* She hugged her tightly and sang, "Jesus loves me, this I know; for the Bible tells me so. Little ones to Him belong; they are weak and He is strong." After hearing it several times, the children hummed the melody and stumbled over the words. Julie knew that something was taking place, but she didn't know what. "Lord, thank You for being with us."

Mahipal volunteered, "I was playing in front of the store where my mother shopped. A man grabbed me and threw me in a car. There were many children kept in one large room. The men sent us to beg, then beat us every night. They said they would kill us if we left. One night, I ran and ran. I found here and stayed. My name is Mahipal Bharat, and I lived at house number 8 opposite to the Eshwara temple, in Geddalahalli 11."

You have your address? Why didn't you go home?"

"I could not find home. No one helped me. I had no money. I had to hide during the day so I would not be killed."

Julie jumped up, dragging the child to his feet.

"Ravi, Mahipal and I are going to take a taxi. Tell everyone they must pray to Jesus to help us get him back home. I need money for the fare. Tell them to pray now."

She and Mahipal ran to the street to hail an auto rickshaw. When she looked back, all the children were in a circle with their heads bowed. When the taxi arrived, Mahipal gave the address. The driver nodded and held up ten fingers.

"Ten minutes, ten miles, ten kilometers, ten rupees? Yes, Lord." The taxi moved slowly with the traffic. They finally transitioned to the country with green fields on both sides and sheep grazing. There were cows, monkeys, dogs, and cats wandering freely.

At first Julie felt relaxed, but then the driver picked up speed. Driving on the left side of the road caused enough anxiety, but the driver passed on hills and at other times took to the shoulder to make way for drivers headed straight toward them in their lane. Julie was kicking herself for not bringing Ravi to translate.

"Slow down, slow down," she shrieked. She tapped his shoulder. He had no intention of slowing down. The more quickly he finished this run, the sooner he could get another one. Large dump trucks painted in bright colors barreled down the road. "O Jesus, help us, help us," she squealed as her driver passed on a blind curve and narrowly missed a minivan.

She put her arm around Mahipal and wrote the word *Jesus* on his palm, then placed his hand on his chest. She held him close and sang over him, then prayed for him to fulfill his destiny.

The driver slowed as he came to a little town. Mahipal's face lit up. He sat up straight and pointed to various houses and little shops and chattered nonstop.

When the driver stopped in front of a small house with bougainvillea growing up a trellis, Mahipal let out a shriek and ran toward the door, opened it, and disappeared inside. Julie stepped out of the auto rickshaw and motioned for the drive to stay.

Screaming, laughter, and shouts of joy spilled from the house. She followed the sound and gazed in the doorway. Tears spilled over her cheeks as she drank in the sight—people with their arms all flung around each other, making a melody of laughter, tears, and sweetness.

Looks like mom, two younger sisters, and an older one.

Eventually Mahipal saw Julie and squealed. He grabbed his mother's hand and pulled her toward Julie, talking all the way. The mother dropped to her knees and flung her arms around Julie's waist, wailing. Julie stood rather uncomfortably for 30 long seconds until she was released. The sobbing mother pulled a gold bracelet from her wrist and offered it to Julie.

"I couldn't, no, but thank you. It was my pleasure." She slid the bangle back on the woman's wrist. The mother led her to the couch and disappeared into the next room. She returned with a rusted metal container, emptied it on to the couch and scraped coins and paper money toward Julie.

Taxi fare! Thank you, Lord. She grabbed a few coins, and smiled. "Dhanivadha." The woman continued to scoop the pile toward Julie, who once again motioned no with her hands.

Julie stood up and hugged and kissed Mahipal as she slowly rocked him from side to side.

"Bless you, Mahipal. Don't forget Jesus really loves you. Amen." She pointed to the word written on his hand.

"Ah-meen," he replied.

Julie, Mahipal will be My humble servant. He will have the grace to embrace wounded, hurting people whom no one else believes in.

His life verse is: "He has sent me to bind up the brokenhearted, to proclaim freedom for the captives and release from darkness for the prisoners....to comfort all who mourn....to bestow on them a crown of beauty instead of ashes, the oil of gladness instead of mourning, and a garment of praise instead of a spirit of despair."[1]

"Thank You, Lord. You have an incredible destiny for Mahipal!"

His mother grabbed Julie's arms and stared deeply into her eyes. The tears in the eyes of two mothers from halfway around the world connected without words. They both smiled and hugged, and Julie almost floated back to the taxi.

"Thank You, Lord. I'm overwhelmed. Mahipal is going to grow up and serve You. Thank You, thank You, thank You for allowing me to participate in this amazing journey. I am emotionally exhausted, but totally exhilarated if that's possible."

Thank you for being obedient, Julie. I'm glad you didn't leave when you had the chance.

Julie smiled, leaned back in the seat, and let her hair fly in the wind. *One down, and 11 to go.*

When Julie returned, it was getting close to dinnertime.

"Ravi, I need you to help with the food, but pick another boy to help us too." Ravi looked around, "I choose Praveen." Ravi explained to Praveen that he'd help pick berries and then go to the market. In his usual show of excitement, Praveen jumped up and clapped. The three headed for the bushes. As Praveen walked, he constantly looked around.

"Ravi," said Julie, "ask Praveen what he's looking for."

"He says he's looking for bad guys and criminals. He wants to be a detective and thinks he's going to solve a big crime," said Ravi.

They picked berries together, and Praveen was full of questions all about Julie and her life and crime in the United States.

He's a little sponge for information, thought Julie.

With the sack of berries in her arms, she spoke to Ravi as they walked, "Ask Praveen what his favorite food is." Ravi asked Praveen, and with a sly look replied, "He says bananas." At first Julie accepted this; then an enlightened smile spread across her face.

"Maybe he didn't understand, Ravi. Ask him again, please."

"Tandoori chicken."

"I have a little change left from taxi fare."

Ravi spotted the wheeled cart and ran ahead. When Julie ordered one piece, Ravi began to pout. As Praveen ate, Ravi crossed his arms and trailed behind.

"Ravi," said Julie, "can you be happy for Praveen when he gets something special?" Ravi looked at the street frowning.

"He's eating special chicken, his favorite. Can you be glad for him?" Ravi still didn't look convinced. Julie laid her hand on his shoulder, "Hey mister monkey, remember how happy you were when you had your bananas? That's how happy Praveen is today. We should be happy for him, too!"

Ravi shook his head and forced a smile.

They bought sandwiches, fruit, and juice. Julie used the toilet, and she was very grateful. "Little things mean a lot. I will not forget Your blessings, Lord."

The two boys carried the food through the crowds. When they arrived at the dump, Sashi was getting the girls in a circle, and to Julie's great surprise and pleasure, Wilson was helping the boys.

"What happened here today, Lord?"

This time she prayed a quick blessing before handing out the food, and this time she really meant it. She smiled at each child as she distributed the food to each grasping, outstretched arm.

"Here you go, Wilson. Eat up! Sapna, this is yours. Enjoy. Sashi, my friend. I'm so glad you're here with us. Shoba, I hope you like today's selection."

After they wolfed down their food, some of the children deposited their sandwich wrappers on the dump, and others dropped them. *Well, we're making a little progress.*

When everyone was done, Julie excitedly recounted, in great detail, Mahipal's joyful arrival back home. The children all laughed when Julie acted out the enthusiastic group hug. "And, I didn't have any money for the auto, but I knew you were here praying, and Mahipal's mother tried to give me a lot! More than I even needed."

"Your God answered as we prayed?" asked Sashi.

"Yes, He did. His name is Jesus, and He answered your prayers."

"Why?"

"Because He loves you, and He wants to be a part of your life each day. He wants to be your friend."

Sashi's face brightened. "He wants to be my friend and talk to me?"

"Yes. He loves you. He created you, and He has a plan for your life." Julie could see that the rest of the girls were listening, and Wilson seemed attentive, too.

Madhu sat working diligently on the seed with the nail. He gave a push and the top of the seed cracked. Julie saw the tears well in his eyes.

"I'm sorry, Madhu." She smiled at him. He threw the seed toward the dump, put the nail back in his pocket, and pulled out a flat, folded square of paper that he manipulated into a silver cube. When he opened it the inside was blue, after a few more folds the silver was the inside and the blue was the outside.

"How'd you do that?"

Madhu smiled and pulled an intricately folded piece of grey paper from his pocket and made a few additional folds. Julie watched as an elephant took shape.

"Madhu. You're so talented!" Julie watched him fold a crane, a frog, an airplane, and a kite.

Out of the corner of her eye, Julie saw movement. She was surprised to see the muscular policeman on the sidewalk watching them. When he realized he'd been spotted, he approached. Praveen shouted something, and all the children scattered behind the hedge, watching from a distance.

"I told you," whispered Praveen, who was always looking for a good conspiracy, "policemen put orphans in jail and then grind them up for food." He paused to look right and left. "They eat them every day!" This exclamation caused the children to run screaming further away.

Great, just what I need, a crooked policeman. What kind of trouble is he going to stir up? wondered Julie.

"Hello, I'm Daya," said the officer, extending his hand. Julie was on her feet and forced a smile, trying to seem more confident that she was. *Amazing, you're off your duff and walking a beat?*

"Can we talk?"

"Sure," said Julie, her arms crossed. "We have two options—stand or sit on the dirt." *I know exactly how you operate. Don't think you're going to get away with anything.*

"Here's fine." He crossed his legs and sat. "Your face looks better."

"What?"

He pointed to his cheeks. "Not, um, red anymore."

Julie nodded. "It finally cleared up." *Thanks for your concern—not.*

"You have orphans."

If he asks me for a bribe, I swear I'll scream. "Yes, I told all of you I was taking care of orphans. You believe me now?"

"We believed you then."

"If you believed me, then why didn't anyone do anything?"

"Orphans don't vote, and orphans don't have money for bribes. That's why orphans never get help. In India those who get help are those who can afford help."

Well, that eliminates us. "What do you want?"

"To help."

"I told you I have no money. My wallet was stolen—remember." Julie rolled her eyes and let out a deep sigh.

"I don't mean me, the police officer, I mean me, myself," he said, placing his hand over his chest.

"And what do you want in return?"

"I want nothing from you in return."

"Oh, well, the orphans aren't for sale. They're not going anywhere. We're a family and we'll fight you as a family." Her voice began to rise. "We already ran off one guy who wanted them to beg, and we're not afraid—"

"I want nothing from the orphans, either. I am a Jesus-follower, and I want to help."

Julie's false bravado collapsed. "You're a, you believe in Jesus?"

"Yes, and He commands we help the widows and orphans."

"Yes, He does." Julie looked chagrined. *I guess some people do it willingly.*

"How can I help the orphans?"

"You really want to help the orphans? You want to help us?"

"Yes. What can I do?"

"We need food every day. I need to find homes for all these children. Their stories are heart-wrenching. They aren't safe here. Can you see if you can find an address for one of our orphans? Her name is Chavvi Reddy; she is eight, and her house is very close to a park with a large fountain."

"I know that park. It's about ten kilometers away."

"She has a loving family, but she was separated from them at a large religious festival."

"That would be the Dasara festival; they celebrate the goddess Chamundi. I will see what I can find. Maybe we can get that little one back home."

"Oh, that would be so wonderful. Maybe I'll take back all the bad things I thought about you," she smiled.

He stood. "And I will start bringing food for the orphans once a day. I will bring it during my lunch. I will also include this street in my route. I will walk it three times a day. If you have problems, I will help."

"Oh," sighed Julie, totally letting down her guard, "that's wonderful. You have no idea how helpful that will be. " Before she could stop herself, she had flung her arms around Daya. He looked slightly embarrassed and took a step backward once he was released from her grip.

"I will come this Saturday and teach, how you say, self-deee-fense, to the children."

"You're really going to help us?"

"Yes. Maybe I will bring some friends later. How many to be fed?"

"Ten, um, 11 if you want me to eat."

"Eleven then. Have you eaten today?"

"Yes."

"I will be back tomorrow on my lunch break with your food." He turned to go.

"One more thing. I hate to ask, but could you bring a bottle of hand sanitizer, the large size?"

Julie went to look for her orphans and found them huddled together behind a garden fence in someone's backyard.

"Ravi, translate for me. Jesus has answered our prayers and has sent someone who will bring us food and help us. His name is Daya. Thank You, Jesus." Julie was so excited she didn't notice that the orphans weren't.

"Let's go! Let's go back to the dump. He's going to bring us food starting tomorrow."

The orphans talked among themselves and decided that it was safe to return since he was gone, but if anyone saw him again the whole group would hide together back in this spot. They all adjourned back to the dump.

20

Julie woke the next morning. "Thanks, Lord, I really slept well. Thanks for bringing Daya to provide food. I wonder if there are berries today?"

The Lord answered, *Why would there be berries today? I have provided food for you in a new way.*

She smiled and made a mental note to slip away later and check the bushes for herself.

It was late morning, and the group was together playing Paper, Rock, Scissors. Julie was startled when Praveen jumped up, pointed, and let out a yell. Fearing it was Mr. Shah she turned, but it was Daya coming with a large bag of groceries.

She walked to greet him, but noticed he was staring past her. She turned in time to see the last orphan disappear around the hedge.

"Now, what got into them?" She looked a little embarrassed. "I wanted them to meet you and of course to thank you for your generosity."

He nodded.

"I bet they're afraid of you because of Mr. Shah. Oh my gosh. You, the police, can arrest Mr. Shah. He steals children and puts them on the street to beg. He just snatched two boys. Three of our boys have escaped from him, and he cut off Kumar's arm."

"People like Mr. Shah pay bribes to the police to be left alone to do their dirty work. But I do not take bribes. I would like very much to meet Mr. Shah."

Tears welled in Julie's eyes.

Daya looked embarrassed.

"Well, I hope you can find your orphans. Enjoy the food," he handed the heavy sack to her.

"I'll be back tomorrow."

"Thank you," was all Julie could say. She headed for the garden.

"I told you," said Praveen. "My brother told me he had a friend who was 11, and he was taken by the police, and the next day my brother walked by there, and in the alley were his friend's clothes. In less than a day they had eaten him."

"Police are bad, very bad," said Wilson. "It was the police who tore down my orphanage. My friend and I escaped, and then my friend died because of the police."

Ravi's brow furrowed. He tried to remember if his parents had told him things about the police. Then he remembered visiting with his mother's friend in an apartment. A neighbor was shot, and he solemnly watched the police arrive and break down the door.

"It's true," shouted Ravi, "they ate my mom's friend's neighbor! They eat live and dead people!"

Several of the smaller girls clung to each other and Nilaya began to cry. Sammy inched closer to Ravi. The whole group startled when Julie's smiling face appeared over the top of the fence accompanied by a cheery greeting,

"I thought I might find you here. Tell them, Ravi, that Daya brought them lots of food. Let's go eat."

"The policeman brought food. Auntie wants us to go back and eat." At that point, Julie grabbed a bunch of bananas and held them up as evidence. That was all that Ravi and several of the other children needed, and they headed for the garden gate.

"Wait," shouted Praveen. "What if the food is poisoned? They eat dead people, too. He could kill us all and then come for our bodies tonight." His eyes narrowed.

The children looked at Julie's smiling face and the food, then back at Praveen while they considered the risk. Hunger gnawed at them, begging to be relieved.

The bananas were wearing on Ravi's resolve.

"Is the policeman still there?"

"No, but he'll walk by later this evening to make sure we're OK. Tell them to come, Ravi." She walked away, carrying the food with her.

"He's not there. Maybe we could just go back and maybe not eat or not eat much," said Ravi. *How much poison can fit in a banana? How much is needed to make me sick? To make me die?*

The hungry, frightened group took several collective sighs and silently walked back. Julie had carefully sorted the food and laid it in piles in a row. Eleven boxes of juice, 11 sandwiches, 11 bananas, 11 apples, and sweets. It was more food than they had seen in their lives all together in one place.

"Ravi, tell them to line up right here. Girls first and then the boys. Then after I pray you can walk and take ONE piece of food from each pile. Close your eyes everyone." She kept one eye open as she prayed, "Dear Jesus, thank You for hearing and answering our prayers. Help us never to forget that. And thank You for loving us enough to provide this food for us. Help us to love You back. And bless our new friend, Daya, the policeman. And keep Bhanu and Kumar safe." Julie was giddy with excitement.

After a brief pause, when the orphans all looked at one another, hunger nudged them forward, and each child filed by Julie, who gave them a large dollop of hand sanitizer. After a quick tutorial on how to rub it in, they quickly grabbed food from each pile and sat down, but no one ate.

Julie picked up her food and took a big bite of her sandwich. After waiting several seconds, the orphans felt safe to eat theirs. When Julie peeled her banana, they all peeled theirs, too. She didn't notice them watching her intently and following her lead. After she had finished all the food, she picked up her sweet.

"I'm stuffed," she announced. "I'm saving my sweet for later."

Praveen had pulled the wrapper off his sweet when Julie had picked hers up. With every ounce of will power he could muster, he carefully wrapped it back up and shoved it in his pocket. Some of the children groaned as they looked at each other, wondering if it was worth the risk. Praveen was one of the oldest, and he knew things other kids didn't know—that policemen eat children. With great effort the children abstained from eating the sweets, all except Sammy, who had immediately popped his in his mouth when Julie reached for hers. All eyes turned to Sammy.

Chavvi pointed.

"Is he going to die?" asked Wilson.

"Sammy, you ate the sweet—it was poisoned!" blurted Madhu.

Sammie's smile faded and panic filled his eyes. He coughed while pounding his chest in an attempt to bring back up the sweet.

"He's dying," yelled Wilson.

The panic in his voice caused Julie to look up.

"He's dying," yelled Ravi in English to Julie about the time that full-fledged panic overwhelmed Sammy. He ran in a big circle as fast as his limp would allow. He cried out in terror while flailing his arms.

A horrified look crossed Praveen's face. It was poisoned! And when he tossed his sweet in the dump, all the rest did the same.

Julie caught Sammy and scooped him up in her arms, and he wailed louder. "Ravi," screamed Julie over Sammy's screams, "what's the matter?"

"The sweet made him sick."

"The sweet? He just ate it. Ask him what's wrong?"

"It's the sweet," Ravi insisted, flinging his arms out for emphasis.

"Oh, for goodness sakes." She turned her focus back to Sammy, who was still wailing in her ear. She bounced him and walked him, but nothing worked.

"Maybe," yelled Ravi to Julie, "you could eat your sweet."

"How would that help?" shouted Julie.

"It just would," screamed Ravi. Since nothing else was working, Julie deposited Sammy on the ground, unwrapped her sweet, and ate it. All eyes were glued to her. Thirty seconds passed as the orphans observed Julie. Then there was a stampede to the dump to retrieve and eat the discarded sweets. Sammy's wails turned to sniffles.

"Am I going to die, Ravi?" asked Sammy.

"No, you won't die," said Ravi, patting his friend on the back.

Julie was befuddled. The perfect lunch had turned catastrophic, and she had no idea why or how eating a sweet had redeemed it.

She looked toward Ravi, who shrugged his shoulders and said nothing. He wondered if she knew the policeman was their enemy. *Why does she keep inviting him? Can I keep trusting her?*

The children played together while keeping a lookout for Daya, who was supposed to return. Except for Sammy, who kept an eye on Julie in case she keeled over; then he would know to do the same.

Julie taught the children a rhyming song. "Touch your shoulders, touch your knees. Raise your arms, and drop them, please. Touch your ankles, touch your toes. Pull your ears, and touch your nose."

The faster it went, the more the children laughed.

"Now do it standing on your right foot," shouted Julie, laughing at their unstable attempts and especially her own.

What a change in these children. It's amazing. The more the children laughed, the more she did, too.

It was Julie who spotted the muscular policeman first.

"Daya, hello! Look everyone, Daya is here!" But when she turned around, all the children were gone. If they had been wearing hats, they would have still been hanging in the air cartoon-style due to the abrupt departure.

"How was lunch?"

"Wonderful!" sighed Julie. Then he noticed the puzzled look on her face.

"Something wrong?"

"Well, I think the children still think you're just another Mr. Shah. That's why they run, but one of them thought he was dying when he ate his sweet."

"Dying? Did he choke?"

"No, he's one of the boys who escaped from Mr. Shah. He was convinced he was dying until I ate my sweet, too."

"Strange."

"Very strange."

"I have wonderful news. I was able to locate Chavvi's address."

"Oh, Daya, that is wonderful news, better than wonderful."

"It's just a few kilometers away. I went by the house and no one was home, but I'll take her now and stay with her until the family returns. Can you get her for me?"

"Wait right here." Julie ran back to the garden where the orphans were gathered. She was bubbling with excitement. "Ravi, translate, please. Chavvi, I know your address. I know where your family lives." Julie flung her arms above her head. "Thank You, Jesus! It's a miracle; you'll be back with your family today."

Chavvi frowned as Ravi spoke, and then her face lit up with joy.

"My family, my family."

"That's right. Say good-bye to everyone, and then we'll go."

One by one the orphans all said their farewells. The girls hugged her, and the boys all spoke something Julie couldn't understand. Sammy stepped forward and gave her a big hug and then stepped back.

"Let's go, Chavvi," Julie extended her hand, and the two walked back to the dump.

The children were still exploring their options for self-preservation.

"What if he eats Auntie?" asked Ravi.

"Who would take care of us then?" asked Sammy.

"She feeds us every day," said Sapna.

"Who would protect us from being eaten next?" asked Praveen.

Sammy felt the anxiety building in his gut, and he began to wail again.

"I'm dying." He collapsed onto the ground.

"You're not dying," said Sashi, kneeling beside him. "We all ate our sweets, remember?"

Sammy paused in mid-cry, his brows furrowed. After a few seconds, he accepted this logic and stood.

"Maybe," said Wilson, "we should attack him the next time he comes, like we did Mr. Shah." He still had memories of bashing out the side window with his walking stick. It had become a highlight of his uneventful life.

"But he brought us food. If we attack him, he won't bring food anymore," said Madhu.

"But Auntie always brought food for us," said Sashi.

"But he brought more food," said Madhu.

"OK, we won't attack him now. Let's see if he keeps bringing food. If he stops, then we'll attack him," said Wilson.

The sober-looking children nodded their heads in agreement.

"Let's go see if he's gone," said Ravi.

Daya stopped by one more time that evening, sending the children flying back to the garden.

"Just wanted to let you know that Chavvi arrived home just fine. Her parents and sisters and brothers were all crying. I've never seen such a reunion. I almost cried myself."

"Oh, Daya," gushed Julie, "thank you so much. I'll sleep better tonight knowing that she's safe and back with her family. You are truly an answer to prayer."

"You might just be the answer to our prayers," said Daya.

You were praying for a bunch of orphans and a grumpy, displaced American? "How's that?"

"I can't say; we can speak about it later. I'm here to protect all of you. Any problems?"

"You mean other than the fact that I'm in charge of all these children who live on a garbage dump, in the open, with no parents to return them to and no idea how to solve this dilemma?"

"Well, other than that?"

"Nope, that's about all the problems I have today."

Daya grinned.

"Well, feel free to lavish food and protection on us any time of the day or night. The children are always here," she smiled, "except when you are."

"I'll be back tomorrow morning to check on all of you."

"That sounds wonderful to me, but I need to get you and them on speaking terms. Maybe for a while you should only come at lunch when you have food, if that's all right."

"Sure. Then I'll be back during my lunch hour with food tomorrow. Have a pleasant evening."

Julie couldn't wait to tell the children the good news. She found them having a serious conversation in the garden.

"Ravi, translate please. It's so exciting," she looked him in the face, and he smiled back, catching her enthusiasm.

"Daya took Chavvi back to her family today!"

Ravi's countenance dropped.

"I, I thought, I thought you were taking her home like you did with Mahipal. You took him in an auto rickshaw! Why did you give her to Daya? Is she gone?"

"Calm down, Ravi. It's wonderful news, he took her, and now she's back with her family."

Ravi turned and spoke to the orphans. Praveen cried out, "He's eaten her, too. She's dead." A collective moan went up. Wilson gasped. Nilaya cried. A look of horror spread over Sashi's face. Sammy inched toward Ravi.

"I thought you'd be happy for her. She's with her family—her family. Tell them again, Ravi. They must have misunderstood."

Ravi looked at the ground and spoke slowly, but the mood didn't change.

"Well, I don't know what's going on, but I feel like I'm on the outside looking in. I can't believe you're not happy." Julie turned back toward the dump. *Maybe they're jealous!*

Bedtime at the dump was a somber affair. There was little talking, and everyone seemed exceptionally skittish.

Ravi lay awake wondering if Julie was going to become another Mr. Shah and if there was anyone he could trust in this unsafe, unstable world.

Julie lay awake thinking. *I feel like I've lived a lifetime in the last few days. I've been from the depths of despair, losing Bhanu and Kumar and hearing the childrens' stories, to total delight delivering Mahipal to his family and everything in between. And now we have Daya to help us, and my stomach is almost full. I'm so grateful and so tired, I don't even have the energy complain about the heat.*

And with that, she fell asleep.

CHAPTER

21

The next morning before the children woke, Julie walked by the bushes just to see if there were berries. Since the first day Daya had brought food, they never reappeared.

She returned and spent about 40 minutes reviewing the Exodus story *Wow, Lord, You really provided food for 40 years for about a million people. I guess providing for our little group each day is really easy.* She spent another 20 minutes praying for the orphans and Michael and Logan. *I don't think I've ever prayed that long in my life!*

After everyone was awake, Julie shared the Exodus story.[1] The children loved the frogs and the gnats and were especially attentive when Julie told how the Lord provided manna every day for them to eat.

Julie led the children in a prayer for the Lord to rescue them from the dump and to rescue Bhanu and Kumar. Ravi translated, and the children repeated. Several of them closed their eyes and prayed fervently. *Wow*, thought Julie, *they're becoming little prayer warriors.*

Through Ravi's translation, Julie had learned more of their stories and about their personalities. From this, she would ask the Lord for a specific plan to help each child.

If she didn't hear anything definite, most days she would take a child for a walk to the market, even though she couldn't buy anything for them or herself. They all seemed to enjoy the special attention and the colorful change of scenery that the market provided.

Julie had been waking earlier than the children and spending time in prayer, asking for wisdom and compassion.

"Lord, You referred to a key to unlock Nilaya's heart. After I scratched her and almost beat her with my purse, she won't trust me. I can't blame her."

It's not just you, Julie. All her life she's been rejected and abused, and no one has loved her well or at all. It's not that she doesn't want to trust; it's that she can't. No one around her has ever been trustworthy, until now. She hates being left out, but she is driven by her fears. But I am going to bind up her wounds and heal her hurts. Watch and see what I do with Nilaya in the next few days. Today I will give her courage to approach you. Welcome her and praise her lavishly. Show My love to her today. I have chosen you to show her a new way.

"How do I show her a new way?"

Consistency and follow through. Each day promise her some small thing; begin very small, a back scratch, a conversation, a walk—and then do it. Over time she will learn a new pattern. And smile. No one's eyes have ever lit up when she came into the room. For now, she must receive My delight in her and My love for her through you.

Julie watched the children play from her vantage point, sitting with her back against the lone tree.

This heat really zaps my energy. So lethargic. All I want to do is rest. She wiped the sweat from her brow. *How do they survive without air conditioning?*

With Shoba sleeping beside her, she dozed off and on and dreamed she heard a baby cry. The next thing she knew, Nilaya was shaking her shoulder, and there was definitely a real baby crying. Julie smiled at Nilaya, who looked at the ground. Nilaya tried to hand the infant to Julie, who paused, slathered hand sanitizer up to her elbows, and then received the newborn that was wrapped in rags and bundled in a light-weight, dirty blanket. Holding the baby with great care, Julie looked into its big, dark eyes.

"You are so precious. Where did you come from, little one?"

"Thank you, Nilaya. You rescued a baby. Thank you so much." She put her hand on Nilaya's arm. Nilaya beamed at Julie's tone of voice, even though she couldn't understand.

"Poor thing, she's probably starving. Oh, Lord, what can we do? I don't have any money. And how are we ever going to keep a baby healthy and clean at a garbage dump?"

After applying hand sanitizer to her index finger, she inserted it in the baby's mouth, and it calmed down.

"Whew, ancient pacifier."

Ravi had just arrived. "Ancient what?"

"Nothing, it makes the baby happy."

"Where did we get a baby?"

"Ask Nilaya. Oh, sorry, maybe not. Someone must have dropped her, him, whatever, off this morning." Julie checked. "It's a girl!"

In minutes all the orphans were surrounding Julie, peering at the baby.

"Lord, show us what to do and how to care for this precious baby. Amen." All the girls wanted to hold her; the boys were more cautious, but still curious. Ever vigilant, Julie used almost the whole bottle of hand sanitizer, making sure that every hand and finger that touched the infant was sterile.

The boys eventually left, but the girls spent hours being little mothers, fascinated by the baby. Julie smiled as Nilaya slid in close so she could keep a hand on the infant. Ravi had stayed as translator so Julie could give instructions.

"Support her neck. Hold up her head. She's so sweet."

The more the girls spent time with the baby, the more captivated they were. They made faces, trying to get her to smile.

"Translate, please, Ravi. Nilaya is a hero. She saved the baby's life. Nilaya, you are a wonderful little girl. I'm so proud of you." Julie reached her arm around Nilaya as she spoke. Nilaya beamed. *Thank You, Lord*, thought Julie. *What a breakthrough.*

"Could I, would you, let me hold the baby?" asked Ravi.

"Of course you can." She positioned him against the tree for back support. Julie was surprised at how tenderly Ravi handled the infant. He cooed and rocked and even sang a lullaby.

"That's beautiful Ravi." Julie stared adoringly at the infant and Ravi.

He looked a little embarrassed, but confessed, "My mother used to sing me this song so I could go to sleep."

Julie smiled. "Now, everyone think of a good name for her." All the girls shouted their own names as suggestions, with the exception of Nilaya, who was silent.

Lord, what do you call her?

Ravi looked up at Julie.

"I have a name for the baby. Could we name her Sharavathi?" Ravi looked hopeful.

"What a beautiful name."

He looked back at the baby.

"It was my mother's name," he said as he ran his fingers over the baby's cheek.

"Since Nilaya found the baby, I think Nilaya should name the baby." Sitting a little taller, Nilaya almost grinned as Ravi translated.

"Nilaya, what do you think about the name Sharavathi?" Looking up, Nilaya nodded, her face brightening.

"Sharavathi she is. Can we call her Shara?" Nilaya nodded again, unable to squelch her smile. Ravi grinned from ear to ear and handed her back to Julie.

Wilson's voice rang out, alerting everyone that Daya had arrived. Before Julie knew what was happening, they were gone to the garden except Ravi, who hid on the other side of the hedge to watch.

Daya sat two large groceries bags next to Julie.

"What? A baby?"

Julie nodded.

"Someone must have left her at the dump early this morning. She's probably less than a week old. Nilaya was digging looking for something to eat," Julie shuddered, "and saw this little bundle move."

"This is not unusual. Couples want to have boys so they will be supported in their old age. Many times they kill the girls and try again."

Julie gasped and reflexively held Shara closer.

"She needs food, and she needs to be cleaned. I have no money to even buy milk and a bottle."

"I will take her," said Daya.

"To the police station?" blurted Julie. "What will they do with her, or to her?"

"The police care even less about abandoned babies than they do orphans. I will take her to my friends at church. There are two sisters, Chanda and Champa, who love children. They will take good care of her until someone will adopt her."

"Are you sure they will take good care of her?" Julie asked, while staring into Shara's eyes and brushing her fingers over Shara's thick black hair.

Daya looked at her as if she had asked the stupidest question ever.

"Yes, they are Jesus-lovers, too, and love children very much. If I take her—"

"Shara, we named her Sharavathi."

"If I take Sharavathi now, I will have time to take her to the sisters on my lunch break. But I must hurry."

Julie breathed a silent prayer and rubbed her nose against Shara's.

"You are so sweet. I wish I could take you home with me. You would be my special baby." She choked back tears as she reluctantly handed the baby to his outstretched arms.

"Don't worry. I promise she will be cared for very well." He left in a hurry.

Ravi observed the whole thing and sprinted to the garden.

"The police eat orphans and old dead people and they eat babies, too!" yelled Ravi. "And he's going to eat Sharavathi. He's going to eat our baby!"

A few of the girls shrieked. Wilson clutched his walking stick and several boys gasped. "I saw him. He took Shara and then ran away!"

"Are you sure?" asked Shoba.

"Yes. I saw him leave with her in his arms."

"What can we do?" wailed Sashi.

Nilaya dropped to the ground and began to cry.

"He's gone," moaned Ravi. "We'd never catch, him even if we knew where he took her. Why did Auntie give him our baby?"

"Did he bring food before he left?" asked Sammy in a hopeful voice.

Ravi nodded.

"It wasn't poisoned yesterday, and if he's going to eat the baby, he's not going to be hungry for a long time, so he wouldn't need to kill us today," said Madhu, who was always thinking.

"But," said Praveen, pointing his index finger, "he didn't know we had a baby today, so maybe the food is poisoned." The older children, now distracted from the baby, pondered this; the younger ones just looked confused.

"Auntie must be very hungry to trade the baby for food," said Sapna.

Ravi spoke up, "But I don't think she *knows* he's a bad guy like Mr. Shah."

"Can't we just go see the food?" asked Sammy, who felt his stomach growling.

"Maybe we can tell if it's poisoned," said Madhu.

The group marched solemnly back to Julie, who greeted them with unbounded excitement.

"The Lord answered our prayers. He not only provided us with food today; He provided a place for Shara. Isn't that great? Our new friend knows two sisters who will take care of Shara."

Julie didn't understand why the group wasn't more excited after Ravi translated for her, but she started laying out food in piles. *Is it my imagination, or is Sashi frowning at me?* When they saw the food, the children's focus left Shara and turned to relieving their hunger.

"OK, let's pray. Jesus, thanks for providing our new friend, Daya, and thanks for the food he brings, and thanks for saving Shara's life. Amen."

There was dead silence.

"Ah-meen," Julie said. She sanitized their hands; then they gathered their food and sat. Once again, all eyes were on Julie. She didn't realize that when she ate her roti, after a few seconds hesitation, everyone else did, too. She pulled a plastic lid off of a foam cup.

"What is this—rice and something?" She smelled it and crinkled up her nose. "Very spicy." She took a small taste, made a face, and put the lid back on the cup. Reluctantly the others did, too.

"It's poisoned," whispered Praveen.

The children were even more alert now. They peeled their orange when Julie did, but waited until she ate a few segments to follow. At the end, she popped her sweet in her mouth. "Oh, that's good. It's lemon."

Sammy, in an uncharacteristic show of will power, waited extra long and was the last one to eat his.

Julie picked up the trash and realized all the foam cups were still full.

"Praveen, you didn't eat your rice. Ravi, yours is full. Nilaya, you didn't eat yours either. Ravi, what's going on?"

"Umm, we did not think it tasted good either. Also too spicy for us." He kept a somber face and could see Praveen staring at him out of the corner of his eye.

"Ravi," chirped Julie, "are you planning to rescue more children? Daya will help us, he will protect us from Mr. Shah. He can rescue Kumar and Bhanu." Julie gathered all the cups and put them in one of the sacks. "I'll keep these for later, and when you want yours just come to me." *They're pretty serious for having eaten such a wonderful meal. Even the bananas didn't seem to cheer Ravi.*

As the afternoon wore on, Julie had the distinct feeling that the children were meeting as a group and she was excluded. *That's unusual; the boys usually play as a group, and the girls gather and play where I am.*

When they noticed her strolling toward them, they quit talking. She walked away, and they started chatting again.

Julie's feelings were wounded. She prayed. "Lord, what's going on? It's like I'm persona non grata all of a sudden."

Talk to Ravi, was all the Lord said.

Julie strolled to the group. They all fell mute and stared at the ground.

"Ravi, I need to talk with you. Will you come, please?" She tried to figure out what to ask. *I guess I'll start with food. Can't go wrong with that!*

"Here, Ravi," said Julie, handing him two cups of rice. "You can have mine, too."

Ravi's eyes grew big, and he shook his head as he scooted away a little.

"Go on, Ravi, eat it. It's not like you to turn down food."

The more she insisted, the more anxious he became.

"What's wrong?" She scooted near him, but he scooted away.

"Ravi?"

"I can't; don't make me eat it."

"OK, you don't have to eat it. Here, I'm putting it back in the sack." She sat quietly while asking the Lord for wisdom.

"What's wrong? Please tell me." Finally the burden Ravi was carrying became too much to bear.

"The food is poisoned, and he ate Chavvi and Shara, and then he's going to eat us, and then he's going to find some old dead people to eat. Why don't you protect us?"

"What? What are you talking about?"

"The policeman."

"Our policeman? Daya?" Ravi nodded and burst into tears.

"Did you know he was bad? Were you going to let him eat us one at a time?"

"Where did you get such an idea?"

After several minutes of prodding, Ravi unraveled the whole story. Julie picked him up, and he collapsed into her arms.

"Oh, Ravi. I'm so sorry you've all been so scared. It's all a big misunderstanding." She explained the situation to Ravi, who gradually stopped crying.

"Go get everyone. Tell them I'm going to eat the rice to prove it's not poisoned."

After Julie explained the misunderstanding through Ravi, she held up the foam cup, smiled, and took a large bite of rice. The orphans watched anxiously. She stopped chewing. *My mouth is on fire.* Her eyes watered, and she tried to hide the burning sensation and stifled the desire to cough.

I'd give anything for a juice box or an ice cube! She resisted the burning urge to spit out the rice and forced herself to swallow. She felt her face flush and perspiration bead on her forehead.

"Ummmm, good," she said through clenched teeth. *I always order mild sauce when I eat Mexican food. I think I'm going to die!* She steeled herself and took another bite, but didn't chew this time. She swallowed it just to get it out of her mouth quickly. *My tongue must be medium-well by now.* The children watched attentively. *My esophagus is permanently scorched. Help me, Jesus.*

After a few moments had passed, the other children all grabbed their cups. Julie sighed in great relief.

"Here," she said, holding up her cup. "Someone can finish mine!" *While I crawl in the bushes and expire.* She watched the children delighting in the rice. *How in the world can they tolerate that?*

"I'm going to go for a walk, and I'll be back in a little while. Tell the children to just relax and play, Ravi. You've all had a rough two days." She turned around, opened her mouth, and fanned it with her hands.

22

In an hour, Julie was back with a smile on her face. A few minutes later Daya arrived wearing street clothes and carrying a grocery sack in one hand and a clean Shara wearing new clothes in the other.

Julie gathered Shara in her arms.

"Oh, it's a clean baby! I love clean babies." She cradled Shara, gooing and cooing and gently rocking. She hoisted Shara to her shoulder, patted her on the back several times, and the baby spit up, covering the entire left side of Julie's dress with formula. Julie stared in unbelief at the large wet spot covered in curdled milk. The tension was broken. The boys shrieked and laughed. Wilson even fell backward on the grass. The girls giggled. Julie held Shara at arm's length.

Sammy looked confused. When the laughter subsided, he whispered to Ravi, who turned to Julie, "Sammy does not understand why someone feeds the baby milk and then you cause the baby to get rid of the milk."

"Tell him it was an accident." There was not a lot Julie could do to clean up, so Daya reached into the sack and pulled out a luscious, rectangular, cream-filled pastry covered with powdered sugar and a cherry on top. Even Julie gasped.

"Is this poisoned?" he asked with a sly smile. "I think not, or I would not do this." Then he took the biggest bite he could fit in his mouth, so big he had trouble chewing. Powdered sugar rimmed his lips. All the children laughed and clapped, and then he handed another pastry to Julie.

"Mmmmm. There is nothing wrong with this!" She opened her mouth wide and shoved the pastry as far in as she could. That was all it took, manners were once again forgotten. It was a mad scramble for the grocery sack and the powdered sugar was flying!

When the last bite was swallowed, Ravi looked at the powdered sugar on Sammy's face and hands and burst out laughing. Praveen looked at the sugar on Ravi's face and did the same. In a minute, they were all pointing and belly laughing their stress away.

Sammy walked up to Daya and reached his two arms high in an invitation to be held. Without hesitation Daya scooped him up and wrapped his arms around him. Sammy's sugar smudged face broke into a gap-toothed grin as he beamed down at the others.

Daya had earned their trust and was soon teaching the boys self-defense, much to their delight.

"This is called Krav Maga. I teach this at the police academy. You will get in shape, be healthier, and have more energy." He pushed up his sleeve and flexed his muscles. The boys pointed and gasped. "I will teach you what actually works. No one can hurt you if you learn."

After class it turned into a free-for-all with the guys against Daya. They jumped on his back; they clung to his muscular legs and tried in vain to restrain him. Daya stretched his arms and flexed his muscles and Praveen and Wilson grabbed hold and Daya lifted them off the ground.

He's a gentle giant, thought Julie. All the girls laughed, and Nilaya crawled on Julie's lap to watch the commotion. Julie's heart did flip-flops as she embraced her with both arms.

Wow, Lord. When You move, things go fast!

Sammy hung on the fringes, afraid to join in the ruckus. Daya scooped him up and placed him on his shoulders.

"Hold on, Sammy." He turned to the boys.

"Sammy and I challenge you all." Sammy clung to Daya's head and shrieked and laughed as Daya caught and then deposited each boy on the ground.

"The winner and still champion," Daya called out as he held Sammy's right arm above his head, "Is Sammy. Yay, Sammy." All the girls clapped and cheered.

"Way to go, Sammy."

"You did it, Sammy." Daya couldn't see it, but Sammy's eyes brimmed with joy.

The boys demanded one more round, and in the end Daya took a dive so they could experience sweet victory. They pinned him and declared themselves the awesome winners.

Thank You, Lord! What a blessing You brought us, thought Julie. Daya sat beside her.

"You're so good with them. They just love you!" Daya's smile turned to a sad expression.

"My wife and I.... The doctors say we can't...no children." Julie laid her hand on his.

"I had two miscarriages after Logan...we, I'm afraid to try again...you'd be a great dad, Daya."

That night she studied the next Scripture, Daniel in the lion's den,[1] and fell asleep praying the Lord would help her to have more compassion.

When the children woke, they relieved themselves by the hedge as always. Julie had managed to convince Ravi, who didn't understand why, but communicated to the other children that for some reason it was extremely important to give Julie her privacy first thing in the morning. *This just doesn't get any easier*, thought Julie, squatting behind the hedge.

After games, Julie could hardly wait to share the story of Daniel and the lion's den.

"Don't forget, the Lord can protect us from our worst enemy." When the story time ended, the whole group prayed for Bhanu and Kumar and for the Lord to make a place for them to live.

As the prayer ended, Daya arrived with food. He barely handed the sack off to Julie before the guys jumped him.

Amazing, they would rather wrestle than eat! I guess that's boys for you, thought Julie.

She flashed back to the conversation she'd had with Michael before she'd left.

"Little boys are all about action and adventure and pirate's treasure. As a former little boy, trust me on this." *My heart is breaking, Lord. I miss my family so much it hurts. Will I ever go home again?* She sat down and hugged her knees and rocked. She was in her own world of pain. *I miss Logan so much. Does he think I'm dead? How badly is he hurting? Lord, are You really taking care of them?* She bit her lip and hugged her knees tighter.

She was snapped back to reality by Daya's voice.

"Julie, before I go back to work, I want to tell you something. Do you remember when I said maybe you were the answer to our prayers?"

"Yes, it made no sense—still doesn't. What do you mean *our* prayers?" As Daya spoke, Wilson made a flying leap and landed on his back.

"Excuse me just a minute." After Wilson was dispatched, Daya said, "My church has been crying out to God on behalf of the orphans, to show us how to help. It's like the Lord sovereignly picked us for this project."

You have no idea! thought Julie. "Here, help me pass out the food, and then we can talk."

When the orphans were eating, Daya continued, "The Lord showed our church that all together we're to get a safe house and train children to love and serve Jesus and to do 'greater works than these.'"[2]

Julie put her hand over her heart and inhaled deeply.

"It's very close. I can take you now to see the house."

"You already have it?"

Julie communicated to the children through Ravi that she was leaving, but would return shortly. She grabbed a sandwich, and she and Daya walked toward the shops. Julie didn't know what she was expecting, but she tried not to get her hopes up. *Maybe an indoor dump—bugs, unsanitary conditions. But whatever it is, it has to be better and smell better than where they live now.*

When they arrived at the wrought iron gate, Daya pushed it open and held it for Julie. She froze; the revelation of His divine orchestration hit her. The Lord had led her to this very house that would be a refuge for the children to be a safe place, as a refuge for her during her difficult introduction to India.

"Is something wrong?" asked Daya, the wide grin fading from his face.

She tossed her head back and laughed.

"Oh, God has such a sense of humor. I slept here several nights."

"How did you get inside?"

"No, I slept right here," she led him to the side and pointed to the small space between the bushes and the house. "The first few nights I was in India."

"You have had no place to stay?"

Julie nodded.

"Now I sleep with the orphans at the dump."

Daya was overcome with emotion.

"You would come all the way from America to help our children, and you slept here and in the dump to do it? God bless you; your kindness is overwhelming."

Well, not exactly, thought Julie, who decided she wouldn't go into the details right now.

"Let's go see the inside!" As she walked by the side of the house, she noticed something. She immediately dropped to her hands and knees and, to Daya's surprise, crawled into the bushes.

"It's my wallet. Everything's here. How?"

She backed out of the bushes and held the brown leather wallet over her head triumphantly. She turned to Daya, "It was stolen from the beauty shop the day I met you. That's why I met you. I came to report my wallet as stolen—oh my gosh. That's how God orchestrated our meeting. I thought it was a bad thing, but He used it for something very good." Julie clutched the wallet to her heart.

"My wallet returned, Nilaya's breakthrough, and a house for the children. Jesus, You are so good to me!" She turned to Daya, "I can't believe the house is ready now."

"It's ready, but not ready." He looked chagrined. "This house became available for rent, and the two sisters volunteered to live here, but the Lord has not provided the rent. We got the house for one month, and while we were waiting for the rest of the money, we received the owner's permission to fix it up. However, if the money never came in, then he had his house fixed for free and returned to him at the end of this month. But, we kept praying the Lord would provide, and we didn't want to waste time. We wanted a place for the children when the perfect time came."

"Now is the perfect time," shouted Julie. "How much would you need a month for the rent, food, everything?"

"It's expensive—20,000 rupees." Julie did the math. *That's a little over $400 a month. I spend that on clothes, cappuccinos, and carryout. I love these children. They need a safe home and people who care.* "I can pay the monthly expenses. I will pay them every month! Promise."

The Lord spoke, *What an attitude change. In the beginning, you didn't care about My orphans at all.*

Oh, Lord, I was only thinking of my own comfort and I didn't know them. I don't mind giving up some extravagances to help meet their basic needs. You've given me a grocery cart full of bread, and I need to start sharing. They've been through so much; they are all my heroes.

And you are My hero for helping them.

With a big smile she said to Daya, "Let's go in."

The porch was swept clean. *If the inside looks the same as the outside, the children will be in great shape.* Daya opened the heavy wooden door and Julie gasped. The house was clean, and all the rooms had been freshly painted ivory. Julie thought of how much time she had spent trying to find the perfect paint colors for each room in her Victorian home. *It looks beautiful in ivory!*

The two sisters Daya had spoken of, Chanda and Champa, greeted Julie like she was a lost relative.

"Oh, you have Shara." Julie held out her arms, and Champa handed her the baby.

"Hello, sweetie. I've missed you." She nuzzled noses again, totally distracted from the task at hand. After she loved on Shara for several minutes, an older gentleman cleared his throat.

"This is Pastor Kandal," said Daya. "This is the Julie I've been telling you about, and she is going to provide the money we need each month for the rent."

"Praise the Lord," shouted Pastor Kandal in respectable English. Julie looked up from Shara.

"I'm glad to meet you. It's so exciting what you and your church have done."

"You are the answer to our prayers, Julie. We can provide the work and staff, but the money we did not have."

"It's an honor. And you are an answer to my prayers for the children's safety." She kissed Shara again. "How long have you been working here?"

"Several weeks, every weekend, some evenings, mornings. Whatever fits people's schedules." Julie's eyes scanned the downstairs. A large dining area with a table and benches. A large living area, with a gently used couch and several plastic chairs.

He touched her arm. "Through that door is the kitchen," he said, with not a little pride in his voice. Although the appliances were old, they were very clean.

"Here is the boys' room," said the pastor, pushing the door open to reveal a room with mats lined on the floor and nothing else. "The downstairs bathroom is around the corner. Chanda will watch the boys; here is her bedroom."

"Let me take you upstairs and show you where the girls will stay." They exited the front door and climbed the outside staircase. There were two large rooms with mats on the floor and a closet with no doors. "Champa will watch the girls; this is her bedroom."

"There are enough mats for everyone with some left over!" said Julie.

"God is so amazing," said Pastor Kandal. "We were working on the building, but not sure how the Lord would provide the money. You had the children, but no place to stay. It took an American and some Indians partnering to make God's dream come true."

Tears welled in Julie's eyes. She reluctantly handed Shara to Daya.

"I know you think I'm some kind of hero, but when I first came here I hated it. I didn't even want to come here. God just made me."

Pastor Kandal looked startled.

"I mean I really, *really* hated it, and I had no idea what would happen with the orphans, and I really didn't care. I couldn't imagine that I would have a part in it. All I wanted was to get back to my family and my comfortable life. All the time I was whining and doubting, you and your church were working on a building you didn't even know if you would get."

She buried her face in her hands and fought back the tears.

"The Lord told me I could go home early, and He would find someone else. I almost said yes. What if I'd gone home?"

"But you didn't go home; you stayed, Julie from America." Julie had her arms wrapped around her torso, still wrestling her emotions for control.

"I came so close to missing out on a life-changing miracle." A tear rolled down her cheek.

"I have read that 'One act of obedience is better than one hundred sermons,'"[3] said Pastor Kandal.

"You might not have liked it in the beginning, but you have certainly proven your obedience by staying."

She took several deep breaths, wiped the tears from her eyes, and with her happiest voice asked, "When can we move the children in?"

"Now that we have the rent, we are ready."

"Thank You, Jesus. I never thought this day would come," said Julie.

"OK, the church ladies will cook a nice hot meal for the children, and we will all eat together!"

"For the children," shouted Julie as they high-fived.

"Pastor, what else do you need for the house?" The pastor looked a little embarrassed. "We need reading materials, and I'd like them each to have their own Bibles."

"Let's go now! The Lord returned my wallet at just the right time! Let's get the supplies, then we'll come home, put them in place, and then get the children!"

"Thank You, Jesus," he shouted, looking at the ceiling.

Julie and the pastor quickly walked to the market. There they picked out books, pencils, paper, crayons, and reading kits.

"Oh, look at the calendars," said Julie. "We can get one for each room, maybe two." She leafed through one showing snow-capped mountains.

"The pictures are so beautiful. They need to know there's more to this world than the blocks surrounding the dump." Together they picked a calendar of the sites of India, kittens, snow-covered mountains, and tropical beaches, and for the sisters, flowers and butterflies. Pastor Kandal tipped his head back and laughed, "You are like, how do you say? A child in a sweet shop."

"I just can't wait to move the children into a nice, safe, clean house. I'll need to buy them some clothes and a new outfit for me to replace what started out as a dress. We'll also need soap and shampoo, to kill lice, combs, and a pair of scissors. We'll need some clothes for our wonderful, sweet baby and diapers. The children will need storage, maybe plastic bins—"

Pastor Kandal laughed, "We will have our hands full, Julie from America."

"—and," continued Julie, barely listening, "I want to get stuffed, soft toys so they have something to cuddle with at night."

"Julie your generosity is so great. I'm not sure I can accept it."

"It's not for you; it's for the children. Jesus sent me here on a mission, and you would do me a disservice if you stand in the way. You've already done your part, getting the house ready when it seemed there was no place the money could come from."

Daya was waiting when they returned to the house with their purchases.

"I'll go tell the children we have a big surprise," said Julie. "We can bring them here, they can clean up, and we can all eat together! And I can shower too, and it will be paradise to wash my hair, my dirty, oily, greasy, disgusting, filthy hair! Let's go now."

Pastor stood up and motioned toward the dump. Julie clapped and jumped up and down, "YES, let's get them now."

23

Julie was so excited she ran, with Pastor and Daya jogging to keep up. She was so glad to see the children. The dump's stench could still knock her over, but she hadn't realized that it was no longer abhorrent to her.

Lord, You are so good. I griped and complained, and all the while You had the plan. I was sleeping next to Your solution. It was just a few blocks away, and I didn't believe You would do it. She paused and looked up. *I never thought I'd say it, but thanks for uprooting me and bringing me to an Indian dump. It's my dump, and these are my children.*"

Julie shouted, "Jesus has done a miracle." The children within hearing distance came running.

"Did He provide manna for us like He did the children of Israel?" asked Ravi, wide-eyed. This caused Pastor, Daya, and Julie to laugh in their punch-drunk state.

"No, Ravi, it's better. Jesus has answered our prayers, and He has provided a large house for you to live in." Ravi stopped translating and looked to Julie, thinking he had misunderstood.

"It's true, Ravi. I saw it myself. It's the house where we picked berries, and we are going to have a big meal there tonight, and you never have to sleep at this dump again because Jesus loves you so much." Ravi translated, and some of the children just stared, not understanding the ramifications, and with others, all pandemonium broke loose, jumping, yelling, and hugging.

"Pastor Kandal and his church members have been working to fix the house, and it's ready. Let's go!"

Everyone was happy, jumping, laughing, and hugging as they moved together as a group down the street. Julie looked back and saw Sapna standing by herself at the dump. Julie motioned, and she slowly followed behind. When they arrived, quiet little Nilaya looked closely at the beautiful flowers growing on the neighbor's fence, and rambunctious Wilson ran up several stairs leading to the second story and jumped off whooping and flailing his walking stick.

Lord, it's not just our fingerprints that You've made different, is it? mused Julie.

Pastor Kandal put the key in the lock, and Julie hushed everyone so she could say a prayer.

"Thank You, Jesus, Your Word says that You take care of the orphans and that You are a Father to those who have no father.[1] We see the promise come true today. Thank You for answering our prayers," she gave Sashi a wink, "and amen." Julie was overcome with the Lord's goodness.

"Ah-meen," they replied.

Julie eagerly anticipated the children's responses. As Pastor turned the doorknob, her face lit up in a radiant smile.

"We will all stay together and go through one room at a time," said Julie. The minute the door was unlatched, all the children pushed their way through. Julie didn't see Sapna still lagging behind.

"This is the family hall," said the pastor. "When you're not in your room or playing outside, you can come here. Here is the dining room where we will all eat, do our school work, and praise Jesus."

Julie caught a glimpse of Sapna standing on the porch in tears, looking in. *Those aren't tears of happiness.* Julie let Pastor continue with the tour, grabbed Ravi, and put her arm around Sapna.

"What's wrong?"

"This is not my house because I don't love Jesus. My father told me that if I stopped being a Hindu, he would have no daughter."

"Oh, Sapna, you have it backwards; this house is not for everyone who loves Jesus. It is a house for everyone who Jesus loves, and He loves you very much, and He wants you here with your friends." Sapna smiled.

"I can stay? I can live here, too?"

"Yes, you can, because Jesus loves you so much!

"Come, let's see the house Jesus has prepared for you." She grabbed the girl's hand. "Did you know the Bible says that Jesus is in Heaven preparing a house for each of us so when we come to Him we will have a special place to live?"[2] Sapna wiped her eyes, and the three caught up with the group in the boys' room.

The boys had flopped on the mats and were rolling, wrestling, and laughing. Wilson sucked in a deep breath and let out a Tarzan-like wail before he jumped right in the middle and grabbed Praveen's leg.

That must be the Hindi word for "Cannonbaaaall," thought Julie.

"I can't resist," blurted Daya as he waded into the group, much to the boys' delight!

"Krav Maga. Show me, Wilson." Daya had an impromptu class, and when it was over the boys were lying on the mats panting, except Praveen, who was asking Daya questions about solving crime.

Julie asked Pastor and Daya to teach the boys to shower, shampoo, and use the toilets.

Don't forget to use the special lice shampoo," prompted Julie.

The girls all went outside and up the stairs. In about an hour, all the children were clean and wearing new play clothes. Julie even taught the oldest girls how to bathe Shara.

Lord, they are so beautiful. It's the first time they've been clean. They look and smell like angels. I'm the only one still dirty. She literally waltzed into the bathroom.

"Running water in the sink. What a blessing! A western toilet, a double blessing." She tossed her dress into the trash can. *Good riddance to bad rubbish, and I do mean rubbish.*

She filled the bucket from the sink and stepped in the shower. *I haven't been clean in weeks.* Initially the water running down the drain was brown as she sponged the dirt from her elbows and knees.

"What I took for granted at home! I just never appreciated what I had until I had to do without. Lord, let me never forget Your benefits and blessings again."

She lathered her hair and emptied the entire bucket over her head.

"Whee, what a luxury. This feels sooo good!" She filled the bucket again. *Arm pits, I think I'll need steel wool to get rid of the smell! Lord, seriously, help me to never take everyday blessings for granted again.* She examined her elbows and behind her knees to make sure the creases were really clean. She rinsed thoroughly with a third bucket of water just because she could.

Julie had bought two everyday Punjabis for herself. She admired the hand-embroidered design on the neckline of the pink cotton top. *So delicate.* She stepped into the drawstring pants and pulled them up. *One size fits all. I think I have about 20 extra inches here*, she thought as she distributed the gathers. *It feels so good to be clean and wearing clean clothes.* Then she stepped into a pair of embroidered sandals. *And at $19.00 for the whole outfit, including the shoes, Michael would be so proud. Michael, I miss you so much, but I'm too happy right now to be sad. Lord, I trust You to take care of my lambs! Please?*

She towel-dried her hair and combed it. *I know what I need to do next.* She had the girls follow her to the porch. She motioned using her fingers as the scissors on her hair, short, medium, or long? Each girl received a combing and a cut. When she lined them up, they looked adorable. *I could adopt them all,* she thought, giving them big hugs.

Next the boys came and all received the "bowl" type haircut.

"You all look like fine gentlemen," she said to Ravi, who relayed the message, causing the "gentlemen" to stand a little taller and push out their chests.

The children were fascinated with the calendars, and they spent time looking at each beautiful page and asking questions of Pastor Kandal. When they were finally done, Julie held up some tacks and let them decide where the calendars would go. They even put the sisters' calendars in their rooms.

There was a knock on the door. Everyone froze. Pastor jumped up, clapping.

"It's the food!" The children ran shouting toward the door, but Julie arrived first.

"Remember, we sit at the table and wait for the food to come to us." She guided them to the dining room, and each one took a seat on a long bench, the boys on one side and the girls on the other. Daya sat on the boys' bench, and Sammy climbed on his lap and announced, "I'll eat with *you,*" and threw his arms around him. Daya smiled broadly. "And I will *eat* you." He nibbled on Sammy's ear and neck as the children pointed and laughed.

Pastor answered the door, and in came a parade of women carrying a veritable feast. As they put the food on the table, the wonderful aromas came up before the children. The pastor instructed them to remain with their hands on their laps.

"Now we will pray. Oh gracious God, thank You for supplying food and shelter for Your children. Thank You for Julie from America and her help. Thank You for all the church members who worked long hours on this house, and thank You for the women who have cooked today. Amen."

"Ah-meen," they shouted.

Julie pulled the top off of a large dish and the smell of Tandoori chicken wafted through the air.

"Oh, Praveen, this is for you!"

"Tandoori!" screamed Praveen pointing. "Tandoori!" Julie and Ravi laughed. The next dish was dahl, then butter naan, a flat bread. They eagerly leaned forward as each lid was removed. "Ohhh, ahhhh," they sounded like children watching a fireworks display.

There was more than enough food. Julie was still lifting lids. There was jadoh, a spicy dish of rice and pork, and several different curries. Many of the children had never seen the different kinds of foods and certainly never in abundance. Pastor and Julie helped with portions as each dish was passed. As Julie moved around the table, she touched, hugged, kissed, or smiled at each orphan. She also introduced the concept of napkins.

Although there was plenty of food, the women did not accept the invitation to eat. They were delighted watching the orphans.

"Slow down, slow down, and enjoy it," said Julie. "Everyone will get full. Keep your elbows off the table, and everyone make sure your napkin is still in your lap." The children ate in the traditional Indian way, with their right hands, not using silverware. Julie found a large cooking spoon in the kitchen, preferring to eat with that.

"This is the best meal I have ever had," shouted Wilson.

"Well, then, thank the Lord and these ladies," shouted Julie.

"Thank You," he shouted toward the ceiling and then at the ladies. Everyone laughed.

Julie ignored her food and watched the children. *Jesus, You are so good. This is probably the best meal they've ever had.* Tears welled in her eyes as she watched Shoba eating. *Lord, how much longer would she have survived? Look at Sapna, she's smiling. She actually looks sweet.*

After dinner, Daya carried Sammy to meet his wife who had brought part of the meal. "This is Sammy," he said. Her eyes lit up when Sammy leaned from Daya with his arms outstretched. She grabbed him and held him tight. Sammy wrapped his legs around her waist, buried his face in her hair, and proclaimed, "You smell good," followed by his big gap-tooth grin.

After dinner the group had a prayer and dedication time for the home, the sisters, and the pastor. Then Julie took the girls and Pastor took the boys and taught them how to brush their teeth and prepare for bed. The concept of putting on different clothes for sleep was hard for Julie to explain. Julie and Pastor went around and tucked all the children in and had a tender time praying for each one of them. Pastor went downstairs for chai, and Julie wanted a little alone time with Ravi.

She sat cross-legged beside his mat and ran her fingers through his black hair. She asked, "Are you still afraid of monsters, Ravi?"

He grinned.

"Not since you prayed for me."

"We have a big God, don't we?" asked Julie. "Your gods were many, but had no power, and our God is three in one, but He is all-powerful." Julie flipped through her Bible and read to Ravi, *"'He holds the ocean in the palms of His hand and He measures the stars with the span of His hands.'³* How big is the sky at night, with all the stars?"

"Too big to calculate in light years," said Ravi, spreading his arms wide.

Julie was surprised. "You're quite the little astronomer, Ravi." He grinned.

"Our God is so big. His hands are as big as the sky. This is the God who loves you, Ravi. Never, ever forget that." She bent to kiss him good night, and he wrapped his arms tightly around her. She could feel his body relax.

"I love you, Auntie."

"I love you more, Ravi."

Lord, how can I ever leave this little one? My heart is breaking even now.

She went downstairs to join Chanda, Champa, Daya, his wife, and Pastor in the dining room sipping chai and talking.

"May I hold Shara?" She gently took her from Champa's arms. "I saw a sewing machine upstairs," said Julie.

"Yes, that is the first step in helping the girls learn a trade. Many women in the church are very talented. We will teach the girls to sew, make purses, and do beading. The boys will learn wood, metal, and leather craft. They will practice each day.

"After everyone knows a trade, we will encourage them to continue in education and become leaders in their society. Regardless of their future positions, we train them to enjoy walking in God's ways. In every aspect of life they learn to carry a spirit of excellence and to see through Jesus' hope-filled eyes for the people and the world around them."

"You need to know that Madhu is so creative," said Julie. "He makes toys from trash and does elaborate paper folding projects. He seems to be a little entrepreneur."

"We will nurture his and all the children's natural giftings," said Pastor Kandal.

"What a gift to these children," said Julie. "I'm catching your vision of what this orphanage can accomplish over the years!"

"I have to confess to you," said Pastor Kandal, "that my faith has not always been strong. There were many days and weeks when I could not see how the Lord could provide the rent. As I worked beside my church members, I worried that I was wasting their time and labor. I wanted to strongly believe, but my faith was weak. I just had to make up my mind to do what the Lord told us and hope for the best. Many nights I was awake worrying." He shook his head and smiled self-consciously.

"I understand," said Julie. "I had lots of pity parties lying under those bushes outside thinking there was no way this was going to work out and resenting the Lord for bringing me here." Julie looked away from the pastor and focused on the door. "I came kicking and screaming, crying and whining—against my will. At first I couldn't see anything good about the situation and even resented the orphans.

"All I cared about was my comfort and cleanliness and how soon I could get back home. But now I'm so grateful. A lot of my selfishness was ripped out by the roots, against my will, and then He filled my heart up with love for these precious children, especially this little one." Julie kissed Shara.

"I'm embarrassed to think how much of my life I've spent totally concentrating on me and my happiness," she took a sip and stared at the cup, "at least what I *thought* would make me happy. Now when I go home, I will leave a large part of my heart here."

There was silence for a moment, then Pastor smiled at her.

"You will return with a large part of our hearts when you go." He placed his hands to his chest and smiled. "I did not know the selfish Julie you speak of, but I like the Julie you are now." Her face brightened.

"We need to go," said Pastor, looking at his watch. "I will be back early in the morning to help with breakfast. There was much food left over. I don't think they'll mind eating the same thing twice."

"I requested the day off tomorrow, and they actually gave it to me, so I will be back, too," said Daya.

"And I also," said his wife.

Champa headed outside and up the stairs to the second story.

"God bless you, Julie from America," said the pastor. He smiled as he stepped into the darkness, then he stopped. "Julie, I think I have heard from the Lord about you. I will tell you, and you must ask the Lord if it is true." With a serious expression, he whispered to her and then disappeared into the night.

Julie closed the door, took a deep breath, and sprawled on the couch, holding Shara and praying. "Oh, Lord. I need to hear from You. Please, please, please."

After about 20 minutes, she peeked into the boys' room. Everyone was asleep stretched out on a mat and snuggled with a stuffed animal.

"They are so beautiful." She went upstairs to the girls' rooms.

"Lord, they are so protected. What would have happened to them if I'd gone home?"

She laid Shara on her mat and entered the bathroom to prepare for bed.

"Pajamas, my own set of clean pajamas." She held them up and smiled at the baby blue cotton gown. "They feel wonderful. I smell wonderful. This is all so wonderful! Thank You, Lord." She combed her shoulder-length brown mane. "Oh, it feels squeaky clean!" After brushing her teeth, she padded into the bedroom and gently lifted Shara to her mat.

"Hi, sweetie. You're all clean, and you have a new home and about a dozen big brothers and sisters to look after you."

"Lord, if Shara tugs at my heartstrings any harder, they'll be ripped right out of my chest." Julie finally quit kissing Shara and stroked her forehead until the baby drifted off to sleep.

"Oh, Lord, this mat feels so good. I can't believe I'm not on dirt. Thank You for supplying all our needs. The dinner tonight was awesome. And everyone was actually full!"

She opened the Bible to see the next verse. "I can't wait to see what You have to say to me tonight, Lord."

"*'I will fight for you.'*[4] That's strange. It seems like the battles are over now, Lord, and it's smooth sailing ahead, but thanks anyway." She closed the Bible and fell asleep snuggled around Shara while thanking and praising Him.

24

Ravi didn't realize it was the Lord who woke him during the middle of the night. As he made his way to the bathroom, he heard shattering glass from the kitchen window. He felt his way through the darkness into the bathroom, closed and locked the door behind him, and crouched in the shower. His heart raced. He pulled the curtain closed. *Footsteps, many footsteps.*

Dear Jesus, You protected Daniel in the lion's den. Will You protect me now?

Ravi recognized Mr. Shah's voice. "You all know what to do. Quick, quick! Adeel and I will go upstairs." Running footsteps disbursed.

Ravi heard the sleepy protests and the gruff male voices commanding the boys to "shut up or else."

Dear Jesus, You can protect me from monsters in my imagination. Can You protect me now? Amen.

The next few minutes were a blur of angry voices commanding the boys to "move, move, move." Ravi heard the heavy adult footsteps and the children's scared voices. Among the sobs, he could identify Sammy's voice, "Help me, Jesus!"

"I see you hiding back there," barked one of the men. There was the sound of a slap, and Wilson's voice cried out in pain.

"Oh, just pick him up," shouted another man.

"Fast, fast," yelled Mr. Shah. Julie's voice rang out, "What do you think you're—" then the sound of a fist on flesh and her voice abruptly went silent.

All the children were herded outside. Cars started and disappeared into the darkness, and it was quiet once again.

Only then did Ravi cry and wail into the darkness.

"Jesus, Auntie, help me." He rocked back and forth with his arms wrapped around his knees. *She can't be gone. She was my new mother. You can't be dead, Auntie. Jesus, don't let her be dead.*

The voice that had told Ravi to walk told him to go to Julie's room. His body trembled as he pulled back the shower curtain and crept in the darkness up the outside stairs. He felt his way to her door. Pictures of his dead mother and father flashed through his mind. He feared their bodies might be there on the floor and with each stride he would step on them.

He was afraid to enter the room; he was afraid not to.

"Jesus, Jesus, help me." He flung open her door and heard a muffled sound. In the dark it sounded like she was dying, croaking out her last breath. A chill ran up his spine, and his breath quickened.

He felt his way to her body, still lying on the mat. *Will there be blood?* He cringed and forced his hand forward. It landed on her shoulder. He could feel her move, and the horrible muffled sound came again and again.

"Don't die, Auntie; Auntie, please don't die. You have to be my new mother."

He touched her face. *What is this? Tape?* He worked his fingernails under the edges and pulled hard. There was a ripping sound followed by a cry of pain.

"Ravi, Ravi, you're OK. I'm so glad you're OK." She sobbed. "So glad you're OK. You're like my adopted son." He lay next to her on the mat with his arms and legs clinging around her in the darkness.

"Ravi, turn on the lights and untie me. I want to hug you back." The light went on, and Ravi was relieved to see only a black eye. Other than being tied up, she looked fine.

In several minutes, he had her arms untied, and she grabbed him and pulled him onto her lap, covering his face with kisses.

"Oh, Ravi. I prayed for Jesus to protect you. I couldn't lose you. I love you too much." She rocked him back and forth and they both wept. "You're safe. Mr. Shah didn't get you. Jesus protected you." After several more minutes and what seemed like a hundred kisses, Julie spoke.

"I have to put you down and untie my feet. I have to see if anyone else is here."

The men herded the whimpering children into the shed behind Mr. Shah's house, startling the five children already there. "Quiet, quiet, we don't want to wake the whole neighborhood," he hissed.

"You can go home now," he said to his accomplices as he slid the bar lock into place from the outside.

Mr. Shah entered his house, stopped abruptly, and ran back to the shed. He flung the door open and burst inside, startling the children. He shined his flashlight from face to face, then from corner to corner. He yelled at the huddling children, his free hand clenched in a fist. "Where's he hiding? Where's Ravi?" When the children looked around and shrugged, Mr. Shah became enraged. He threw his hands up in the air, kicked at the dirt, cursed, and left in his rusty green car, with tires squealing.

Inside the shed, Bhanu and Kumar received hugs. Sashi led the children in a prayer meeting. Each child prayed to Jesus for help.

Julie and Ravi untied the two sisters, one upstairs and the other down.

"Where's Shara?" asked Ravi.

"They must have taken her after they hit me." They all ran back to Julie's bedroom.

Julie looked stricken. "Jesus help us," she cried, staring at the vacant spot on the mat.

"We have to rescue Shara and the children," shouted Chanda.

"Where did they take them?" wailed Champa.

"We need to pray," blurted Julie. "The Lord will fight for us and the children! Lord, please guide us. We don't know what to do." Julie listened so hard that her face was scrunched, but she didn't hear the Lord's voice. "Aaarrrgggh," she clenched her fists. "We need to pray harder." She stood and paced. Her desperation was apparent. She looked at Chanda and Champa. "Have you heard anything?" They solemnly shook their heads.

"I know what to do," announced Ravi.

"Ravi," said Julie, "I know you want to help, but we need to hear from the Lord. Oh, Lord," began Julie, "please show us Your ways. Guide us and protect the children. Lord, we're begging, we don't know what to do unless You reveal it to—"

"But—"

"Not now, Ravi." *Please, Lord, speak to us.* As Julie paced, Chanda and Champa looked at Ravi. They both smiled, which was enough encouragement for Ravi to blurt out, "I know what to do because Jesus just told me what to do!"

"Oh, Ravi, I'm sorry. What did Jesus tell you to do?"

"We should go to Mr. Shah's house right now."

Julie gasped. *Oh, Jesus, can that be You? We could get captured or worse.* "Ravi, are you sure? Are you sure it was Jesus and not your imagination?"

Ravi didn't answer. He ran out the door, motioning for everyone to follow. Julie was alone in the bedroom. She quickly followed Ravi, Chanda, and Champa outside and down the dark stairs.

Fear had crept into Julie's thoughts. "Maybe we should wait for Daya. He'll be here in the morning. He can help."

Driving toward the orphanage, Mr. Shah yelled to nobody, "I had a thriving business until Ravi showed up. I'll make him pay. He'll pay for all the kids he stole from me, and then I'll make him pay some more." He hit the steering wheel. "I'll show him what happens when you double-cross me. No one double-crosses me and lives to brag about it." He cut the lights and pulled to the curb.

"Wait," said Ravi. "Jesus just said we should go out through the backyard."

Oh, for goodness sakes, what difference does it make? thought Julie. But the sound of a slamming car door changed her mind. "Go, go, go." They ran into the backyard, out the gate, and ran for several minutes.

"Wait, we can stop now," panted Julie. She looked around, and they were on the street. "Maybe we will recognize where we are." Julie looked around, trying to get oriented.

OK, Jesus, I need to hear what to do. Now would be a great time to speak.

Julie, I am speaking. I'm just not speaking to you right now.

But, Jesus, I'm responsible for these people, she pointed to Ravi and the sisters. *And I'm responsible for the orphans. I have to know Your plan.*

Julie, I was under the impression that I'm in charge of rescuing the orphans and that I can do that any way I please. Trust My leadership through Ravi. It's time to grow his faith muscle.

She took a deep breath. *OK, Jesus, You've provided for us. I choose to trust You.* "Which way, Ravi? Lead us."

"This way," Ravi gestured emphatically. Julie had to hustle to keep up with them.

Mr. Shah had climbed back through the broken window and inspected every room, every closet, and any place a small boy could hide.

"Ravi," he sung out in a pleasant voice. "I have sweets for you." He narrowed his eyes. "Where are you, my son?"

He exited the back door and saw the gate standing open. He kicked the house, cursed, and stormed back to his car.

After several more right and left turns, Ravi pointed.

"That's the house. His car is gone. Let's go."

Julie wiped her sweaty palms on her pajamas and took several deep breaths. Ravi led the way to the shed in the back and slid the lock. *Jesus, Jesus, Jesus, please protect us all.*

The four of them stepped silently from the moonlight into the darkness.

"Thank You, Jesus, for answering our prayers!" shouted Wilson. Pandemonium broke loose as the pajama-clad orphans swarmed their four rescuers. "You came to get us," squealed Sammy. Bhanu threw his arms around Julie, and Ravi hugged Kumar.

Julie breathed a sigh of relief when she saw Nilaya sitting, rocking Shara. "Thank You, Jesus."

Mr. Shah was ready to pull in his driveway when he noticed the door standing open. He parked on the street and crept to the shed. Inside the orphans were still rejoicing. When he saw Julie and Ravi, he let out a mocking laugh. *This is too good to be true.*

Mr. Shah's silhouette in the doorway plunged the kids from delight to terror. He stood with legs spread and his hands on his hips.

"Enjoy your party, because tomorrow morning *it's over!*" He scowled at Ravi as if remembering his transgressions, then drew his finger across his neck in a slashing motion. He slammed and locked the door and laughed all the way to his bedroom.

Julie's legs buckled under her. She hit the floor. *What does he mean, "tomorrow morning it's over"?*

The silence was broken by crying. First one child, then the next. The three original captives clung to each other and watched the new arrivals.

"What's he going to do to us tomorrow?" wailed Kumar.

"We're going to die," cried Madhu.

Chanda and Champa knelt and embraced the two boys.

"It's all right. Jesus will protect us," whispered Champa.

Sammy squeezed Ravi as hard as he could. Before Julie could get her wits about her, Ravi shouted, "We all need to pray. Jesus will tell us how to rescue ourselves. Remember how He rescued Daniel from the lions?"

"That's right," said Julie. "He can surely rescue us. Ravi, tell them to hold hands in a circle and pray. Have everyone praying now."

Slowly the balance shifted from crying to praying. A gift of faith flooded the room and the voices grew louder and more confident. A few of the children were on their knees, having entered into travail.

Madhu noticed a primitive, heavy crutch made from a tree branch lying beside one of the original captives. After chatting with the boy, he held it up.

"I can dig under the door. Then I will crawl out and unlock it."

"I'll look for something else to dig with," said Praveen. He returned with a small metal dish and a short stick about 12 inches long.

"Ravi, tell everyone to keep praying, and Wilson and Praveen, you dig, too."

Praveen and Wilson joined Madhu scraping at the dirt.

"Faster, faster," pleaded Julie. "Ravi, keep the others praying."

The monkey was sitting on the foot of Mr. Shah's bed. Mr. Shah was having trouble sleeping. His mind kept flipping back and forth to what he would do to Ravi. *I have to make him an example. I can't risk any of these new ones being defiant. Should I do it slowly? Knife? How to instill the most fear? Make them think I'm going to kill them all?*

What about that pesky woman who lives at the dump? Who would miss a homeless woman in this town? No one. She'll be the second to go.

He fluffed his feather pillow and flipped it to the cold side. *This Ravi deal might just turn out fine. I have about ten new workers overnight, and after I finish with him and the woman, none of them will consider disobeying—ever.*

After 15 minutes of frantic digging, a pile of dirt was mounded by the door.

"Let me try now," said Wilson.

"You won't fit. Get Nilaya!" shouted Madhu. "Nilaya, wiggle under the door, then I'll hand you this stick and you can slide the lock." Nilaya lay on her back, pushed with her legs and wiggled her head and shoulders into the night.

She stared up and saw Mr. Shah, monkey perched on his shoulder, glaring down at her. He cursed, then spit in her face, and with his boot against her head, shoved her back under the door. She screamed in pain.

The door flung open. Mr. Shah burst in. The monkey leapt to a rafter. The children cowered together, standing in the middle of the dark room. Kumar fell to the ground, locked in a fetal position. Sammy's eyes were transfixed with horror. Julie felt a sickening wave of terror rising up inside.

He stood menacingly, his hands on his hips and his legs spread. A carved ivory knife handle protruded from the sheath attached to his belt. Julie, Ravi, Sashi, Madhu, Chanda, and Champa continued praying silently.

He paced in front of them, pounding his fist into his open palm.

"So you thought you could escape from Mr. Shah? I should kill you all right now for your disobedience," his eyes narrowed with contempt. He turned toward the children, crossed his arms, and paused to let the thought strike them. "I should kill you all, right now!"

Just then Shara let out a shrill, piercing wail followed by loud crying. Mr. Shah sent her a scorching look.

"Take that baby over there and shut it up now before I shut it up myself!" He pointed to the corner of the building behind him. He patted the knife at his side. "Now!"

Before Julie could intervene, Nilaya scampered to the corner. When she arrived, Shara immediately quit crying. *That's strange*, thought Julie. *She sounded like she would cry for hours.*

Mr. Shah glared at the children again and smirked, "I'm really quite a nice man until you cross me. I can be your best friend or your worst enemy." He patted the sheath on his hip. "Ask Ravi, Sammy, or Kumar. They'll tell you that I sat them at my table and fed them the best food and treated them like a son. Isn't that right, boys?" Sammy and Ravi shook their heads.

"I said, 'Isn't that right, boys?'"

"Yes," they squeaked.

"For some reason, Ravi didn't want to stay with me, and next thing I knew, others were gone. There are few things I despise worse than a thief," his lip curled in disgust. He took several steps toward the group and backhanded Ravi across the face. The children's eyes widened in alarm. Blood dripped onto Ravi's shirt. Julie's face grew ashen.

"I hate it when people steal from me." He spit out his words with contempt. "I can't let that go unpunished; next thing you know, I'd have no business." He fixed a smoldering eye on Ravi.

"Everyone would think, 'I can steal from Mr. Shah and nothing will happen.'" He cracked his knuckles. "I have to set an example. I'll show you what happens to anyone who crosses me." His eyes raked the room as he pulled the knife from its sheath and held it up, pretending to examine it. He slid his finger down the long, curved blade.

He smiled maliciously. "Ravi. I think I'd like to talk with you." He kicked Ravi in the ribs, grabbed him by the arm, and jerked him forward. Ravi, his face contorted in pain, was bent double clutching his ribs. Julie flew to his side.

Mr. Shaw looked at her with contempt, took a step closer, and spit in her face.

"Who are you, and why are you always in my way?" He gave Julie a shove that sent her sprawling. She wiped the spit from her face and stood up, took a few steps forward, and thrust out her hands pleading with Mr. Shah.

"Ravi, are you able to translate?"

Looking directly into Mr. Shah's steely eyes she spoke, "Take me, please! Let Ravi go. He's a little boy. Take me, let them all go." She made a sweeping gesture with her arm. "You can make more money with me," she swallowed the lump in her throat and continued, "than all these children combined. You don't want them. You want me.

"I stole Ravi from the street corner. It was me." She fought to keep her voice steady. "And I helped him steal Sammy and Kumar, too. Ravi was just my puppet. Does he look like a leader? I'm the one who's in charge here. This is my gang," her heart hammered in her chest. *Please, Jesus, don't let him hurt Ravi.* She continued, "It's me you need to deal with, not Ravi. Pleeaase," she pleaded, "let them all go, and I'll, I'll work for you." She looked at Ravi. "Tell him, Ravi. Tell him what I said." Mr. Shah shifted his steely gaze to Ravi.

Ravi was still hunched over holding his ribs. He tried to straighten up. Tears streamed down his cheeks, and his body shook. *Auntie loves me and all the children. She would sacrifice herself for all of us just like Jesus did.* Ravi knew there was only one thing to do. With all his effort, he stood up and stared directly into Mr. Shah's eyes. In his most convincing voice he spoke, "She says she will take all the children and leave and promises with her whole heart to never, ever tell anyone what has happened here tonight. Please let her and the others go."

Mr. Shah snorted. "Tell her she's next." He turned toward Julie and hissed, "You're already a dead woman."

Tears flowed down Ravi's cheeks. He turned to Julie and patted her arm.

"Auntie, he says he's going to think about letting you and everyone go. He'll decide in a minute."

Julie could feel her body stiffen in apprehension as she waited for Mr. Shah's next move. She closed her eyes, *Jesus, please fight for us. We need You. You have good plans for Ravi's life. I know You do. Help us.*

When she opened her eyes she saw Nilaya had left Shara in the corner and was tiptoeing up behind Mr. Shah.

What's she doing? Mr. Shah will take her out with one punch. Oh, Lord, please don't let him kill little Nilaya.

The other children saw her, too. She was about 15 feet away. Praveen began to fidget. Madhu inconspicuously scraped up a hand full of dirt. The monkey watched.

Mr. Shah lunged at Ravi and held him in a headlock against his body. Ravi stiffened. He poked the knife against Ravi's throat, the pressure indenting his flesh. Julie shrieked, "No," and lurched forward. Mr. Shah glared at her with total disdain and pushed harder on the knife. She could see the fear in Ravi's eyes, and she stepped back, raising her hands in surrender.

Nilaya tiptoed closer.

Mr. Shah glared ruthlessly from child to child, demanding all attention in the room in preparation for his next action.

"Watch closely, children, and don't ever forget, THIS is what I do to anyone who disobeys me." He pulled the knife away from Ravi's throat, getting ready to plunge it in when Nilaya stepped close and crouched behind his legs on her hands and knees.

Wilson and Praveen surged forward and toppled him backward over Nilaya. Still in his grasp, Ravi went down, too. Madhu flung the dirt at point-blank range, blinding him. Mr. Shah released Ravi and the knife to scrape at his eyes. He tried to cry out, but could only produce a violent cough.

Wilson, Praveen, and Bhanu all let out a war cry and were on top of him in a flash. The monkey screeched from the rafter. Julie saw the knife land and retrieved it. She clutched it in both hands in front of her, watching the brawl on the floor, unsure how to help.

"Jesus, will fight for us!" she yelled.

"Yes," yelled Sashi and the other girls, who began crying out in prayer.

Fists were flying. Mr. Shah, still coughing and with eyes squinting closed, flailed and boxed at the air, but rarely landed a punch. Unable to see where the next blow was coming from, he folded his arms in front of his face to protect against the boys' direct hits.

The Lord whispered to Chanda, *Daya is at the house now.*

"I'll get Daya," she shouted as she ran out the door.

Julie was still holding the knife, praying. *Lord, what should I do?*

It's under control, Julie. Just trust Me.

OK, Lord, I know You have a future for each of these precious children. I know You promised You would fight for us.

Mr. Shah's bloodcurdling scream filled the air as Sapna bit into his leg. While Wilson, Praveen, and the others held him to the ground, Ravi brought the brawl to an end when he whacked him in the head with the "Y" shaped end of the crutch, knocking him cold.

The shrieking monkey leapt onto Mr. Shah's chest and repeatedly punched him in the face.

Ravi pulled the monkey off. It climbed into his arms, tipped its hat, gave Ravi a candy, reached in other pockets and handed Ravi a toothbrush, a safety pin, and his Silly Putty®! Tears welled in Ravi's eyes.

"We need to tie him up," shouted Praveen, "but we have no rope."

Madhu stepped forward. "I know what we can use."

A few minutes later, a car door slammed, and Daya burst through the doorway looking intense, his gun drawn, followed by Pastor Kandal and Chanda.

Daya looked at Mr. Shah on the floor, and his intensity faded. Pastor Kandal put his hand on Daya's shoulder and pointed. Pastor laughed; Daya howled. Chanda blushed and put her hand over her face.

Mr. Shah's pants were wrapped several times around his ankles and tied and his shirt was wrapped and firmly tied, binding his wrists.

"He wears funny underwear," laughed Wilson, pointing to the white boxers with red hearts.

Chanda held Shara, who was miraculously sleeping.

Daya cuffed Mr. Shah and hoisted him over his broad shoulders.

"Come on, Sleeping Beauty, you're going to wake up in jail." Before exiting, he turned and gave the guys thumbs up. "You are all awesome warriors!"

Julie was still hugging Ravi, who was hugging back ferociously.

As Daya exited the group clapped, shouted, high-fived, and hugged. Tears flowed.

Nilaya beamed as Wilson and Praveen boosted her on their shoulders, and the whole group sang and applauded.

Kumar led Pastor Kandal to the four other captive children, a boy blind in one eye, one without a foot, and a girl without a hand. They all accepted a big hug from him.

"We have a safe place for you to live. Mr. Shah is gone, and he will never hurt you again. You can come with us, and we will be your new family. You will be safe and well fed."

Julie used her new pajamas to wipe the blood from Ravi's face.

"Ravi, translate," said Julie. "Get everyone in a circle; we need to thank the Lord."

Nilaya was the first to pray. "Jesus, thank You for telling me to sneak up behind that bad, bad man...."

C H A P T E R

25

All the children slept until the afternoon. That gave Julie time to pray, give thanks, and read the next Bible story.

Daya stopped by and brought the good news that Mr. Shah would be tried on 13 counts of kidnapping, and the children never had to worry about him again.

"But doesn't he bribe his way out of these things?" asked Julie.

"Those days are gone. I filed the paperwork myself, and he will stand before a judge who is honest and loves justice." Daya added with a sly smile, "And, he is a member of our church!" Julie flung her arms over her head and let out a whoop.

The group had dinner leftovers, and everyone ate until they were satisfied. Praveen had double helpings of Tandoori chicken, and the boys excitedly, and in great detail, told Daya the story of how they had overpowered Mr. Shah using the Krav Maga moves he had taught them.

"You are all champions!" shouted Daya, pumping his fist in the air.

That evening, with Ravi translating, Julie read the story of Gideon[1] and how the Lord had kept whittling away at the number of soldiers available to fight.

"So the Lord sent 22,000 soldiers home, and there were 10,000 left. The Lord told Gideon that he still had too many soldiers. God didn't want them to believe they had won the battle in their own strength. So God sent everyone home except 300 soldiers.

"They didn't even carry weapons, just trumpets, jars, and torches. How would you like to go into battle with just those? The 300 soldiers surrounded the enemy camp by night, then broke the jars, blew the trumpets, and yelled, and the enemy retreated with Gideon and his men in pursuit. It was a supernatural victory.

"In our case God defeated the enemy with a crying baby and Nilaya! It's a miracle. We were all part of a true miracle. I want you to never forget this lesson. You can trust Him—always."

"And He also provided food for us when we were at the dump. Another miracle!" added Sashi.

The children poured out their gratitude. Nilaya climbed on Julie's lap and wept. Kumar snuggled in on one side and Ravi on the other. Julie treasured it all in her heart, her eyes moist with tears.

Lord, never let me forget this moment ever. Please never let me forget the way You provided food for us and how You saved our lives and You did it using the weakest of the weak. Lord, You did fight for us! And nothing is impossible for You, and thank You for teaching me that I can absolutely trust You.

The children all showered and changed into their pajamas, even though they still didn't grasp the concept. Then they had a late snack and were off to bed.

Pastor Kandal repaired the window.

Julie went to sleep with Shara in her arms. At 4:15 A.M. the Lord woke her.

My beloved Julie, My orphans' lives are changed and so is yours. You've accomplished what I called you to do. You can return home the day after tomorrow.

Julie's hands flew to her heart. It was the message she'd been waiting and praying to hear, but now that she had fallen in love with the orphans, the thought of losing them from her life seemed unbearable.

Thank You, Lord, I think. It's like I'm attached to two families now. I can't bear the thought of not having both. She leaned close to Shara and breathed in her smell. Tears fell.

"Oh, sweetie, I love you so much."

Julie lay awake for an hour, praying and pondering. *It's really good/bad news. I miss Michael and Logan so much, but I'm amazed that I could learn to love these children so deeply in such a short time. I know they'll be well taken care of; I won't have to worry about that. I wonder if I'll ever see any of them again? I promise to pray for each of them every day.*

When she woke the next morning, Julie put on the second Indian outfit she had bought: drawstring pants and a long tunic in blue chiffon with delicate embroidery around the sleeves and neckline. *Simple, yet elegant. So glad to be rid of that dress!*

Chanda and Champa were in the kitchen teaching the girls how to prepare breakfast when Julie came down. Champa was overseeing Sashi and Shoba as they prepared dosas. Chanda had the rest of the girls at the table grating coconut for chutney.

"It smells wonderful in here," said Julie. *Lord, they all look so happy and clean.*

Life will be very different for them, Julie. Their physical needs will be met, but more importantly, their spiritual and emotional needs will be cared for. They will be loved and nurtured, and as they learn to spend time in My presence, their emotional wounds will be healed. They will learn to hear My voice and receive their value from Me.

I have exciting plans for each of them. They will grow up believing My Word is true, and they will be mighty warriors in the Kingdom. I can use everything for good,[2] even what these precious ones have endured.

"Lord, You can do exceeding abundantly above all I can ask or think."[3]

I'm delighted you finally realized that, Julie.

After breakfast, it was time for school. Julie was unable to understand anything that was going on. Pastor Kandal was the head instructor, and other women from the church had volunteered to help teach the children, since going to a good school costs money.

Next was a Bible story time. Pastor Kandal taught the story of the Good Samaritan.[4]

"It's important that you learn to have compassion for others the way that compassion has been shown to you."

With Ravi translating, Julie led art class. She had the children pray and then draw what the Lord had shown them. She was taken aback at their pictures. A staircase leading to Heaven. A key unlocking a heart. A picture of Jesus with His arms outstretched.

They hear well, thought Julie.

Champa took the children to play dodgeball in the back. The children were delighted when Julie played, and both sides wanted her on their team.

At lunch period they had aloo vada, a deep-fried potato served with chutneys, and bananas for dessert.

"This is a perfect day," shouted Ravi, and everyone agreed.

Daya dropped by after school and continued his Krav Maga lessons with the boys.

"You are experts now. Maybe you should teach me!"

Julie had gotten permission to borrow Ravi.

"I need you to translate. I want to buy something."

"What?"

"A large, carved wooden screen. It's really beautiful." *And I want to take it as a memento of India*. She couldn't broach the subject yet.

Walking back, Ravi asked, "Where will the screen go?"

"Ravi, it's actually a present for my husband. Remember, I'm from America. I have a husband and a son your age. The Lord sent me here to help all of you find a home."

"When are your husband and son coming?"

"They're not. I was just sent here for a certain period of time. And that period of time is up." She took a deep breath. "Ravi, let's sit down and talk."

The bedtime routine went smoothly. After praying for each child, Julie lay down with Shara. *And, Lord, what about what Pastor Kandal said? Was that from You? I'd be so happy if it was.* As Julie prayed, she dozed off, and the next thing she knew, it was morning, and she had her answer.

"Thank You, Jesus!"

Morning was a somber time—time to say good-bye. The group huddled around Julie in the living room. One by one, the children came forward to thank and hug Julie as Ravi translated. Many of them had made cards or pictures.

Julie, I am smiling over these children's futures. They are all beautiful, they are all a blessing, and they were worth fighting for. I have given them extraordinary gifts, and they will be worshipers and mighty warriors for My Kingdom. They will be caring and compassionate toward others' needs, and through loving others, they will love Me well. Today is their graduation day and yours.

Nilaya came boldly forward and hugged Julie. She looked her in the eyes and said, "I love you, Auntie." Julie felt a lump in her throat.

"I love you, too, Nilaya. You are my hero for finding Shara and being the bravest little girl I know. The Lord used you to save us all, and you didn't even know Krav Maga." She winked at Wilson and Praveen, and they laughed.

Julie remembered Nilaya with her injured ankle lying in the street looking terrified. *How could I have been so angry with such a precious little girl? Lord, I was a mess. For the longest time she couldn't make eye contact or talk. What a charming smile she has. What a change in this little one. Lord, bless Nilaya.*

Nilaya is blessed. She has a keen sense of what is right and will not easily be swayed from the truth. She has pure motives and is quick to meet others' needs. She will walk and commune with Me and bring My presence into all of life.

Here is her verse: "My sheep hear My voice, and I know them, and they follow Me: and I give unto them eternal life; and they shall never perish, and no one shall snatch them out of My hand."[5]

Sapna approached Julie with a big smile. Julie wrapped her arms around her. *Lord, this filthy, angry little waif, swimming in a man's t-shirt, biting people when she didn't get her way, is all smiles now.*

Yes, and she'll learn new ways to deal with her anger. She will become an encourager, speaking the right words at the right time to bring hope to the hopeless.

Here is her verse: "You shall love the Lord your God with all your heart and with all your soul and with all your mind…and….love your neighbor as yourself."[6]

"I will miss you, Auntie."

"I will miss you, too, Sapna." Julie smiled; she still bore the scar on her leg.

"I'm sorry I bit you."

"I forgive you, Sapna. Every time I see the scar, I will remember you with great fondness."

Sashi was next in line and gave Julie a big hug.

"Thank you for coming to teach us about Jesus. I dreamed last night that Jesus appeared and told me not to worry about my future. That He would take care of me."

Julie's voice quavered.

"And He will, Sashi. He will. Never forget your prayers helped bring about a miracle. You have the heart of a servant, you are a diligent helper, and you will become an awesome woman of God."

"Mithra, Auntie, mithra, Sashi," she said, laying her hand on Julie's chest.

I will give Sashi the highest level of spiritual authority because she will not abuse it. She has a strong desire to serve Me and walk in holiness.

This is her verse: "All authority in heaven and on earth has been given to Me. Therefore go and make disciples of all nations, baptizing them in the name of the Father and of the Son and of the Holy Spirit, and teaching them to obey everything I have commanded you. And surely I am with you always, to the very end of the age."[7]

When Julie hugged Shoba, she could feel her bones. *She's still so emaciated. If I'd gone home, would she even be alive?*

You saved Shoba's life, Julie. She will be My songbird who worships Me face to face with a thankful attitude. She will bring praise, joy, and thanksgiving to people's challenging situations.

Here is My verse for her: "Enter His gates with thanksgiving and His courts with praise; give thanks to Him and praise His name. For the Lord is good and His love endures forever; His faithfulness continues through all generations."[8]

Shoba handed Julie a drawing of a table covered with food.

"God will supply our daily bread," she said.

"Yes, He will, Shoba; yes, He will."

Her countenance used to be so sorrowful. She has such gentleness about her now. Shoba was to receive double portions on food until she gained 15 pounds.

Praveen was next. He was trying to be brave and not cry, but he wasn't succeeding. He flung his arms around Julie and buried his face in her shoulder.

"Auntie, Auntie."

"It's OK, Praveen. It's OK. Jesus loves you even more than I do, and He's always with you all the time. Go to Him, and He will comfort you when you're sad. And you can relax and let your guard down now that you know that Jesus will fight for you!"

Praveen has the gift of leadership. I will give him strategic wisdom keys, and show him My plans for individuals, cities, and nations.

His verse is Psalm 37:23. "The steps of a good man are ordered by the Lord, and He delights in his way."[9]

After several seconds, he released his grasp, took several deep breaths, and stoically walked to the back of the group.

Wilson approached next, also choking back tears. He stared at the floor until he wrestled his emotions under control. After several seconds of silence, he looked Julie in the eyes and thrust his walking stick toward her.

Julie sucked in a deep breath and put her hand over her heart.

"Oh, oh, Wilson," she stammered, "I can't take your walking stick, but thank you so much." She threw her arms around him; the stick clanked to the floor, and he held her tightly.

"You are so kind and generous. You would give up your most precious possession for me. You are just like Jesus."

Wilson is a caregiver. He loves others and desires to protect them. He knows My heart and will reveal it to others.

Here is his verse: "Learn to do right! Seek justice, encourage the oppressed. Defend the cause of the fatherless, plead the case of the widow."[10]

Wilson finally released her and looked directly into her eyes again. She picked up the stick and handed it back to him and then kissed his forehead. He smiled and walked to the back of the group with Praveen.

Kumar approached Julie and handed her a drawing of a heart inside a heart with a third, smaller heart inside.

"That's beautiful, Kumar. What's it mean?"

"Well," he pointed to the outside heart, "this is mine and this one," he pointed to the second heart, "is Jesus' heart because He lives inside me now."

"What's the smallest one?"

"That's your heart because I will always remember you right here." He pointed to his chest.

She knelt down and looked into his eyes. "And I will also carry you in my heart, Kumar."

I will give Kumar a spirit of adoption. He will minister to orphans with the goal of seeing Mumbai transformed one child at a time, by caring long-term for each child's emotional, spiritual, and financial need. Here is his verse: "He will turn the hearts of the parents to their children, and the hearts of the children to their parents."[11] Kumar smiled, paused, then walked away as Madhu approached. He pulled a white cotton string from his pocket with three large brown seeds hanging in the middle. He held it out to her and smiled.

"Oh, Madhu," gushed Julie, slipping it over her head. "What a beautiful necklace. I know you worked hours on this." Madhu beamed. "It's my new favorite necklace. Thank you so much. I'll always treasure it."

Madhu will be My intercessor. He will help change difficult people, situations, cities, and nations by the hours he will spend on his knees.

Here is his verse: "Be joyful in hope, patient in affliction, faithful in prayer. Share with God's people who are in need. Practice hospitality."[12]

Bhanu walked to Julie and threw his arms around her.

Lord, it's amazing what a little bit of kindness, love, and acceptance can do.

Yes, Julie, and this transformation is just beginning. As Bhanu's heart heals, he will become more vulnerable. He will eventually befriend the hurting and walk them through their pain and introduce them to Me.

His life verse is: "A man that hath friends must shew himself friendly: and there is a friend that sticketh closer than a brother."[13]

Bhanu released her and smiled. It was a sad smile, but it had replaced his permanent frown.

"I like the new Bhanu," said Julie, tickling him under his chin. "I love to see you smile." When she said that, he did.

Daya and his wife sat on the couch with Sammy sharing their laps.

"Julie, I believe I am the most grateful of all," said Daya. "Not only was my faith increased by seeing God miraculously answer our prayers for the orphanage, but I gained the best son in the world." He tossed Sammy in the air and caught him. Sammy squealed with delight. Daya's wife smiled broadly.

"Yes, I owe you a debt of gratitude I can never pay," he continued. Her face flushed with happiness.

"You have a wonderful son. I'm humbled to have been a part of you three becoming a family," said Julie.

"I will be teaching here," said Daya's wife, "so I will bring Sammy each day for school. He will not miss his friends. The Lord has worked a miracle for our family. Thank you for your obedience." Julie smiled and nodded.

Sammy handed Julie a card, which showed a picture of Mr. Shah behind jail bars. She held it up and everyone laughed.

"My dad put him in jail," said Sammy. Daya gave him a big hug. "That's right; he won't bother you anymore." Julie smiled. She collected all the pictures and carefully placed them in her battered, stained, green designer bag.

Sammy will develop a keen sense of justice and love the underdog. He will learn to hear My voice and be quick to see what I am doing in a situation.

His verse is Micah 6:8: "He has told you, O man, what is good; and what does the Lord require of you but to do justice, to love kindness, and to walk humbly with your God?"[14]

"Let's pray for Julie's safe journey and thank God for bringing her to bless us. Thank you, Julie from America," said Pastor Kandal, "for obeying God's voice to help these wonderful, amazing children. Their destinies are different because of you."

As the children prayed, Julie was overcome by emotion.

I feel like my heart is being crushed in my chest. How can I leave these precious ones?

Their wonderful prayers and their obvious affection for her moved her to tears.

Lord, I am a blessed woman. I'm surrounded by children who love me and whom I love. For the first time in my life, I am really rich.

When the last child finished, the whole group shouted, "Ah-meen!"

"We need pictures," said Pastor Kandal as he held up his cell phone. The children gathering close to her made her cry all the more.

"Everybody smile," said Pastor.

Right, thought Julie. *I feel like I might never smile again.* She rummaged through her purse and came up with her phone.

I wonder? She looked at the bars—fully charged. She grinned. *Lord, You are too funny!*

"Pastor, will you take pictures of these wonderful, precious children for me?" *I might need them to prove to my husband where I've been all this time.*

After all the good-byes and hugs, with occasional smiles breaking through the tears, Julie heard the auto rickshaw honk.

Lord, I guess this is it. She took a deep breath, and the whole group huddled around her as she made her way outside. When she was seated in the auto rickshaw, Pastor Kandal handed Shara to her; Ravi climbed in the other side, and Daya wedged in the wooden, tri-fold screen.

"I love you all. I miss you already," cried Julie, looking at each of their faces. Ravi waved. The children ran along beside the auto rickshaw shouting and waving as it eased away from the curb.

Julie pulled her Bible from her battered purse. "Look at this Scripture. I was praying last night about bringing you and Shara home with me, and when I woke this morning, this was the verse the Lord gave me for today: '*God sets the lonely in families....*'[15] I was hoping, hoping, hoping, but when I read that, I knew it was Jesus telling me that we are family, forever."

CHAPTER

26

"To the train station please," she said, putting her arm around Ravi and pulling him close.

Hello, love; to the train station it is.

Julie looked at the driver. "Mr. Dove?"

Yes, indeed! I told you I'd help you get home when the time was right. He smiled as He held up His pocket watch. *Julie, I am glad to know that you grew to love your Father's lambs. And you are bringing two of them home. And, love, don't worry about the adoption paperwork; everything has been carefully prepared.* He gave her a wink and said to Ravi, *The Bible compares Jesus to a shepherd and His followers to sheep.[1] You, Ravi, are one of Jesus' precious lambs. He has a wonderful plan for your life.*

"How do You know my name?" He turned to Julie. "How does He know my name?"

"He has been sent by the Lord to take us to the train station." Turning to Mr. Dove, she asked, "Is that train the same? I mean, are the *passengers* the same?"

"If you are referring to your dining partner, yes, Julie, He's waiting." She clapped her hands and let out a whoop that woke Sharavathi. She clasped Ravi's shoulder and gave him an affectionate hug. "He is there for us; He's waiting for us." A puzzled Ravi asked, "Who, who?"

"Jesus!"

"Jesus is on the train? A plane is much faster." Julie laughed.

Jesus lives in Heaven, said Mr. Dove. *He sits on a throne next to His Father God. He has billions of angels serving Him, and He can appear anywhere He wants any time He wants. He's on the train because He wants to spend some time with you.*

When the auto rickshaw arrived at the deserted station, Mr. Dove parked and carried the screen. The train was at the far side of the platform.

Ravi, hurry ahead; someone's waiting for you on the train, said Mr. Dove.

Ravi looked to Julie.

"Go, run fast." Julie could see Jesus watching through the window. Ravi jumped up on the steps and entered. She hurried across the deserted platform carrying Shara and heard wild laughter as she climbed the steps, followed by Mr. Dove.

Ravi was in Jesus' arms with his legs wrapped around His waist. Jesus was spinning, and they were both laughing hilariously.

I am restoring the smile to your eyes, Ravi.

I've never heard such pure joy, thought Julie. Soon she had tossed back her head and had joined the sweet mayhem. She didn't know how long they laughed, but Jesus came to her holding Ravi on His right hip, and He embraced her with His left arm. Shara snoozed contentedly. He gave Julie the longest hug. His embrace felt like warm, refreshing oil flowing over her, soothing away all concerns and tensions.

I am the joyful, happy God, and together we will dance on your problems.

She looked into His eyes and was engulfed in unconditional love. Tears ran down her cheeks as the waves continued to wash over her. She looked at Ravi, who had his head on Jesus' shoulder. He was quietly crying, too. They clutched each other and wept in love and joy until Jesus wiped their tears away. Then Jesus picked up Sharavathi with His left hand and held her to His chest.

Let's all sit and have something to eat, said Jesus, motioning toward the booth. Ravi's eyes lit up, but changed to disappointment when he saw a carafe of grape juice and unleavened bread. He sat down at the booth and snuggled up next to Jesus. Julie slid in directly across from them.

Jesus laid Sharavathi across His lap. As He tore the bread into three pieces, Ravi caught sight of the nail scars. He gasped.

Ravi, this bread represents My body, which was crucified so you could be free from sin. Eat this so you will not forget that My broken body delivered you from sinfulness into righteousness.

He laid His left hand on the table. Julie and Ravi automatically touched it as they ate the bread, and they began to weep again. Jesus filled three glasses from the carafe.

He held up His glass. *This is My blood that was shed for your sin. You are totally forgiven. The cup stands for deliverance from death into life. Drink this so you will not forget that I provided salvation for you.*

As they drank the juice, more tears flowed. Julie and Ravi were overwhelmed by the revelation of His love and sacrifice for them. Ravi broke the silence, "I wish we could stay here forever."

Ravi, I'm always as near to you as I am now, even though you can't see Me. What we just did is called the Lord's Supper, and you can take it every day so you never forget the sacrifice I made for you. He put the glass down.

Ravi, you have a special calling on your life. Before I formed you in your mother's womb, I called you to be an evangelist. I am moving you from disappointed to appointed.

You will place many peoples' hands in Mine, and you will become a lover of My Word and a man of prayer and worship. I will place in you wisdom, love, authority, faith, and hope. But you need to grow up being loved by a family for all this to happen. How you do like the new mother I chose for you?

Julie's face broke into a huge smile as Ravi said with excitement, "She is the best mother in the world."

Jesus replied, *Yes, she is the best mother in the world for you.*

Jesus took Julie's hands in His own. *Julie, I'm so proud of you. Your heart is so soft because you followed My commands. You are leaving India a different person than when you arrived. I have called you to mother, love, and educate Ravi, Logan, and Sharavathi. You'll train them in My ways and help them grow in their spiritual gifts. You will be a builder for the next generation and lay a firm foundation for all your children. You will be a happy family, and your husband will love and enjoy Ravi and Shara just like he loves Logan.*

I saw your tears over the miscarriages, and I stored all of them in a bottle.[2] Julie began to cry. *These two wonderful children are My healing answer to your incredible pain. My dreams for you are more than you could ever imagine, and I will enjoy watching you and your expanded family grow, dance, laugh, and fulfill your destinies.*

She looked into His eyes, "Oh, thank You, Lord. I never believed my broken heart could ever heal. I thought it was just too wounded. After the second miscarriage, it felt way past wounded; it felt shattered."

I know, Julie, but now your heart will heal because it is filled up with love. Only My love can dissolve your excruciating grief.

"I can't wait for my new family to meet my old family."

That's you, My friend, He said, putting His arm around Ravi's shoulder. *You must be hungry. I took the liberty of preparing some food; let Me serve you both.*

"No, Lord," Julie blurted.

No, Lord? Haven't we been through this before? He smiled. *Julie, you made Me so happy as you took care of My lambs.*

"Lord, I have the ability to make You happy?"

Can Ravi make you smile, be happy, laugh, or be proud?

"Yes, but I never knew, I mean...."

Oh, I enjoy and love My children so much more than any earthly parent does. He gave her a radiant smile.

"In that case, Lord, I want to be the reason for Your smile."

You are, Julie. More than you know.

Mr. Dove arrived pushing a cart with curry and cardamon-colored stoneware. He bowed, tipped His hat, and smiled, *Hopefully everything is to your satisfaction, love.* Then He left.

"Those were the dishes in my dream!"

I still speak through dreams, Jesus said with a mischievous grin.

"Wait, what's that mean?"

It will become apparent shortly. She began to speak, and He held up His hand, signaling her to let it go. Then He winked at her as He lifted the lid off the chafing dish.

"Real food," cried Julie with delight. "Roast and mashed potatoes and gravy and corn on the cob. My favorite meal from childhood."

It's your mother's recipe.

"I was just thinking I'd fix it when I arrived home. You really do know all my needs and my desires, don't You?"

I know them before you do. Before you call, I will answer.[3] *Every solution for all My lambs was already worked out and waiting to be implemented before I sent you to India.*

"Really?"

Really. I called you after Pastor Kandal and the church began to work on the house. You just had to be available.

"In the beginning, it felt like pulling teeth every day."

He poured three glasses of apricot nectar.

That's because you didn't trust Me and trust that I could solve the problems. Every hard circumstance is an invitation to partner with Me. You carried a lot of the pressures because you didn't believe that I would do what I said. If you had believed that I had a solution for every problem, then you could have relaxed the whole time.

"Looking back now, it seems easy to trust. When I was living through it, it seemed impossible. I couldn't make things work out logically." She pointed to her head.

"And, Lord, I've been thinking about how You told me that You can use everything for good, but I didn't believe that. Going to India against my will seemed to be a horrendous tragedy. I couldn't see one positive thing about it, but it turned out to be the high point of my life. And you used my stolen wallet, another thing I thought was unredeemable, so I could connect with Daya. You really can use what seems to be a bad situation and make it positive."

And I didn't just have a solution for these situations, but I have a solution for all your situations for the rest of your life. I take joy in sneaking up on you with great answers. Each day when you wake, I have it all planned. Keep your mind on Me. Trust Me, and you will live in perfect peace. And I do mean perfect.[4]

"Help me to remember that, Lord."

Come to Me each day and I will. Every day is an invitation to grow with Me, even in the most mundane circumstances. You might just be surprised by how I define daily success for you. He carved the meat and laid it on Ravi and Julie's plate. Julie bowed her head to pray, then smiled and looked up at Him. "Thanks." She turned to Ravi, "Practice using your silverware." Ravi fumbled with the fork.

Julie took a bite. "Oh, it's better than mom's!"

Ravi eventually got a bite and cried out, "This is the best thing I've ever tasted. What is this?"

It's called beef, Ravi. It's going to be your new favorite. Julie caught Jesus' eye, and they both laughed.

Here, try some mashed potatoes and fruit salad. I believe there are bananas in it, He said with a smile. Ravi scooped the food in his mouth with his right hand as fast as he could. Jesus touched his shoulder.

Slow down, My friend. There's always more than enough at My table. No one will ever take your food away again. I want to see you really enjoying it.

When Julie picked up her corn on the cob,

Ravi laughed and pointed. "You are eating like an Indian." He laid his silverware down and used his right hand.

"What does success look like for me each day?" asked Julie.

How do you please a good father, Julie?

"I-I don't know. I didn't... I tried, but I couldn't."

You hold up your cup and ask for more!

"What?"

You please a good father by holding up your cup and asking for more.

"Can I have more beee-f?" asked Ravi, holding up his empty plate. "It tastes good!"

See, said Jesus, looking toward Julie with a big smile. *Ravi, let me help you. You may have all that you want.* He piled more food on his plate.

"I don't know what *beee-f* is, but I sure like it."

As Ravi grabbed a bite, Jesus said, *Swish it through the mashed potatoes and then dip it in the gravy.* Following His instructions, Ravi popped it in his mouth.

"Ummm."

Jesus turned back to Julie, *Who would you be if you'd never been wounded? How would you act if you didn't have a desperate need for attention or if you didn't fear punishment or if you didn't do what you think other people expect? You don't have to perform or try to be anything you're not. Why not be the genuine Julie? I love your Julie-ness.*

She looked puzzled as this truth penetrated her soul.

It's all good. I am the God who loves to redeem—lost time, mistakes, and brokenness. Today's missteps become tomorrow's victories. Your past can't rob you of your destiny because I can redeem anything you bring to Me. No child of Mine draws a bad picture or prays a bad prayer. If I had a refrigerator, your picture would be on it.

"I've never thought of it like that, Lord." Julie loaded her fork with a bite of roast beef.

Success is learning to not lean on your own understanding, to not strive in your own strength. I delight in being your strength, source, and wisdom. I make easy on-ramps. Put your hand in Mine, and we'll walk out each day together.

Spend time with Me, and you'll receive a healed vision of Me and of yourself. You are not a pauper, but a princess. I am not a harsh father, but a proud parent who loves you every minute of the day.

"But how can You—?"

I see you through the finished work of the cross. Period. Your righteousness is established, and anything that says it's not is a lie, a deception from My enemy.

"Lord," said Julie, smiling as she held up her glass, "I'd love some more."

And I'd love to accommodate you, He said, picking up the pitcher. *What did you learn on this trip, My beautiful one?*

"I learned that all people are precious, no matter what nationality, age, class, economic status, or level of cleanliness. They are all created in Your image and are all precious. Lord, I have totally changed the way I evaluate, I mean, the way I judge people, You know, by the exterior. I'm so sorry; please forgive me."

I do forgive you, and I will help you to remember to lay down your judge's robe and look through the eyes of love. Each person is precious enough for Me to die for. I will help you to see My face in every person you meet.

"Thank You, Lord. I need that. I guess I focused on people's faults and flaws, not on who You created them to be. I just never saw their potential."

Jesus nodded, then glanced at Ravi and smiled. He was in his own world chewing on a large bite of roast and sighing.

What else have you learned?

"I learned to love the Bible. I never realized all the miracles You performed or how much You loved people. The more I read, the more I got to know You. And I actually learned to pray. Before I just prayed boring rote prayers. I never realized I could actually connect with You."

You can always connect with Me through prayer.

"And about money. I think I've probably spent more on one outfit than the average third world family earns in a year. I loved money and all my possessions and clothes. It was a god before, wasn't it?"

It replaced Me.

"I didn't realize how it consumed me until it was suddenly gone. I had no heart for the needs of others. All the problems I saw on the world news didn't seem any more real than a movie with actors. Once the TV was off they were totally gone. This trip really opened my eyes to the amount of tragedy and pain that goes on. I'm going to support our precious orphans, and I'd like to give to other places, too."

No one ever found true happiness from trusting in money, but many have found true satisfaction from giving it. There are many causes to support, but I will guide you.

"And, Lord, I'm going to stop buying so much stuff. I don't need it; after a week, the newness always wore off, and it never made me permanently happy." She fiddled with her napkin. "I can see that I loved things and used people. My new goal is to love people and use things. Thanks for putting up with me, um, my stubbornness, selfishness, and immaturity."

Of course, I totally forgive you, Julie, and from now on, you'll concentrate on storing treasures in Heaven.[5]

"What a paradigm switch. It's so clear now." She absentmindedly ran her finger over the seeds on her necklace.

I see you have some new jewelry.

"Yes, isn't it lovely? I'm going to wear it regularly so the memories it carries will always be close to my heart."

But it's not a designer piece, nor is it made with precious stones.

She smiled, "You're wrong, Lord; it's both. It was designed especially for me, and it's very, very precious."

Ravi continued to eat.

"Ummm, this po-tat-oes is so good. It's almost better than bananas!" Jesus smiled as He nodded and tousled Ravi's hair.

Ravi, I'm glad you mentioned bananas because I picked our dessert with you in mind. It's called banana cream pie.

"Banana cream pie," cried Ravi. "It sounds wonderful."

Some might say it's "heavenly," said Jesus, serving a piece to him.

Ravi took a big bite.

"*This* is the best thing I've ever tasted!" He licked the whipped cream off his fingers and grabbed another big bite.

Jesus and Julie laughed at his delight.

What else, Julie?

"I've learned that You move through prayer. I learned that I saw more with my eyes closed than with my eyes open."

Meet Me each day on your knees, Julie. Everyone wins on their knees. Prayer is one of the most powerful forces in the universe. Prayer on one side of the world can cause Me to move someone from the other side of the world, He said with a wink. *You were the answer to Ravi's desperate prayers.* Julie's eyebrows shot up in surprise. Ravi looked confused. Between bites he said, "But, Jesus, I never prayed to You until Julie was here."

But, Ravi, I heard your prayers, and I selected Julie to come here to learn some lessons she needed to know and to adopt you and Shara. It all started with your prayers.

"Are you saying Ravi's prayers to his Hindu gods really caused You to move me halfway around the world?"

My heart was moved with compassion for him. And aren't you glad?

"Oh, Lord, I wouldn't have traded the experience for anything, especially since I have Ravi and Shara, and the lessons I've learned and the time I've gotten to spend with You."

And you can spend time with Me any place or hour. My ear is always attuned to you.

"Lord, I've been thinking. My heart's not really in retail anymore. It used to be such a thrill to accessorize the new fashions on the mannequins..." she paused, "just perfectly." She grinned at Him and continued, "Somehow I don't think it's going to be much of a thrill when I get back."

Jesus nodded.

"So I was thinking maybe Michael and I could downsize. Sell the house, get rid of a lot of excess stuff, and then I could afford to quit my job and be a full-time mom to my wonderful family."

Jesus smiled and looked deep in her eyes. *You have made a wise choice—to sow seed on good soil.[6] Enjoy the unknown, Julie. Learn to die daily to doubt and fear. Don't be afraid of a world that is already afraid; be at peace. What do you feel physically?*

"What do you mean?"

Notice your body. What do you feel?

"I don't know what You mean. I don't feel anything."

That's right, He laid His hand on top of hers. *You're living for the very first time. No clenched jaw, no more tension in the neck, and no more migraines. I am the Prince of Peace.[7] Do you know what that makes you?*

"No."

It makes you the Princess of Peace!

She smiled. "I'm not tense. My shoulders aren't tight. I'm actually relaxed. Life is going to be so different."

Yes, because you've learned that you can trust Me, and you've learned how to battle the enemy. Fight the good fight of faith.[8] *Do you know what a good fight is, Julie?*

She shook her head.

A good fight is one you win! This life is a marathon, not a sprint. The enemy will return again and again. Remember what I said about taking every thought captive? If it's not from Me, resist and rebuke it and state the truth to yourself, out loud. Your mind will become a beautiful, peaceful place for you to live.

"Yes, Lord. I'm ready to do hand-to-hand combat with Your enemy for my life and my family. And I haven't forgotten about putting on the whole armor of God each morning to resist those fiery darts.[9] With Your help, I will walk as a confident warrior."

Excellent, Julie, you are well on the way to being an overcomer![10] People learn best in the furnace of affliction, and you now possess gold refined by fire,[11] the purest form there is. You will no longer tread water, but you will walk on it. What else did you learn?

"That my self-worth doesn't depend on me being perfect, which is good because I can't be perfect. Soooo, I guess I can quit trying." She grinned. "Lord, I'm so glad I learned this now, not in my 60s. I was constantly exhausted— mentally, physically, and emotionally."

I'm glad you did, too, Julie. Aim for a spirit of excellence, never perfection.

"I'm learning to believe that I don't have to perform for You to love me."

I love you because I love you. I don't stop loving you, even if you have what you would call "a bad day," any more than you would stop loving Ravi. The finished work of the cross. Period.

"That takes the pressure off, doesn't it?"

Yes, relax in the gift of My love and My righteousness. Knowing how I feel about you eliminates striving. I celebrate you and your future. I purchased your victory 2,000 years ago on the cross. As long as you don't give up, you cannot fail.

"I always thought that Christianity was set up so I could never succeed."

Julie, your sincere heart toward Me ensures that you can never fail. Did you know that you have never once disappointed Me?

"Lord, I didn't think You could lie!"

I can't, and you haven't. Disappointment comes from hoping or expecting one thing and getting something less. I chose you knowing every day of your life and every sin you'd ever commit, so it is impossible for you to disappoint Me, ever.

"Lord, You're amazing! You love using flawed people, don't You?"

If you hadn't noticed, Julie, it's still the only kind I have, and yes, I'm crazy about them.

After everyone was sufficiently full and Ravi and Julie had talked on and on about the trip, the children, the food, and the future, the train came to a stop. Jesus said, *I believe this is your stop.*

"But I don't want to leave You," blurted Ravi.

You can't leave Me because I never leave you. I am with you always, even until the end of the world.[12]

"But it's really nice to *see* You, you know, in the flesh." Julie touched His hand.

Seeing is not reality. My Word is reality and truth. I am always with you; I will never leave you nor forsake you.[13] *I don't just send you back; I launch you into your destiny. You will know My leadership like never before. And your compassionate heart will love people like never before. Now it's time for you to get back to your family and introduce these two wonderful new members. This meeting is what you've longed for.*

She felt her stress rising. Before she could catch it, her mind was back in the old pattern. *What will my family think? I've been gone so long. How will I explain it? And I'm bringing home two new children!*

It'll be fine, Julie. One final test for you—trust Me on this one. Now take that thought captive. Resist and renounce it, and replace it with the truth.

"I resist and renounce this lie that Michael and Logan will be upset with me in Jesus' name, and I replace it with the truth that our reunion will be wonderful."

Excellent, Julie. Knowing the truth is what sets you free.[14]

He turned her around and escorted her to the back of the train.

Trust Me; remember how I had everything planned in India? I have everything planned here, too.

"OK, Lord; I trust You." He handed Shara to Ravi and gave Julie a final, long hug.

"Thank You, Lord. I have two new children and didn't even have to go through labor."

He looked deep into her eyes. *Yes, but it was costly.* They both grinned.

"But so worth it. I am so grateful that You didn't let me miss the time in India. Thank You for teaching me what I didn't want to learn!

"Here I go to my joyful reunion." She headed for the door.

Jesus put His arm around Ravi. *Let her spend a little time with Michael and Logan, and then she will introduce you. Ravi, do you realize I sing with joy over your life?[15]*

C H A P T E R

27

Julie caught a glimpse of Logan and Michael on the deserted platform and ran down the steps. She flung her arms around them both.

"Wow. Is this the latest fashion in New York? It looks a little Asian," said Michael, examining her. "Where'd you get the, um, *necklace?*"

"Oh, isn't it wonderful? It's my new favorite piece of jewelry."

"You look a little different," said Michael, cocking his head to one side.

"Oh, Michael, you have no idea." She smiled and hugged them again.

"It's so good to see you two. I've missed you both soooo much. Please don't be upset with me."

"Why would we be upset?" asked Logan.

"Because I didn't call, but you need to know that I thought about you every day, and I missed you both so much."

"Don't get over-dramatic; you make two days sound like an eternity," said Michael.

"Two days—*what are you* talking about? I've been gone for weeks."

"Weeks—*what are you* talking about?"

Logan looked to his dad and made the "crazy" hand signal.

"What's today's date?" asked Julie

"It's Sunday the 26th."

"August 26th. That means I've been gone a little over a month."

Michael's eyes widened.

"August? It's the 26th of *July.* You've been gone two days."

"It can't still be July. Don't joke about this." Michael held out his watch, and she fell silent.

"I think you shopped a little too long and a little too hard."

Julie realized the truth of the timing and laughed uproariously. Logan and Michael exchanged glances.

"Michael, trust me. Really, I've been in India."

Mr. Dove came down the stairs carrying the folding screen.

Julie, wait, you almost forgot this.

"Where'd you get that? It must really have cost a fortune." Mr. Dove bowed slightly and said, *Julie purchased it in India for a very reasonable price. You must be Michael,* he said extending his hand. *She purchased it for your office.*

Michael gawked in silence. "It's amazing. Did you say she purchased it in *India?*"

Mr. Dove nodded. *Mumbai.*

"It's hard to explain," said Julie. "I didn't end up shopping, but I do have two gifts, two amazing, precious and wonderful gifts for all of us. I'll explain in detail later, but for now, just trust what I say, even though it sounds impossible."

At that point, Ravi came down the steps holding Sharavathi. Julie ran to them. "These are the gifts I have for us. This is Ravi and Sharavathi." Julie was nearly giddy. "They were orphans, and now they're ours."

Logan looked at Michael.

"See, Dad, I told you. I told you this morning about my dream!" He turned to Julie. "A man came and held me and said I'd have a brother and a little sister—and that's HIM." Logan pointed to the platform on the train where Jesus now stood with His arms stretched wide. Logan scampered up the stairs and into the waiting hug.

"Oh, my God," exclaimed Michael.

Yes, replied Jesus, looking at him.

"Oh, sorry. Didn't mean...." Jesus smiled and turned His attention back to Logan.

You are going to be the best brother ever to Ravi and Shara. I have so much fun planned for the three of you. You will be marvelous comrades, inseparable; you'll have many awesome adventures together.

"This is just like my dream," squealed Logan. "You held me just like this!"

I did, said Jesus. *And, Logan, I will continue to speak to you in the night through dreams. You will learn to hear My voice clearly, whether it comes as loud as thunder,* He looked toward Julie, *or whether it is a tiny, small whisper.*

You will be a helper and will grow in love and kindness. You will be a tenderhearted encourager. I will show you the hidden pain in each person's heart. You will make sure no one is overlooked. You, Logan, will be the voice that tells others to "look up!"

"Wow," said Logan. "Mom, did you hear that?" Julie was too choked up to respond.

There's more, Logan. When you grow up, you will bring My presence and compassion to the secular marketplace. Because you have a hopeful heart, wherever you walk, you will help rid your world of despair—you will lead others into hopeful happiness. Logan raised his eyebrows, and Julie was ready to jump with joy.

"Amazing," said Michael.

Jesus took Shara from Ravi and walked down the stairs. He held her close and smiled as He gently stroked her cheek.

Julie and Michael, would you like to know a little about your daughter's future? He looked at Shara. *And you, little one, will grow up to be a woman of destiny, a powerful force in My Kingdom. You're going to cause great fear in My enemy. You will not draw back, but you will run headfirst into obstacles. I will help you soar. You will hear My voice clearly, and you will shatter doubts, fears, and lies.*

I will tell you My secrets, and when you speak them, it will set the captives free—free from addictions, fears, depression, and anxieties. I will fill you up with the knowledge of My Father, and you will feed others with this knowledge. You will rescue people from the miry clay and plant their feet upon the Rock.[1]

Julie wept and clung to Michael.

"We have an awesome future, and our children will surpass us. Our ceiling will be their floor."

An older, petite woman tried to hold open the door while pushing a cleaning cart onto the other end of the platform. Jesus looked at her and smiled warmly; then turned His attention back to Michael.

Michael, I want you to know that your sister's wreck wasn't your fault.

Michael's body stiffened and tears welled in his eyes.

"But she left angry. If I hadn't argued—"

Michael, I said it wasn't your fault. You didn't realize she was leaving anyway. She had made plans to meet her friends at the mall. You had no way of knowing that. When she left the house, she started praying, and she had forgiven you—she was over it very quickly.

No one knew that a dog ran in front of her car, and she swerved to miss it. She didn't leave because of you; she didn't die because of you.

Jesus wrapped His arms around Michael. After a minute, Michael's tears began to flow; then his sobs turned into wailing.

"She was only 16."

It wasn't you; it was her inexperience at the wheel. She couldn't regain control.

"All these years I've felt so guilty."

I'm here to put an end to that today. No more of those thoughts. Julie can teach you how to deal with them. I want to break your condemnation and grief, Michael. You've carried these heavy burdens far too long.

Jeannie is with Me, and she wouldn't have it any other way. She's Jeannie like you've never seen her before. She's full of life, love, and energy. No more adolescent angst, depression, or insecurity battles. Every second of every day she lives in complete joy. She wouldn't want to come back to Earth. I'm telling you the truth, Michael. I'm here to set you free today.

Julie smiled, "Trust Him, Michael. He's always right!"

Julie, I believe you should all head home; you have an awful lot to talk about, and I have another get-together starting now. I want to remind you to trust Me. I have it all under control. He smiled, handed her Shara, then cupped her cheeks in His hands and kissed her forehead. *You are beautiful, My beloved.*

He said good-bye to Michael, Logan, and Ravi and then jogged toward the brown-haired woman who was squeegeeing the windows.

Hello, Lovera, let Me help you with that.

Mr. Dove turned to Julie, *Well done! It was a pleasure to help you find His lambs. Their lives will never be the same. Michael, Ravi, and Logan, you have a wonderful life ahead.* He looked at his pocket watch. *I'm off to My next appointment,* and tipped his hat before entering the train. *Cheers.*

"Here, Michael, would you like to carry her? I'll get the screen," said Julie. She gently handed him Shara, who awoke and stared deeply into Michael's eyes.

"Her?" said Michael, already feeling smitten. "'Her' just sounds so wonderful. Come along, precious; you're daddy's girl now." He kissed each cheek and ran his hand through her thick hair. "She's so beautiful—dark skin, black hair, and look at those beautiful, big brown eyes."

"What do you think of your little sister, Logan?" asked Michael.

"She's got a suntan."

Julie put the strap of her dirty, damaged bag over her shoulder and they turned to go. Logan asked Ravi, "Have you ever seen this before?" He opened his hand to reveal a wad of Silly Putty®. Ravi's eyes lit up as he reached into his pocket and pulled out his egg.

Endnotes

CHAPTER 3

1. See Jeremiah 1:5.

CHAPTER 4

1. See Ephesians 1:4 NKJV.

2. See Matthew 10:30.

3. See Revelation 4:5 NKJV.

4. See James 4:14 NKJV.

5. See Psalm 103:15-16 NLT.

6. See Song of Solomon 1:5.

7. See Matthew 28:20 NKJV.

8. See John 8:12 NKJV.

CHAPTER 7

1. See Numbers 22:28-30.

2. See Acts 8:26-39.

3. Paraphrase of Matthew 25:14-28 MSG.

CHAPTER 8

1. Romans 8:28.

2. "Number of World's Hungry Tops a Billion," *World Food Programme;* http://www.wfp.org/stories/number-world-hungry-tops-billion; accessed on May 11, 2011.

3. See Matthew 15:35-37.

CHAPTER 9

1. "9 Mind-Blowing Facts: Information that Will Amaze You From Quora Users," *Huff Post Tech;* http://www.huffingtonpost.com/2011/06/02/mind-blowing-facts_n_870706.html#s286685&title=Over_3_Billion; accessed on August 1, 2011.

2. See James 1:27a NCV.

3. Peggy Joyce Ruth, *God's Shield of Protection Psalm 91,* (Lake Mary, FL: Creation House, 2007), 35.

CHAPTER 10

1. See Psalm 55:22.

2. See Isaiah 40:12 NKJV.

3. Proverbs 3:5-6 NKJV.

CHAPTER 11

1. See Isaiah 55:8 NKJV.

2. See Isaiah 55:9 NKJV.

3. See Ephesians 6:11 NKJV.

4. See 2 Corinthians 10:5 NKJV.

5. See John 8:44b.

6. See John 14:6.

7. See Psalm 2:4.

CHAPTER 12

1. See Revelation 21:27 NKJV.

CHAPTER 13

1. See 2 Corinthians 12:9 NKJV.

2. See John 15:5.

3. NKJV.

CHAPTER 14

1. See John 16:33 NKJV.

CHAPTER 15

1. See Numbers 13:18-31.

2. Andrew Malone, "The real Slumdog Millionaires: Behind the cinema fantasy, mafia gangs are deliberately crippling children for profit," Mail Online;http://www.dailymail.co.uk/news/worldnews/article-1127056/The-real-Slumdog-Millionaires-Behind-cinema-fantasy-mafia-gangs-deliberately-crippling-children-profit.html; accessed on June 2, 2011.

3. Ibid.

4. See 1 Corinthians 12:4-11.

CHAPTER 16

1. See Exodus 16:14-31; Deuteronomy 8:16 NKJV.

2. See Psalm 103:2.

3. See Numbers 11:7-9.

4. See Deuteronomy 29:5.

5. See Matthew 6:11.

CHAPTER 17

1. See Psalm 34:7 NKJV.

CHAPTER 18

1. http://arollingcrone.blogspot.com/2009/01/child-beggars-in-india. html; accessed on June 1, 2011.

CHAPTER 19

1. Isaiah 61:1-3.

CHAPTER 21

1. See Exodus 7:1–12:39.

CHAPTER 22

1. See Daniel 6.

2. See John 14:12 NKJV.

3. Dietrich Bonhoeffer, quoted on Christian Quoting; http://www. christiansquoting.org.uk/quotes_o.htm; accessed February 5, 2011.

CHAPTER 23

1. See Psalm 68:5.

2. See John 14:3 NKJV.

3. See Isaiah 40:12 NCV.

4. See Deuteronomy 20:4.

CHAPTER 25

1. See Judges 7.

2. See Romans 8:28 NKJV.

3. See Ephesians 3:20 ASV.

4. See Luke 10:30-37.

5. See John 10:27-28 ASV.

6. See Matthew 22:37-39 NKJV.

7. Matthew 28:18-20.

8. Psalm 100:4-5.

9. NKJV.

10. Isaiah 1:17.

11. See Malachi 4:6.

12. Romans 12:12-13.

13. Proverbs 18:24 KJV.

14. NASB.

15. Psalm 68:6a.

CHAPTER 26

1. See John 10:2-14.

2. See Psalm 56:8 NKJV.

3. See Isaiah 65:24 NKJV.

4. See Isaiah 26:3 NKJV.

5. See Matthew 6:19-20 NKJV.

6. See Luke 8:4-15.

7. See Isaiah 9:6.

8. See 1 Timothy 6:12 KJV.

9. See Ephesians 6:11 NKJV.

10. See Revelation 2:26.

11. See 1 Peter 1:7.

12. See Matthew 28:20 NKJV.

13. See Deuteronomy 31:8.

14. See John 8:32.

15. See Zephaniah 3:17b.

CHAPTER 27

1. See Psalm 40:2 NKJV.

About Jackie Macgirvin

Jackie welcomes your feedback on *The Designer Bag at the Garbage Dump* and invites you to read her blog at http://jackiemacgirvin.com. She is available for speaking engagements, humorous or regular.